The darke... was as silen... objects along the floor cast long, mingling shadows, their shapes lost in a general haze of deep greys and blacks.

The creature waited. Only his eyes moved, darting quickly along the floor from one side of the room to the other, searching.

A large grey and brown rat scurried out from the shadows beside the fireplace and across the floor. When it paused momentarily near the mountainous pile of garbage to sniff at an empty tin can, the creature sprang, hands reaching out in front of him, fingers curled like hooks. Slightly off-balance when he leaped, the creature slid along the floor and collided with the mound of garbage, sending it scattering. The rat escaped easily and disappeared into the shadows again.

THE BEAST WITHIN

WITHIN

Edward Levy

Hamlyn Paperbacks

A Hamlyn Paperback

Published by Arrow Books Limited
17-21 Conway Street, London W1P 6JD

A division of the Hutchinson Publishing Group

London Melbourne Sydney Auckland
Johannesburg and agencies throughout
the world

First published in Great Britain by
Hamlyn Paperbacks 1982
Reprinted 1985

Printed and bound in Great Britain by
Anchor Brendon Limited, Tiptree, Essex

ISBN 0 09 940980 1

TO MY DAUGHTERS, LYNDA, DANA AND KAREN — three bright, warm, comforting lights in an otherwise cold, dark world.

PROLOGUE

Man is the dominant species of life on this planet, due to his superior intellect and dexterity . . . Man is, for the most part, a civilised, naturally gentle species, seeking to live and prosper in the company of his own kind . . . Because God loves mankind, He has given man the potential to evolve from his tree-dwelling, fruit-and-nut-gathering beginning to become master of this world, building an advanced technological society to match his intellectual and cultural capabilities . . . Man, or rather man-*kind*, is rapidly approaching the utopia that is his destiny.

These are the things we all are told.

None of this is true.

No matter how intelligent, sophisticated, or civilised man may have reason to believe he is, within each of us there dwells a beast, a nightmare creature so bloodthirsty and depraved, so vile and terrifying, that our mind must, for sanity's sake, find a way to deny its existence.

Many teachings of organised religion, for example, are contradictions, inversions, of this truth about man's basic nature. Precepts such as 'Thou shalt not kill' and 'Love thy enemy' are paradoxical concepts unto themselves, because no amount of philosophising can change fact: the beast that dwells within each man is a killer.

All around us are examples of this beast coming to the surface, if only we make in our minds a safe place from which to view reality as we otherwise refuse to know it.

Take the mass murderer, for instance, who is not satisfied with merely killing but is then strangely compelled to hack or tear his victims to pieces, then can give no plausible explanation for his behaviour. We know the real measure of our fascination with him.

Tradition excuses the soldier in battle from admitting to the overpowering exhilaration he feels in killing his fellow man. A man such as this is usually decorated as a hero, but the opportunity to unchain his inner savagery is his real reward.

The successful hunter who sits in the firelight with his fellows after gutting a deer talks about the stalk and the shoot but will find a way around the lusty pleasure he felt at the warmth and wetness on his blood-stained hands. And none of the men who listened will ask him, knowing as they do that the only difference between themselves and a carnivorous 'beast' that kills and rips its prey apart with fangs and claws is the choice of weapons.

The denial of the beast-in-man is not an inherited quality; it must be taught and learned. In the world we know, the imprisonment of the beast begins at birth.

But what if this process is arrested? What if the *man* is imprisoned, so that the animal will within him might be set free? If we were to do away with the civilisation man has erected to keep his beastliness *confined* — strip away the technology, the comforts, the moral and ethical taboos — then to what state would man revert?

In the right circumstances, it is possible for the beast to grow and strengthen from within; to push outward past the overlay of personality and merge with — then dominate — physical and psychological appearances. In some cases, the phenomenon has proven to be hereditary; the stronger the influence of the beast has developed in the parent, the more readily it will predominate in the offspring.

Not every human being has glimpsed this truth, for it is usually seen only in a moment of great primal rage or animal pleasure and recedes into the dark realm of the better-left-forgotten after the storm of instinctual responses has passed. Those who doubt the existence of this beast, take a moment to gaze at yourself in a mirror, studying closely the eyes that look back, concentrating on what *seems* to be looking out at you from behind them — then try to deny, even to yourself, the presence of the beast within you . . .

PART 1

1

The August sun beat down unmercifully on the small field, scorching it with an almost furnacelike intensity. The few green plants hardy enough to push their way up through the parched, cracking soil were soon baked dry of their moisture and life and stood in wilting clumps along the furrowed rows.

Henry Scruggs pulled his mule to a halt and wrapped the reins around the handle of the wooden plough. He took a deep, tired breath — the hot, dry air burning his throat — and pulled a large handkerchief from the back pocket of his overalls. Removing his sweat-soaked straw hat, he wiped the rivulets of perspiration that ran down his face and neck. He ran the cloth through his sweat-plastered hair and thick beard, then wadded it into a damp ball and stuffed it into the pocket again. The intense heat radiating up from the hard-packed soil made his feet feel roasted inside his boots.

'That's enough for today, Mildred,' he said, noticing that the animal's sides were heaving from the heat and strain and foamy drool dripped from her mouth. 'Ain't no reason killing ourselves on a scorcher like this.'

He gave the mule's sweaty neck an affectionate pat as he unhooked the plough harness from the bridle, then slowly trotted her away from the wooden plough and over to a dense clump of trees that bordered the field. He left the mule in the shade, grazing on the only patch of moist, green grass, and trudged back across the field to inspect the plough.

He dropped to his knees in the dry, rocky soil and looked closely at the bent and deeply scarred cutting blade. He shook his head in disgust at the way the wooden yoke holding the metal blade had splintered and cracked. 'Lord,' he said, clasping his hands in front of him and closing his eyes against the blinding glare of the sun. 'Lord, I know you must have had good reason for making so many rocks, but why did you have to dump them all on my land?'

Rocks, he thought bitterly as he got slowly to his feet again and brushed the powdery dirt from his knees. Rocks got to be God's own curse on mankind. They make the farming damn near impossible.

It had taken him the better part of eight months just to clear and plough his north field. It had been backbreaking work — some of the rocks had been so large that he had had to spend hours on each one, digging it up and dragging it away by hand. Each spring, he would set to work clearing his fields of rocks and readying the soil for planting. The following year, somehow, his fields would be full of rocks again. He was convinced that God had given the rocks the power to multiply and grow. He was also firmly convinced the rocks were God's way of testing his fibre and his strength.

His mother, a puritanical and religious woman, had taught him that human beings were basically vile, blasphemous creatures with wickedness embedded in their souls. There were no limits, she had said repeatedly, to the depths of depravity into which man would sink in order to satisfy his hunger and lust for the flesh. The seeds of deceit, treachery and carnal lust were firmly planted within the human soul, to take root and grow within the human spirit like a twisted and gnarled weed, choking off all goodness and decency. The only way to attain righteousness in the eyes of God was to fight temptation; only then could man claim his rightful place in the glorious Kingdom of Heaven. This was what was strictly taught to Henry Scruggs as a child, and this was what he had fervently believed for the last fifty-two years of his life.

Leading the mule back across the field, towards the farmhouse and the enclosures behind, his mind began drifting off into one of the few pleasures he allowed himself: thinking about and remembering his parents. To his mind, they were probably the only truly righteous and God-fearing people he had ever known. They were perhaps strict, straitlaced people, condemning with every word and gesture the evils and temptation that cursed mankind, but to him, they had had the light of God's own truth shining within them. And they had taught these truths to him, forcing them into his consciousness and memory with a repetitive fervour like the beat of a drum.

Some of the lessons had not been pleasant. He could still remember vividly the time — he was around fourteen years of age — when he had begun to experience strange new feelings and sensations within his loins. He had gone out to a stand of trees behind the barn, and after dropping his overalls, had begun stroking himself vigorously. His father had caught him at this, and after cutting a long, springy switch from the bough of a tree, had pointed out the evils of what Henry had done while nearly flaying the skin off his back and buttocks. It had been a painful lesson at the time, but he knew now that it had been done for his own good.

He had been born on this farm, born in the very bedroom that Sarah and he now shared. His parents had come from Missouri and had settled in this northwestern corner of Arkansas back in 1865. His father had told him the story many times of how they had come down out of the Ozark Mountains of southern Missouri and onto a rich plateau. They had found themselves on a fertile delta formed by two slow-moving creeks branching from the White River. The soil was extremely rocky, but looked to be excellent for farming and the raising of live-stock.

His father had laboured hard through the first summer and winter, clearing the fields he had staked out for himself and building a house and barn out of the all too abundant supply of rocks, mortared together by a mixture of lime-stone, sand and water that he had found in great supply along the banks of the creek. This house and barn, by Henry's calculation, had already stood for over sixty years.

This farm was the only home he had ever known, or ever wanted to know. Far from the main road, it was almost completely isolated from the world beyond. The only thing remotely resembling a road or path leading to his farm was a wagon trail that he himself had made during his few-and-far-between trips to Pea Ridge, the nearest small town, which he had to visit from time to time for supplies.

During his infrequent visits to Pea Ridge, he always found himself shocked by the immorality and sin that he found there. On one particular occasion, Tom Hunter, the local feed store owner, had wickedly suggested to him that they 'Go on down to Sylvia's Place to have a few drinks and grab some leg.' Horrified by the suggestion, he had loaded the supplies in his wagon as quickly as he could and had returned home to the safety and seclusion of his farm.

My pa was right, he thought bitterly to himself as he led the mule past the side-by-side graves of his parents. People must be the wickedest things God ever put on earth . . .

Sarah Louise Scruggs twisted her long, chestnut-brown hair into a loose rope and piled it on top of her head, then tied a bandanna to hold the hair in place. This was something she had to do whenever she went down into the root cellar for stored vegetables. If she didn't, she would emerge with her hair thick with dirt and cobwebs and horrible little crawling things.

It all seemed so hopeless, she thought, as she gripped the leather pull-ring in both hands and pulled the trap door open. What kind of life is this, she wondered desperately, asking herself the same questions and thinking the same thoughts that she had thought over and over again in the past six years. Why had she done it? Why had she agreed to marry a man like Henry? To live a life of loneliness and drudgery; to do endless chores; to be continually cleaning this uncleanable, filthy house . . .

She carefully felt her way down the wooden steps set into the square hole Henry had cut in the wood-planked floor, and into the dank, musty root cellar he had built 'for her' down under the house. She hated the root cellar, as she hated the entire house. Why had she ever listened to her papa, when he had told her to marry Henry Scruggs?

'But I don't love him, papa,' she had said: 'I don't even know him except to say hello to at church.'

'Sure you know him, girl. He's been our neighbour three mile down the road for — seems like forever,' her father had said. 'He's a good man, Sarah. A God-fearing man. He'll take good care of you.'

'But, papa, he's so . . . old,' she had pleaded. 'I don't want to marry an old man.'

'He's the same age as me, and I ain't old.'

'But, papa — '

'Sarah, you do like I say, marry him,' he had said, an edge in his voice. After a moment his voice softened. 'You do like I say, girl. I'm just looking after your own good.'

Sarah knew that 'looking after her own good' wasn't all that true. From the pieces of conversation she had caught while Henry and her father sat out on the porch and talked, she was pretty sure that the two of them had made some kind of a deal.

Unable to think of a way out, she had agreed to marry him two weeks later. Henry Scruggs had acquired a nineteen-year-old wife; a housekeeper, a worker. Her papa, somehow, had acquired two milking cows, a fine sow ready to drop a litter of piglets, and three sacks of potatoes. And she? She had acquired a life of misery and loneliness.

They had come back to his farm that first evening after the marriage ceremony. They ate the supper she had hastily prepared for him. Then he sat in his favourite chair in front of the warming fireplace and thoughtfully puffed on his pipe.

She had come to him then, feeling nervous and shy, but at the same time filled with the feeling of exhilaration she had never experienced before. She sat by his feet and gently put her hand on his knee in a small gesture of affection. 'I'll try to make you a good wife, Henry,' she had said, looking up at him, trying to find some reassurance in the harsh lines the fire cast on his face.

'I expect you will, child,' he said, the corncob still clamped between his teeth. He continued staring straight ahead into the fire.

'Oh, I'll try so hard to make you happy,' she said, trying hard to turn anticipation into something like joy. 'Just . . . be patient with me, 'til I learn your ways. I'll be a good wife to you, Henry. I'll work real hard with you to make this a good farm. I'll have your children — '

'I want no children from you,' he had said quietly, but with finality. 'Don't need 'em.'

'The way I hear, they can be kinda hard to prevent,' she had said, looking up at him shyly and giggling. 'Less you — '

His entire body stiffened noticeably. 'I'll not have you bringing wicked talk into this house,' he said slowly between gritted teeth, his face contorting with anger. 'This is a Christian home. My ma and pa built this house, every stone of it, with their pure love for Jesus Christ. You'll not taint it with talk of your hungers for the flesh.' He stood up so abruptly that she fell back, sprawling on the floor.

'I didn't mean nothing sinful,' she pleaded, staring in sudden terror at his huge frame towering over her. 'But, we're married now. I thought you'd want to – '

'I told you to shut your filthy mouth,' he shouted, drawing his arm back as if ready to slap her.

Suddenly, vividly, she could see herself being taken apart limb-from-limb by those huge, powerful hands, but, oddly, she wasn't afraid. 'If your ma and pa was so damn pure,' she shouted back defiantly, 'where'd *you* come from?'

He stood for another few seconds staring down at her, his face livid with rage. Then he turned on his bootheels and stalked out of the house, to sleep that night in the barn . . .

This was how they had spent their wedding night, she remembered bitterly, as she felt around in the dust and gloom of the root cellar for the bushel basket that held the dried corn. He's never even touched me since. I was pure as the Virgin Mary when he married me, and that's the way I'll die. She gathered some corn in her apron and carefully felt her way back up the wooden steps, closing the trap door behind her.

Six years we been married, she thought again dismally, and he don't even want to touch me. All he ever talks about is how this here is a sin, and that there is a blasphemy, and how God'll damn us for this or that. Well – God damn him!

Sarah mashed the dampened corn kernels to a thick, gooey consistency, then spooned it into a pot of boiling water on the stove. The heat radiating from the wood-burning, cast-iron stove made the already stifling air in the small kitchen almost unbearable. She could never figure out why, but Henry really seemed to enjoy the corn soup on hot days like this. It was one of the few things he found no fault with and was well worth the effort and discomfort of preparing – if it pleased him.

She left the kitchen, finding only minor relief from the oppressive stuffiness in the relative coolness of the rest of the house. She stood by the open window for a moment, hoping to catch a slight breeze; the air was hot and still. Must be one hell of a scorcher out there for him to quit work so early in the day, she thought, watching Henry as he trudged from the barn. He stopped at the water pump, and after pumping the handle vigorously, plunged his head and shoulders under the splashing stream. How much like a wet bear he looks now, she mused to herself, then wondered if now was a good time to try talking to him again — the last thing she wanted was to have another argument with him. If only he would listen to her once in a while she was sure that things would be better for them. But she had learned a long time ago that he had a way of completely shutting out conversations and ideas disagreeable to him, and retiring within himself for long periods of time, feeling safe and protected by his own righteous thoughts and beliefs. His spells, she called them, and they were almost as unnerving as his rages.

Henry came through the door, still shaking water out of his hair and beard. 'Hotter'n blazes out there,' he said, slicking his hair back out of his face with his hand. 'Mildred darn near collapsed.' He sat down heavily in his chair and took a deep, tired breath of the stale, hot air. 'Don't know how you can stand being inside on a day like this.'

'I can't stand it, Henry. I never could,' she said, still staring out the window.

'Well, I figure the hot spell'll break in maybe another week or two, then — '

'That ain't what I mean, and you know it!' she shouted, turning from the window to face him. 'It's the way we're . . . living — it's everything!'

'Now, Sarah,' he said in a tired, almost annoyed voice, 'you ain't gonna start that again.'

'I *am* going to start that again,' she shouted, no longer giving a thought to the anger it would surely provoke. It was as if the dam holding back all the unhappiness and frustration had finally broken, and the words poured uncontrollably from her mouth. 'Just you look at us — we fry in the summer — we freeze in the winter — we live like the poorest white trash what ever drew breath! You spend half your life out in that God-forsaken field, digging and planting by hand — and what's it ever got you? You barely grow enough to keep us alive! And what you do grow rots in a minute down in that cellar of ours, because it's so blamed hot and stuffy down there! I been wearing this same dress for two years now! It's the only thing I got! I keep patching and sewing it just to keep a rag on my back, else I'd be

17

walking around here naked —

'Now, you ain't got no cause to be talking like that,' he said, staring at her in disbelief. This was the first time she had ever actually shouted at him. 'We got plenty of — '

'We ain't got shit!'

Henry came slowly out of his chair. 'Sarah, I'm warning you,' he said through clenched teeth, his face beet-red with anger. 'I ain't never yet laid a hand on you. But if you don't stop that vile talk — '

'I didn't mean to rile you with what I said, Henry,' she said quickly, as soothingly as she could. Shouting, she knew, was not the way to get through his stubborness and make him listen to her. But she had had enough. 'It's just that . . . that I can't live like this no more. We gotta at least talk about it. But any time I try, you just get all riled up and tell me to shut my mouth.'

He seemed to calm down somewhat. He sat down again in his chair and looked reflectively at her face. 'What's bothering you, girl?' he asked softly.

'For one thing — I'm so lonely out here I could just scream,' she said with an exasperated gesture. 'Do you realise I ain't seen my papa but once since the day we got married? I don't know if he's alive or dead. We ain't had a single soul come by this farm in the last two years — nobody! At least from time to time you take a trip to Pea Ridge — '

'That ain't no place for you,' Henry said with finality.

'Why ain't it?' Sarah asked, her voice rising again. 'At least you get to talk to people — other human beings. Me — all I ever got to talk to is them damn chickens out there.'

'The kinda wicked people living in that unholy place ain't the kind a girl like you should be mixing with. Next thing you know, they'd be teaching you their evil ways.'

'Henry, I know right from wrong. Ain't nobody gonna teach me nothing I don't wanna to learn.'

'Them people's got Satan guiding their hand. They can turn your head towards the ways of evil 'fore you know it. You ain't going to Pea Ridge, and that's all I'm saying 'bout it.'

Sarah could see the futility in this course of conversation. She decided to take another, more urgent tack. 'How about us . . . living right here on this farm?' she asked tentatively.

'What about us?' Henry asked, looking a little surprised.

'I mean you and me — us,' she said nervously, stumbling on her words.

'What about us?' he said again.

'Well, just . . . you and me,' she stammered. 'We're married — we're living in this house together — but there ain't no closeness between us. It's like there's a high stone wall built right between us.'

'We're close,' he said with a shrug of his shoulders. 'We're talking right now, ain't we?'

'That ain't what I mean. I mean — other things. Can't you understand?' she said, almost in tears. The frustration she felt threatened to choke her.

'No. Guess I can't,' he said, shaking his head. He looked genuinely confused by the conversation.

'I wanna have a baby!' she blurted out, unable to control herself any longer. 'Henry, please listen to me,' she pleaded desperately. 'A baby would give me something to love and take care of. It would make us a family — a real family, not just you and me no more. It'll be wonderful — you'll see. Henry, please — I want it more than anything in the world.'

It was as if Henry's face had turned to stone. Unflinching, unmoving, he stared at her with eyes filled with revulsion, then anger.

'Henry, I know how you feel about having kids,' Sarah said pleadingly, 'but couldn't you just think about it? Couldn't we just talk about it?' She stood quietly, staring down at him, hoping and praying that he could understand her real need.

Henry's face softened into an almost forlorn look. 'Sarah,' he said slowly and deliberately, 'I've tried to guide and learn you in the right ways. I can see now that you've turned your face from God — '

'I ain't turned my face from God! I love God! God ain't got nothing to do with this — excepting it was Him what designed people for making kids! Ain't nothing unholy or dirty about creating another life — one you can love and take care of.'

'I don't wanna hear — '

'You *gotta* hear it, Henry. We gotta talk about it. We was

married under the sight of God. He blessed our marriage, remember? Wasn't we blessed?'

He slowly nodded his head affirmatively.

'Then there ain't nothing wrong with two people, blessed in marriage by God, enjoying each other's body — as long as they love each other. Can't you see that, Henry?'

'It still be lusting after the flesh. It's a sin and I won't be swayed — '

'I ain't trying to sway you into no sin, Henry. Get that idea outa your head.' Her voice was a mixture of pleading and exasperation. 'But, well . . . don't you never got no . . . like, feelin's . . . when you're laying beside me in bed at night?'

'Naw, never,' he answered firmly.

'Well, I sure do,' she admitted, watching his face carefully. 'Sometimes, at night, I lay there — feeling your body almost touching mine — and I get to feeling . . . mighty attracted to you, Henry. It's like I'm caught up with a fever — a funny, hot, tingling feeling, all over my body. Some nights, it near drives me plumb crazy. I wanna wake you up and tell you — but I'm scared to. Didn't you never feel like that?'

He was looking at her strangely again; the same look of revulsion now mixed with a kind of pity. 'No — and I never will. That feeling you're describing's the Devil, getting inside you and filling your mind and body with evil. I don't want no part of it.'

'It ain't evil!' she shouted, trying desperately to make him understand. She felt that if she didn't get through to him now, she would spend the rest of her life as miserable as she now felt. 'If it was evil and dirty like you say, God wouldn't have made you a man and me a woman. He woulda made us all the same. Then we wouldn't have no feelings about nothing. He made us like we are so we could give love and pleasure to each other — and have us a family.'

'Sarah,' Henry said softly, as though he were speaking to the child she wanted, 'tonight we'll read the Bible together, and I'll show the right way to God. God don't want two people, married or not, to be groveling and rolling round together like a couple of lust-filled animals. What you're talking is evil and disgusting. In my eyes, everything about you is disgusting.'

'You think I'm disgusting?' Sarah screamed at him hysterically. 'You think my body is disgusting?'

'I don't wanna talk no more about it,' he said, turning his face from her and staring into the empty fireplace.

'You think my body's disgusting?' she screamed again. Her fingers went to the three buttons holding her skimpy dress closed. In a quick movement she unfastened the buttons and spread the front of the dress wide, exposing her nakedness. 'Look at me, Henry!' she shouted defiantly. 'Look at my disgusting body!'

'Leave me be, Sarah,' he said, his face still turned towards the fireplace. 'I don't wanna talk no more.'

'Look at me, Henry!' she screamed. 'Goddamn you, look at me!'

Henry slowly turned his face from the fireplace and stared into her eyes, his face now a mask of uncontrolled rage. The bulging, hate-filled eyes travelled slowly down her exposed body, lingering only briefly on the smooth, pink contours. Then, with a bellow or rage, he was out of the chair, his right hand flashing out to slap her across the face with its full force. Sarah reeled backwards from the force of the blow and collided with the wall with a bone-jarring thud, then slumped slowly to the floor. Blood, oozing from the left side of her mouth, dripped from her chin, and ran in a thin red line onto her breasts.

'Evil, corrupt bitch! Have you no shame?' he bellowed, towering over her and glaring down at her. 'Satan has surely possessed you! There is no place in God's eyes for the like of you! You'll pay for your transgressions by suffering an eternity in the fiery pits of hell.' He stalked to the door and yanked it open. 'I'll not spend another night in the same room as you! Not 'til you've cleansed your soul and have God's pure light shining within you!' The door slammed hard behind him.

Sarah was not sure how long she lay there. She had not completely lost consciousness, but had teetered on the brink for an undetermined amount of time. Her brain was filled with swirling shadows and bright, flashing lights. Her body felt numbed and useless.

When full consciousness returned to her, with it came pain. The almost unbearable pain in the back of her head and along the left side of her face made it impossible for her to focus her eyes. She felt the rough wood of the floor beneath her hands, and carefully pushed herself up to a sitting position, then drew her knees up tightly into her stomach.

Long minutes later, the pain in her head subsided enough for her to attempt to stand. Her legs were still very shaky, but by using the wall for support, she managed to get to her feet and move towards the kitchen. She made her way to the water pitcher on the table and poured a cupful. Taking a drink, she swirled the water around inside her mouth, hoping to rid herself of the gritty, bitter taste, then spat it into the basin.

After wetting a cloth and washing the blood off her face and body, she made her way into the bedroom. She lay carefully on her back on the bed and stared up at the wood-planked ceiling and thought about her life.

The thought of spending the rest of her life on this dusty God-forsaken farm with a man like Henry, cruel, strict and unyielding — to never know love and companionship from a man — these were things far too horrible for her to comprehend.

I've got to get away from here, she thought desperately to herself as her eyes welled up and tears spilled down the sides of her face. Somehow — someway — I've got to get away from here . . .

2

The stifling heat of mid-August dissipated quickly as the air cooled during September and set the scene for the almost torrential rains that swept down across the Ozark Plateau from the north during the first part of October. The flooding water so engorged the White River and its tributaries that they nearly overflowed their banks. During this brief deluge, the parched, dry soil was thoroughly saturated. Now, with the passing of the rains, the delta valley sprang forth with a multitude of green vegetation of every imaginable sort — and land had drunk its fill, and now it was alive again.

Henry Scruggs swung his axe one last time, and embedded its sharp edge in the tree stump. He bent slightly forward at the waist and revolved his arms slowly over his head in an effort to relieve the tension and fatigue that had built up in his shoulders from the heavy work. The fence bordering his property had been badly in need of repair, and he had spent the last three days at the chore of splitting and shaping the wooden rails. It had been backbreaking, but it needed to be done. Although there was a definite chill in the air, his body, bare to the waist, glistened with perspiration from his labour. It was work such as this that kept him, at fifty-six years of age, in a fine muscular condition such as a younger man might envy.

That's the last of them, he thought contentedly, as he eyed the ample pile of log rails. Now, just to set them in place, and I'm done.

It was true. With the repair of his fence, he had completed all the maintenance chores around the farm before winter. The roof on the barn had been patched and sealed with pitch, the corrals and animal pens had been repaired, the well had been cleared of rocks, and the farmhouse now had a new porch. The fields had been weeded and cleared of rocks for the last time this season, and the crops were coming up full and rich with life. This would be a good year for his crops; he could tell. Yeah, he thought, as he dragged the new fence rail to replace one that was hanging, cracked and rotted; this would be a very good year for the farm.

There was an obvious change between Sarah and him, a change for the better as far as he was concerned. After spending a week sleeping in the barn, he had returned to the house. He had found Sarah subdued and quiet, only speaking to him when he spoke first. Other than her quietness, the only evidence of that fateful incident was a large, purple bruise on the left side of her jaw. Quietly she cooked his meals, cleaned the house, and did her chores; as a matter of fact, he couldn't recall hearing a single complaint from her in the last three months. They had even taken to reading the Bible together in the evening, and she could now recite most of his beloved scriptures by heart. He was sure now that she had been possessed for a time by the forces of evil, and that he, through his strength and belief, had ridded her of that evil. God had seen this, and had rewarded him this season with a rich, bountiful crop.

There had been that time last month when, expecting a long and cold winter coming up, he had had to make a trip into Pea Ridge for supplies. Sarah had begged and pleaded to be allowed to come along. This, of course, was out of the question; how could he trust her not to slip back into the grip of sin that she had only recently escaped? He had told her no, and she had accepted it docilely. He was sure that before winter had passed he would have her a normal, God-fearing Christian again.

The sun was hanging low in the sky as he fitted a new rail into the last section of broken fence that ran along the outskirts of his property, along the wagon road. He was glad to have the fence completed; this should hold up for at least another year. Also, by the position of the sun and the growling in his stomach, he knew it was almost dinnertime. He wondered abstractedly what she had prepared. Whatever it was, he knew he'd enjoy it, he always did. Sarah was a good cook, better than his mother had been. As a matter of fact, he admitted to himself, he had never really liked —

He heard something — some kind of a noise or call. He looked around in surprise; who was there around this deserted area to be calling him? He heard it again; a low voice calling, 'hello.' Then he saw the man, walking towards him from far down the road.

Sarah added a bowl of cut vegetables to the pot simmering on the stove. She stirred the contents slowly, thoroughly mixing the vegetables with the meat already bubbling in the broth. Early that morning, Henry had butchered one of the young piglets, and she had used the meat to fashion a kind of pork stew. Eating the pork stew usually sickened her with its greasiness, but Henry loved it. 'This stew, and a loaf of corn bread, could be the staples of life, far's I'm concerned,' he had often said. She far from agreed with him but, if it made him happy . . . She had made that her prime concern lately; keeping him happy and contented.

When he was contented, there were no admonitions, no anger, no insults shouted at her and, above all, no cruelty. She had made it her business to keep him in a passive and contented frame of mind by anticipating and doing everything that she knew he would approve of, like their nightly Bible-reading sessions. She not only read the Bible, but had taken the time to memorise the scriptures and verses — had even made sure she was memorising *his* interpretation of those scriptures and verses, odd as they were.

She could vividly remember the times when she was a little girl, and her mother had sat and read that same Bible to her. The stories and verses had been beautiful; filled with faith and love and righteousness; truly something she could take to her heart. Henry's interpretation, on the other hand, was filled with hell-fire and damnation; this one being a sinner and transgressor, that one being a fornicator of little children, and everyone, it seemed, being damned by God. The Bible, which had once been a beautiful and loving thing to her, had been turned, by Henry, into an ugly and hateful piece of literature. But she had read and memorised it the way he chose to see it — because it made him happy.

He also approved of her saying a prayer to God before she went to sleep at night. But the prayer she so fervently mumbled with hands clasped in front of her was not the kind he would have hoped for. Every night she prayed with all her heart and soul that tonight would be the night that her husband died peaceably in his sleep. Upon waking in the morning, before even opening her eyes, she would pray again to find him lying dead beside her. The discovery each morning that he was not would ruin her day.

She looked out the window at the sun, just setting behind the hills in the west; he would be coming home soon. She looked around the room. The house was clean and tidy, the dinner was finished, and there was a cheerful, warm fire going in the fireplace. Good. He would have nothing to complain about today.

She had just placed the Bible on the small table beside his chair where he could reach it easily and was filling his pipe with tobacco when she heard the familiar sound of the pump handle and then the water gushing into the trough. Her husband was home. She tried to quell the nervous, jittery feeling she always seemed to feel at this time, and went to the door to meet him.

Her first response upon opening the front door was that of total, numbing shock. A man — a most handsome man — was walking towards the house, talking animatedly to Henry. She could not believe her eyes. A tall, good-looking man, hair the colour of polished rust, dressed in clothes she had only seen in the Sears catalogue. Here, on this God-forsaken farm, about to walk into the house and meet her.

Closing the door quickly, she turned on her heels and ran into the bedroom. Snatching up the hand mirror she had inherited from her late mother as a wedding present, she looked at herself, hating immediately what she saw. She tried running her fingers through the knots and snarls of her hair; she owned neither a comb nor a brush. Not much better. She looked down at herself and groaned. This dress! How could she let anyone see her in this dress? Oh, it was clean enough; she washed it every time she knew Henry would be away from the house for a while. But still, look at it! The left sleeve was torn, and she had lost the bottom one of the three buttons the night Henry had slapped her. With the bottom button missing, the opening in the front came high up almost to her thighs, almost to her — Well, she thought dismally, I'll just have to be real careful if I sit down, that's all.

She was contemplating sewing up her torn sleeve, when she heard the front door open and close, then: 'Sarah, where are you? We got us a visitor.'

'Damn,' she muttered. Reluctantly, she opened the door and left the bedroom.

'Sarah, come here girl, and meet Mr Connors,' Henry said, by way of introduction. 'He'll be taking supper with us tonight.'

Connors smiled an almost radiant smile that somehow made Sarah feel weak in her knees. 'Please, call me Jimmy — all my friends call me Jimmy.' He turned to Henry. 'Mr Scruggs, you certainly have a beautiful daughter.'

'That ain't my daughter,' Henry corrected him curtly, 'that's my wife.'

'Oh, I do beg your pardon,' Connors said, quickly covering his surprise. He let his eyes quickly sweep over her from head to toe. 'Mrs Scruggs, it is truly a pleasure to

26

meet you.'

'You sure do talk funny,' Sarah said with a giggle. She felt a blush of nervous embarrassment sweep over her face and neck.

'Sarah, watch your mouth,' Henry warned angrily.

'Oh, that's quite all right, Mr Scruggs. I attended school in England, and I guess my speech patterns do sound a bit foreign here in Arkansas.' He continued to stare at Sarah, a little more than would seem polite.

Sarah could not take her eyes off his face. She was fascinated by his neatly combed moustache, which seemed to wiggle and jump when he spoke — like a rusty-red caterpillar riding on his upper lip. In comparison, his hair had a neatly dishevelled look — as though he carefully combed and curled it with a small rake. And his eyes — those piercing blue eyes; they had a way of looking right inside your head; into your soul. Again she could feel the flush of embarrassment; the way he was looking at her . . .

'I cannot express my sorrow for the imposition I've caused you good people,' Connors began explaining, 'but my Ford broke down on the road — '

'Your what?' Sarah asked, puzzled.

'My Ford,' Connors said, looking at her curiously. 'A Ford automobile. My dear lady, this is nineteen twenty-seven; I would think everyone in this day and age knows what an automobile is.'

'Yeah, I seen them, when I was in Pea Ridge,' Henry said, happy in spite of himself at his worldliness. 'Let's you and me go set by the fire and warm ourselves. Give Sarah a chance to get dinner on the table.'

Henry pulled another chair in front of the fireplace, then sat in his favourite chair and lit his pipe. Connors sat down and lit up a long, thin, oddly sweet-smelling cigar he had extracted from a silver case.

'What brings you to this here part of the country?' Henry asked, puffing contentedly on his pipe.

Sarah busied herself setting the table, straining to catch any bits of conversation from the fascinating stranger.

'I'm touring through this part of the country showing and selling an item that a lot of people ignore and do without, but everyone needs and should have. Bibles, sir. Beautiful, personalised Bibles.'

'I got me one,' Henry announced proudly, pointing to the shabby-looking book with its broken binding. 'Couldn't live without it.'

'So I see,' Connors said. 'Is that the King James version?'

'Naw, belongs to me. Belonged to my ma and pa before me.'

Connors smiled politely. 'I didn't mean who does it belong to. I meant is it the King James version of the Bible, as opposed to another version.'

'Don't rightly know what kind it is,' Henry admitted, after thinking about it for a moment. 'Didn't know there's more than one kind of Good Book.'

'There is, Mr Scruggs. Many kinds,' Connors assured him. 'There's the Old Testament, the New Testament — ' He picked up the old Bible and skimmed through it. 'You have the King James version here. Now, as a personal favour, because you nice folks have been so hospitable to me, I can have delivered to you a brand-spanking-new-Bible, with your name printed across the front in beautiful gold letters. And you can have it at cost, Mr Scruggs. *At cost.*' He smiled at Henry enthusiastically. 'How does that sound to you?'

'How much you talking about,' Henry asked, appearing to weigh the offer in his mind.

'Only five dollars, Mr Scruggs. Complete and delivered.'

Henry gave Connors an incredulous look. 'I ain't got near that kind of money. And if I did, I'd buy myself a new pair of boots.' He picked up his Bible again. 'Ain't nothing wrong with this one. It serves me just fine.'

'But wouldn't you like to own something really fine that you could leave as a legacy?' Connors asked, pushing the matter. 'Something beautiful that you can hand down to your children.'

'Ain't got no children,' Henry said simply. 'Never wanted none.' He was too busy with Connors to notice the look of hate that Sarah shot him from where she was ladling stew into the plates at the table.

'Oh, that is a shame, Mr Scruggs,' Connors said, turning around and giving Sarah an appraising look. 'If ever I've seen a young woman designed to have children, it's your lovely wife there.'

28

Sarah had not missed the compliment or the attention Connors was paying her. One glance at Henry's face told her that he did not approve of the direction the conversation had taken. He had turned sullen, and was now sitting back in his chair, puffing slowly on his pipe and staring mutely into the fire.

Connors, also, could not miss the rapid change in Henry's disposition. Quietly he got up from his chair and came over to Sarah. 'Was it something I said?' he asked in a conspiratorial whisper.

'Naw, he just gets kinda moody sometimes,' she answered with a shrug. 'He'll snap out of it after a while.' She returned the pot of stew to the stove.

When she turned around again, Connors was standing right behind her. He stood for a moment looking down at her, locking her eyes with his. 'You are a very beautiful woman,' he said in a low, deep voice. 'But, of course, you know that, don't you?'

'No, reckon I don't,' she answered in a shy voice. She could feel the flush of embarrassment returning to her cheeks.

'Mrs Scruggs sounds so — formal,' he said, his eyes still holding hers. 'May I call you Sarah?'

'Yes, go ahead.' She had a queer, fluttery feeling in the pit of her stomach, and her knees felt as if they were made of rubber. She leaned back slightly to steady herself against the door frame.

'Well, Sarah, I have something in my travelling bag I'd like for you to have — if you'll accept it.' He turned and went to a canvas valise and from one of the side pockets he extracted a silver cross, mounted on a mother-of-pearl backing and hanging from a silver chain. He was very careful not to allow her to see the seventeen identical crosses he had tucked away in the bag.

'This cross belonged to my grandmother,' he said, holding it up in front of her. 'I vowed long ago to only give it to a woman beautiful enough to be worthy of it.' He held the cross out to her. 'I want you to have it.'

Sarah was stunned and speechless. No one had ever given her anything as beautiful as this. 'Oh — no, I couldn't,' she stammered. 'Well, maybe I could,' she retracted. 'I better ask Henry.'

'Here, let me put it on you first,' Connors suggested. Going around behind her, he slipped the chain around her neck.

Whether Connors did it by accident or on purpose, she couldn't be sure, but as he worked the clasp, she could feel him press the length of his body against her back. The nearness of him filled her with an excitement she had never experienced before. She closed her eyes against the feeling. When he locked the chain, and his fingers touched her throat and the back of her neck, she thought she would faint.

'Henry! Henry, look!' she squealed, rushing to where her husband sat still, staring into the fire. 'Look what Mr Connors just gave me!'

Henry's eyes went from the cross dangling around Sarah's neck to Connors. 'Very pretty,' he said, after a moment, 'but it ain't necessary. She don't need nothing like that.'

'Nonsense, sir,' Connors said with a dismissing wave of his hand. 'See how beautiful it looks on her. And I feel it's the least I can do to repay the friendliness and hospitality you're extending to me. Please, Mr Scruggs, let her keep it.'

'Yeah, Henry,' Sarah pleaded. 'Please lemme keep it.'

'Go on and keep it, if it means all that much to you,' Henry said, getting up and moving to the dinner table. 'Now, if you're done fooling with that stuff, let's eat supper.'

All during dinner, Henry remained in his sullen, almost gloomy mood. If he spoke at all, it was only to answer some question in monosyllables. Most of the time he stared into his plate as he ate.

Sarah, on the contrary, was cheerful and full of life. She talked incessantly, pumping and urging Connors to continue talking about himself. She seemed especially fascinated by talk of his travels.

'I've travelled the length and breadth of this wonderful country of ours,' Connors boasted, putting his fork down and pushing his empty plate away. 'I doubt if there's a city or town that I haven't visited at one time or another. I've been everywhere, from the big, beautiful cities like

Chicago and San Francisco, right down to the little one-horse communities like Pea Ridge.'

'Gosh,' Sarah said, her eyes wide with awe and wonder. 'I ain't never been nowhere.'

'In my teen days,' Connors continued, 'I spent many years abroad, travelling in countries such as England, France and Germany. That was, of course, before the big war.'

'What war was that?' Sarah asked. 'I ain't heard about no war.'

'Why, the war to end all wars — the Great War.' Connors looked at Sarah and Henry through disbelieving eyes. 'Don't you people get any news at all, living out here?'

'Naw, guess not,' Sarah answered, shaking her head. 'Tell me about it.'

'England, France and the United States — the Allied countries, went to war with Germany. It was really a terrible thing — lasted years. It was in all the newspapers.'

'Was you in the war, too?' she asked, looking at him almost reverently.

'No, thank heavens. I was back in the United States by then, which was all for the best, as far as I'm concerned — they managed to do just fine without me,' he explained, hurrying quickly past the subject of his wartime involvement. 'The shame of it is that France, and especially Germany, truly beautiful countries when I visited them, are now a total shambles due to the war.'

'Tell me about France. I heard about that place before,' Sarah asked.

'Ah, France,' he said, nodding and smiling at her. 'You'd truly love it there. There has never been a country so full of love and happiness. It is said that the city of Paris never sleeps, and I can testify to that fact, personally.'

'Sarah, you want to get us some coffee,' Henry said testily.

'Sure, Henry,' Sarah answered, snapping out of her fantasy about bright lights and happy people.

As Sarah leaned over to pour Connors his coffee, her left breast brushed against his shoulder. The contact, through the thin material of her dress, made her nipple tingle strangely. The touch was purely accidental and she hoped Connors hadn't noticed. But she found out quickly that he

31

had, because he dropped his right hand casually down behind her and gently squeezed the cheeks of her buttocks. She successfully fought her surprised reaction, even though the caress made her dizzy with sensation. She continued slowly to pour his coffee hoping to God Henry wouldn't notice how her hands were shaking. She shot a quick look at Connors, but to all outward appearances, he seemed completely engrossed in balancing his spoon on the side of his plate. She felt the hand move down slightly, the fingers gently probing at the top of her inner thighs. Given her choice, she would have stood there all night, but seeing that his coffee cup was filled almost to overflowing she took a deep breath and casually straightened up and went around the table to fill Henry's cup. When that was done, she turned back to Connors, and studied his features carefully. Suddenly, she realised the truth about herself. This stranger in her home, this handsome stranger — he was the man she had dreamed of all her life — and she would give herself to him, body and soul, if he asked. At first the thought terrified her; she had never felt such a complete wanting for any man; then her fear was replaced by another realisation — if he was the man of her dreams, she was sure that he could sense her feelings, which was why he had done what he had done. She knew that something would happen between them, the only question seemed to be — when?

'Can I get you anything else?' she asked, looking him squarely in the eye and smiling slightly.

'No, thank you. That should suffice for now,' Connors answered, his voice thick with feeling. 'You've been more than hospitable to me already.'

Henry was still in the grip of the 'spell' that had beset him in front of the fire, and he had not taken notice of the innuendos between his wife and Connors as he sat staring moodily into his coffee cup. Sarah was sure that somewhere in his mind he had already pictured the ground opening up, and the entire wicked and evil country of France being sucked down into an eternity of damnation. So much the better; she had enjoyed her brief semi-aloneness with Connors.

'You can bed yourself down in the barn tonight,' Henry said abruptly, startling Sarah and making her drop the cup

32

she was holding. 'But you gotta be up and away early tomorrow morning. I got a lot of chores to do, and I don't want to be tripping over you.'

'Agreed, Mr Scruggs, and thank you,' Connors replied. Getting up from his chair at the table, he went to his valise. 'You've allowed me to give your wife a present by way of repayment for your hospitality,' he said, taking a new gilt-edged Bible from the travelling bag. 'Now I would like you to accept this, along with my gratitude.' He handed the Bible to Henry.

Henry looked through the book raptly. 'I'll just do that,' he said, nodding. 'Thank you.'

'What're you going to do about your automobile?' Sarah asked, as Connors picked up his travelling bag and went to the door.

'Oh, I suppose if I can walk as far as Bentonville, I'll hire someone to come back with me and tow it into town to be fixed,' he said, shrugging. 'What other choice have I?' He took Henry's hand and shook it firmly. 'Again, thank you for your friendliness, and for sharing what you have with me.'

Something in his words and voice made Sarah blush slightly as she also extended her hand to him.

Connors took her hand. 'As for you, Sarah, it has truly been a pleasure.' He pressed her hand warmly to his lips. 'I bid you both a good night.'

Sarah was too flustered to reply as he went out the door and closed it softly behind him.

Sarah lay wide-awake and motionless on her side of the bed, afraid to do anything that might wake Henry up. She had lain there for what seemed like hours, listening to him snoring and grunting and grinding his teeth − oh, how she hated when he ground his teeth; it would rasp on every nerve in her body. The muscles in her arms and legs ached with cramp and tension, but she dared not move − for him to wake up now would ruin all her plans.

This was the chance she had been waiting for, to get away from Henry, from this loathsome farm, from a life she knew she detested with every fibre of her being. The one chance she could ever hope to have for any kind of real happiness was at this moment asleep in the barn.

She would go to him, beg and plead if she had to — do anything he asked — as long as he took her away with him, away from Henry and this farm.

As carefully and quietly as she could, she slid off the edge of the bed. As her feet touched the floor, Henry let out a loud snort and rolled over on his side. Her heart froze; if he woke up now — ! She remained stock-still for what seemed like an eternity, but finally his rhythmic snoring began again.

She looked quickly around the bedroom, looking for anything she wanted to take with her. She realised that there was nothing — nothing belonging to her that she would want to take — except the damn dress she was wearing. So much the better — she would leave with nothing because, as far as her life was concerned, she was leaving nothing behind.

She quietly tip-toed out of the bedroom and into the front room. There was nothing in here she wanted, either. She said a silent good riddance to everything she hated, then went out the front door, carefully latching it again behind her.

Connors lay contentedly on a pile of hay, his hands folded comfortably behind his head. He gazed up at the shadowy rafters of the old barn and smiled to himself — she'll come, he thought smugly — they always did.

Travelling the farm route as he did, he had met countless young wives or older daughters who, completely discouraged and disgusted with the humdrum lives they led, looked upon him as some sort of knight-in-shining-armour. All you had to do is give the natives a trinket or two, he thought, laughing to himself, and invariably they would come seeking him out for some excitement to fill their otherwise drab lives, and, he patted the pile of straw on which he lay — a good roll in the hay.

There were some parts of the game he played that he found boring. Almost without exception, when the little honey was lying in his arms, he would have to patiently listen to grotesque stories about how this one's husband was mean and cruel to her or that one's boyfriend who lived down the road was cheating on her. There had been some foolish girls who believed that after letting him have them

34

once, he would be all ready to take them away to the city for a life of gaiety and never-ending thrills. One had actually suggested that he kill her husband and marry her — imagine that!

But he made good sport of it. He would agree with them, sympathise with them, console them, and tell them what they wanted to hear — until he was through with them. At that point, he would kiss them tenderly on the cheek, pat them on the fanny, and tell them to go back to their husbands or boyfriends — then he would get the hell out of there, before some enraged male came after him with a shotgun.

He was not at all surprised when the barn door creaked open and Sarah slipped quietly inside.

'Mr Connors, you awake?' she whispered.

Smiling to himself, Connors pretended to be asleep.

Sarah stood for a moment, allowing her eyes to adjust to the shadowy interior of the barn. 'Mr Connors, wake up. I have to talk to you,' she said. Finally, she reached down and touched his shoulder tentatively.

He went through the motions of waking up, stretching his arms over his head and yawning. 'Why, Sarah,' he said in his best sleepy voice, 'I was just dreaming about you.'

'Dreaming? About me?' she asked, kneeling down by his side. 'What was you dreaming?'

'What would I be dreaming about, if I were dreaming of a beautiful woman like you?' he answered smoothly.

'Mr Connors, you got to listen to me, it's very important,' she said, her voice straining to emphasise the urgency through a whisper.

'Why, of course I'll listen to you, my dear,' he said, gently slipping his hand around her waist. 'Tell me what's troubling you.'

'When you leave tomorrow morning, you gotta take me with you,' she said pleadingly. 'If you don't, Henry's gonna kill me. I just know he will.'

Connors groaned inwardly. Oh, no, he thought, not another one whose husband is going to kill her. 'Why, of course I'm going to take you with me,' he said, as if it went without saying. 'I had intended to ask you to go away with me from the first moment I saw you. You're the kind of woman I've always needed.'

'You did . . . I am,' she exclaimed excitedly. 'Oh, Mr Connors, thank you!' She leaned over and kissed him wetly on the mouth.

'We'll go up to Chicago,' he whispered. 'You'll love Chicago, it's so full of beauty and excitement — and love.'

'Oh, Mr Connors! Oh, yes!' She bathed his face with kisses.

'We'll leave just before dawn's first light,' he suggested. 'That will give us the rest of the night to . . . get to know each other better.' He gently unfastened the top button of her dress, and both of her breasts sprang free.

'Oh, Mr Connors — it'll be so wonderful — I'll be so good to you . . . oh, Jimmy, thank you, thank you,' she rambled excitedly.

He carefully undid the last button and the dress opened completely.

She seemed to notice for the first time what he had done. 'Oh, Jimmy, no — not here — not now,' she said, looking down at her exposed body.

'Oh yes, now, Sarah. I want you . . . now . . . ,' he whispered, slipping both hands inside her dress and around her.

'But I ain't never done this before: I'll need time to —'

'You've never made love before?' Connors asked in total disbelief. 'And you've been married for — how many years? Surely you're joking — '

'I ain't joking. It's the truth,' she admitted. 'Henry's kinda . . . odd that way. He don't believe in doing none of that stuff.'

'Well, my dear. You've come to the right place,' he said, pulling her down on top of him. 'You're about to get lesson number one.' He rolled them both over, putting her on the bottom.

'Be careful of my dress,' she whispered, wrapping both arms around his neck, 'it's all I got.'

She returned his kisses and caresses with a surprising passion that soon overcame her lack of knowledge. It was, he thought, time that she learned. He rolled off of her and laid on his back. 'Unhook my belt,' he instructed, 'then the buttons on my pants.'

'You do it, Jimmy,' she said timidly. 'I don't think I could . . . '

'Go ahead,' he urged. 'I can assure you — it won't bite you.'

Gingerly, she unhooked his belt buckle, then slowly undid each of the buttons. As she undid the last button, his erect penis sprang out and stood up straight and tall.

'Golly,' she said in obvious awe, inspecting his manhood closely, 'I ain't never seen nothing like that before. Oh, I seen my little brother when he was taking a bath — but it sure didn't look nothing like that.'

'Touch it, my little dumpling,' he urged. 'Pet it, if you like.'

Carefully, she touched it lightly with her fingertips. 'Ooooh, it feels all smooth an' silky — like under a pig's belly,' she squealed. She took it in both hands and gently began rubbing it. 'Oooh, I like the way it feels,' she announced happily.

'Well, don't like it too much,' he said, between clenched teeth, 'or we're going to waste the whole night — right in the palm of your hand.'

He took Sarah in his arms and kissed her tenderly; gently, he guided her thighs apart and positioned himself between them. He entered her with remarkable ease; there was only a brief moment when her body flinched and she cried out softly, then the full length of him was within her. He began slow, rhythmic strokes, being as careful as he could not to hurt her. Very soon, the upward strokes of her buttocks were matching his with the movements of love.

Her passion was fiercer than he expected, and twice as she writhed and twisted beneath him, he felt her body shudder in orgasm while his passion was still building.

Finally, he could feel his own climax approaching and he slowed his strokes slightly, savouring every sensation, building as slowly as he could.

As his own powerful orgasm erupted and he briefly entered a private world of sexual release, there was a loud slam of the barn door being thrown open. Still in a state of euphoria, he turned his head in time to see the hulking form of Henry Scruggs towering over him and hear his incoherent bellow of rage. He also caught a quick glimpse of the long, thick axe handle the huge right hand was swinging at him, before his head exploded in a profusion of brightly flashing sparks, followed by an engulfing pitch-blackness.

3

Consciousness slowly seeped back into Connor's brain like a wispy, swirling mist, eddying through the avenues and recesses of his mind, then fading again, to be replaced by indeterminate periods of blackness. The brief periods of conscious feeling consisted almost totally of pain; a searing, almost unbearable agony in his head that threatened to wrench his sanity away — then nothing again . . .

Consciousness and pain returned. A scream rose in his throat as a flash of torment shot through his brain. The scream was choked off as, with his sharp intake of breath, his mouth and throat were strangled by a suffocating cloud of dusty grittiness. He coughed violently as the dust entered his lungs; which sent new waves of torture coursing through his head. He lay perfectly still in his agony, praying that unconsciousness would claim him again and eliminate his suffering. This time it did not.

Instead, after what seemed like an eternity, the terrible pain subsided slightly. Slowly he opened his eyes, blinking several times to clear the dust from his lashes and eyelids. He could see nothing but shadowy darkness for as far as he could rotate his eyes; but it was still enough to assure him of what he had already suspected, that he was lying face-down on some kind of dirt floor. He turned his head slightly in order to get a better look at his surroundings, paying the price of another burst of liquid fire through the back of his head. He groaned audibly at the shooting pain, then looked around.

He could barely see where the dirt floor he lay upon met some kind of stone wall. The wall went up, out of his field of vision; obviously, to meet some kind of ceiling. There were other shadowy objects along the wall, but he couldn't make out exactly what they were — some kind of wooden boxes or crates, perhaps. He slowly turned his body over and moved into a sitting position, being as careful as he could not to move or jar his head any more than was necessary. As he moved his legs, there was a jingling, rattling sound and a slight pressure on his left ankle. Looking down, he discovered a chain, twice wrapped around his ankle and fastened with the oldest lock he had ever seen. The chain stretched a short distance across the dirt floor, to where it was sturdily bolted to the centre of a thick wooden beam set into the wall. He took the chain in both hands and pulled with all his strength — the chain held fast.

He looked around dumbly, his mind still not fully comprehending his situation. The area he was in was roughly fifteen or twenty feet square, with an overhead roof of wood planking that he estimated only to be about five feet above him. The mortar where the rough stone walls met the plank ceiling was cracked and separated at a few places, allowing thin shafts of light to enter, and accounting for his only light source.

Numbly, he wondered what he was doing in such a dank, filthy place, then came a sudden flood of recollection; he and Sarah in the barn; the looming figure of Scruggs standing above him; the swinging axe handle . . . With his recollections, came the even more numbing terror of realisation; he was chained to the wall in this hellhole. He was a prisoner!

He became aware that he was naked, that his body was covered with a multitude of cuts and bruises, as if he had been kicked and beaten many times. His limbs felt stiff and sore, but the only real pain was in his head. He tried to stand, but when he did, a nauseating dizziness swept over him and he hit his head on the wood planking above him.

He lay on his back on the hard-packed dirt floor and tried desperately to think. He found rational thought or planning to be impossible, because his mind kept returning to the same horrifying questions; was he condemned to starve and die in this filthy place? Would this madman Scruggs keep him alive only to torture him continually? He was gripped with an irrational feeling of panic, which started as a small, tight knot in the pit of his stomach and spread through his body, flooding his mind with terrifying fantasies. This couldn't be happening to him, his mind screamed. This couldn't be happening . . .

He came awake suddenly with a moving, tickling sensation in his hair and along the side of his face. He realised that he must have either fallen asleep or passed out from pain or fear. The tickling sensation continued. Insects were crawling on his face! he realized. They were in his hair! He brushed his hand along the side of his face and his hand came away sticky with blood. His head was still bleeding. Gingerly, he ran his hand through his hair on the back of his head; the area felt damp and spongy. He wondered abstractedly if his head was cracked open and his brains were oozing out.

He was gripped with a strong feeling of unreality; this was all just a horrible nightmare, and he would wake shortly. He laughed out loud; he knew that this wasn't real, it *couldn't* be real.

He heard the heavy clump of footsteps on the planking above him. He realised for the first time that the ceiling above him was actually the floor of the house. He was under the house in some kind of storage cellar. He heard the wood creaking on the other side of the cellar, and suddenly a trap door was lifted and fell to one side with a bang, revealing a short stairway. He squinted into the bright sunlight pouring through the square hole. It was Sarah, coming to release him, he thought.

He held on to this hope until he caught sight of the heavy work boots coming down the steps. Connors had never felt such total fear of any man as he felt for Henry Scruggs at that moment.

Scruggs sat down on the bottom step and clasped his hands around his knees in an almost childlike position. He grinned at Connors.

'So, you finally come around, huh?'

Connors tried desperately to keep the panic out of his voice. 'What is the meaning of this? Why are you keeping me captive down here?'

Scruggs continued grinning at him. 'Aw, you know why, don't you?' His face turned hard and mean. 'You ain't stupid, are you?'

Connors decided to try a different ploy. He tried to stand up to give himself more stature, but could only achieve a half-crouch. 'All right, Scruggs, so your wife came after me,' he shouted. 'So what? No real harm done. It didn't mean a thing to me, believe me. I'm not trying to steal anybody from you.'

Scruggs kept his voice matter-of-fact. 'Oh, I know you done screwed my wife – I seen you. But there's more to it than that.'

Connors felt the fear returning. 'What more could there be? You caught me, and you beat me up – while I was unconscious, I might add. What more do you want?'

Scruggs seemed to find humour in the question. 'What more do I want?' he chuckled. 'Why, I want to help you – help you find the light of God.'

'What does God have to do with this?' Connors shouted, his voice shaking. 'Your wife comes out to the barn and like to smothers me to death, then in return you damn near broke my head with an axe handle, you kicked me and beat me while I was unconscious, and you threw me down here for heaven knows how long! Isn't that punishment enough?'

'Ain't nearly punishment enough,' Scruggs replied. His face turned serious again. 'Y'know, she told me everything. I ask her the questions, and she give me the answers. We went out to the barn, and we had our own little trial before God – sort of a trial by fire, you might say. And she told me everything.'

'She – told – you – what?' Connors asked softly, his voice faltering.

'How the two of you was in league with the devil,' Scruggs shouted between gritted teeth. 'How you both sold yourselves to Satan for the evils of the flesh! She told me all of it!' He began nodding his head solemnly. 'Oh, she screamed a lot when the devil was driven from her body, and her soul was cleansed by the fire. Then she found her everlasting peace in the arms o' God.'

Connors was almost speechless with horror. 'You – killed her?'

'I wouldn't never kill her,' Scruggs said simply. 'She was my wife, and I guess I loved her. It was the devil being burned out of her body what killed her.'

'You're insane!' Connors screamed. 'You're out of your mind!'

'Why, because I can recognise the ugly face of evil when I see it?' Scruggs demanded, getting up from where he was

41

sitting and starting up the steps. He pointed an accusing finger at Connors. '*You're* evil! You're the vilest animal ever to crawl on the face of the earth. You'll repent your sins before I'm done with you!' He disappeared up through the hole in the floor, to return a moment later carrying something bulky over his shoulder. 'You wanted her — now you can have her!' he shouted, throwing the limp body of his wife down the steps and slamming the trap door closed.

The first thing to assail Connors's senses was an over-powering, sickening odour of cooked flesh. He couldn't believe what was lying in the dirt before him. He crawled forward, straining the chain that bound him to its maximum, until he came within reach of her. He stared at the body dumbfoundedly.

Only curly stubble remained where most of the hair had been burned from her head. The fingers of both hands were curled and charred. The flesh on both her breasts and thighs were scorched and blistered. Then he looked in shocked horror at her face — or what was left of it; at the bulging, sightless eyes, the lips drawn back over her teeth in a last silent scream of death. He felt the revulsion and nausea rising within his throat, and he bent forward to relieve it in a series of racking convulsions.

When the nausea had subsided, he fell limply over onto his side, and lay still. His eyes filled with tears for the first time since he was a child, and he wept softly, repeating over and over again to himself, 'This can't be happening to me. Dear God, this can't be happening.'

Connors gripped the chain tightly in both hands and planted his feet securely against the beam for better leverage. He pulled; the muscles of his body stiffened and flexed with the exertion. No good; his hands, sweating from the exertion, were slipping on the chain.

On closer inspection, he had discovered that the chain was not merely bolted to the beam, but was fastened to a metal eyelet through which the bolt passed. It would have to either be broken off cleanly or literally be wrenched from the beam.

All of his life, Connors had regarded death as something to be dealt with in the far-distant future — certainly nothing to think about now. After all, he was young and strong and he had a lot of living and loving to do. Maybe someday, a long time from now, when he was old and tired and had had enough of life, then, perhaps, he would lie back comfortably and allow death to take him. But, surely, not for a long, long time.

The stark reality of that very possibility was at that moment beginning to dawn on him. He realised that if he did not somehow escape this hellish prison, this would be the place he would die.

Wrapping the chain around both hands for a better grip, he strained against the beam; his taut body nearly lifting off the ground with his effort. It was no use — all that he had accomplished was to nearly break the bones in his hands as the chain squeezed them tightly.

He released the chain and fell limply onto his back. It was no use, he realised. He was trapped here with no possible escape — fettered to the wall like an animal. A feeling of resignation came over him — there was no way he could free himself, and no way in hell that that maniac, Scruggs, would ever change his demented mind and release him. He was doomed to live whatever life was left to him here; to be tortured and starved, beaten and horribly mistreated, until —

No! he thought suddenly, rising up on his hands and knees again, not as long as there's a breath of life left in me.

He gripped the chain again and, planting his feet against the beam, began pulling with every desperate ounce of strength he had.

Connors lay huddled in the corner of the cellar, his body shivering violently. With the onset of winter, the earth was the first thing to absorb the cold. Soon, the surface of the ground would freeze and a thin layer of ice would form. Now, as his naked skin touched the hard-packed ground, the intense chill was transmitted to his body, seeping into his bones.

Even worse for him than the torment of the bitter cold was the agony of his slow starvation. What had started as terrible hunger pangs seven or eight days ago had spread and intensified as the days had passed, until now it was an uncontrollable, all-consuming need. He must have some kind of food, or he would be dead soon.

Scruggs had come back down into the cellar a week ago, screaming and cursing at him, saying that he was nothing more than an animal, a wicked and disgusting animal. And as such, he would make sure that Connors lived like one. 'Like any other disgusting beast,' Scruggs had raved, 'you get hungry enough, you'll eat anything!'

Scruggs had come down to the cellar every morning after that. He'd bring with him a large bowl of water, and nothing more. He'd set the bowl down just within Connors's reach, then turn and go back up the steps, chuckling to himself and reminding Connors again that, 'Animals'll eat anything.'

Connors had rushed to the bowl and drunk its contents thirstily. But, of course, it had not been nearly enough; his body cried out for some sort of solid nourishment.

Connors had not fully understood the meaning of Scrugg's ravings at the time; he did now. But even now, in his weakened and irrational condition, the thought sickened and revolted him. Many times in the last few days he had started across the dirt floor, only to turn back with the grim resolution that he would rather die of starvation than do such an unspeakable thing. He had been wrong.

Connors slowly uncurled himself from the fetal position in which he lay and began crawling hand over hand across the dirt floor. When he reached the end of the length of chain, he stretched his arm out as far as it would go — just far enough to wrap his fingers around the outstretched arm of the corpse that still lay at the bottom of the steps. It took all of what little strength he had left to pull the rigid body towards him, then drag it over to where he had lain.

Ignoring the body's stiffness from rigor mortis, the unspeakable putrid odour of bodily decomposition, he sank his teeth into the unyielding, yellowish flesh of the thigh . . .

Connors released the chain, then crawled over to the shackle to inspect if he had done any damage. His constant pulling and yanking had had absolutely no effect at loosening or in any way bending the shackle or the bolt. But his violent efforts had, in fact, moved the entire beam a fraction of an inch away from where it had been permanently set into the stone wall and dirt floor. He looked closely at the new cracks and chips surrounding the beam, and felt a slight rush of cool air on his face. The beam was still set deeply into the ground, and extended up the wall and securely through the floor of the house. He knew he could never move it any more than he had, but at least that little bit was — something.

He renewed his efforts at the chain again, not so much because he thought he would ever break it, but more because he had found that if he continued to move around and was active, he did not feel the biting cold of the cellar as much.

The nights were the coldest, when he would rest and try to sleep after exhausting himself the entire day. He would lay shuddering from the cold through most of the night, and wake in the early morning, his arms and legs numbed from contact with the freezing ground. As soon as feeling returned to his limbs, he would again set to work pulling and twisting the chain.

Some nights, he would lie for hours listening to the sound of Scruggs's heavy footsteps as he paced the floor above him. What was he doing up there? he'd wonder dismally. Thinking of new tortures and torments for me? Scruggs had not come down to the cellar, not even to bring him water, for nearly a week now. Maybe he thinks if he just ignores me down here, I'll die, he decided. Well, that won't happen — not as long as I've got one ounce of strength left, one breath of life — !

He quickly dropped the chain as he heard the sounds of the trap door being lifted. He scurried across the dirt floor to the shallow hole he had dug for himself in an effort at some kind of protection against the cold. He lay on his side and put a miserably unhappy look on his face — which was not hard to do. He had already learned that the more miserable he looked during Scruggs's taunting visits, the better it seemed to go for him.

Sunlight flooded the cellar as the trap door opened with a bang, and Scruggs came down the steps, this time carrying a bowl of water. He set the bowl down where Connors could reach it, then returned to sit on his usual perch: the bottom step. He looked around the cellar.

'If I'd knowed you was gonna keep such a filthy place,' he said with a chuckle, 'I never woulda let you move in.'

Connors said nothing. He lay still watching Scruggs intently. He had learned the hard way that to shout back at Scruggs or demand to be released — to say anything at all — was to incur his instant and insane wrath.

'You been repenting your sins like I told you to?' Scruggs asked seriously. His eyes fell upon the partially eaten corpse. 'Well, I see you been eating regular,' he taunted. 'When that's all gone, I'll see if I can find you some more tasty little tidbits. What do you prefer, dead rats or pig crap?' He laughed almost menacingly. 'Don't you worry none. I got no ideas about starving you. You're gonna be down here a long, long time.'

Connors still said nothing.

'Talked to God last night,' Scruggs said seriously. 'He told me I was doing real good, punishing you for your sins. That makes me happy — knowing I'm doing the good work.' He looked at Connors closely, at the sores and pimples that covered his face and body. 'You sure don't look so good, boy,' he said, grinning at Connors. He pointed to Connors's ankle, where the chain had chafed and cut into it. 'Have to keep my eye on that — be sure it don't get infected and turn gangrene — else I'll have to cut it off and put the chain on the other one,' he laughed. 'We gotta take good care of you, boy.' He got up and started up the steps. 'Well, don't go nowhere — and I'll be back tomorrow to see how you're doing.' The trap door closed again with a bang.

Connors quickly went back to frantically pulling and twisting the chain again. He could see the truth in what that lunatic had said. Unless he could do something in order to free himself, he would, indeed, be down here for a long, long time.

4

Henry Scruggs sat quietly in his straight-back chair on the front porch of the house, staring vacantly out at the field, now overgrown and choked with weeds and rocks. For the past two years, he had decided not to clear or plant his fields. What was the use, he thought. With God claiming Sarah as he had done, there was no longer any need to keep up the pretence of trading his crop yield in town.

He had never merely traded his produce, but had always sold it at a good price for cash money. Then, after buying only the barest of essentials, had always had quite a bit of money left. He had never told Sarah about the money, fearing she would only want to spend it foolishly on things like new clothes and furniture. Instead, he had hidden it in a hole he had dug in the far corner of the barn, along with the tin box full of paper money his pa had left him when he died. Counting the money, he had discovered he had a little more than two thousand dollars in the tin box — more than enough, he figured, to keep him in supplies for the rest of his life.

He had also discovered the convenience of keeping great quantities of canned goods on hand. The canned foods, when opened, provided him with a clean, untainted food supply — no more eating half-rotten fruit and vegetables for him. He had three sows that, through the efforts of an amorous hog, had provided him with all the young piglets he needed for meat. Also, he had two cows that faithfully provided him with milk. All in all, he figured, he had more than enough of everything he needed to keep him well supplied for a long time to come. And the best part of it, he thought happily, is that he didn't have to do any more hard work for it.

He had missed Sarah greatly at first, even after seeing what treachery and evil she had held in her heart. During an intimate conversation with God — he had had many such conversations since then — it had been explained to him that Sarah had been nothing more than a challenge for him, in order to fully test his moral strength and righteousness. He was told that he had passed the test admirably, by turning his face from her and not succumbing to her vile suggestions and propositions. With no further need for testing him, God had taken her to him for purification, leaving Henry to lead a solitary life of peace and goodness.

He thought back to the time shortly after he had lost Sarah. On an impulse, he had hitched the wagon and gone to speak with her father. He told him the heartbreaking story of how Sarah had up and run off with a travelling man who was passing through. Her family looked saddened by the news, but really hadn't seemed very surprised, telling him that she had always been a wild girl and they'd always been sure she'd come to no good. He left them after making the solemn promise that he would let them know if he ever heard from her again.

Some months later, he learned from God the true origin of the wickedness he held prisoner in the cellar, and his heart almost burst with pride. God had told him that Satan himself had taken human form and had visited his farm, not only to further tempt him, but also to personally reward Sarah for her wickedness in trying to seduce him into hungering and lusting for her flesh. By recognising this evil entity and subsequently trapping and imprisoning it in his root cellar, he had personally rid the world of its evil — an evil he never again intended to release.

The knowledge and pride of what he, above all other men, had accomplished — the total ridding of all evil in the world — that he had personally been blessed by God — also helped to bolster and harden him against living with the almost unbearable odour emanating up through the cracks in the wooden floor and filling the interior of the house. At first it had sickened him terribly: the sight and odour of the piles of human excrement that covered most of the dirt floor in the cellar, the smell of uncounted urinations, the stink of decomposing animal and vegetable matter . . .

Again, God had come to him, explaining that the foulest odour of all came from the evil creature itself — that it was, literally, the stench of evil and corruption extruding from

48

its very pores. It was, Henry Scruggs was sure, what hell itself must smell like.

At first, it had seemed impossible for him to breathe within the choking, eye-burning air of the house. Then, as time passed, his olfactory sense dulled considerably, and now he hardly noticed the odour at all. If, on occasion, it was so strong that he could actually taste it, this would only serve to remind him of the blessed work he was doing for mankind.

The sun was just dipping behind the hills in the west as Henry Scruggs got up from his chair. He picked up the bucket of slop he had scraped from the bottom of the pig trough, his pigs having refused to eat it, and entered the house. It was time to feed his captive.

The small, grey field mouse scurried across the cellar floor for a short distance, then froze in its tracks, eyes darting everywhere, whiskers twitching as its tiny nose sniffed for danger. When it felt assured of its safety, it continued along the floor again in search of food. The mouse had come in through a small, jagged hole underneath the steps, as many other small animals had done; the root cellar being an ideal hunting ground for small bits of corn or wheat.

Connors lay motionless, his body tensing as he watched the mouse make its careful way along the floor. As it neared him, his hand shot out, fingers closing quickly around the startled little animal. With a practised motion, the thumb and forefinger of his other hand gripped the mouse's tiny head and twisted hard. He sat up, grinning happily as he inspected his furry little prize, then quickly stuffed it into his mouth and began chewing zestily.

Simple words could not adequately describe the torment he had suffered in the past two years. The meagre bits of nourishment made available to him could only be described as nauseatingly inedible, but he had eaten them, had eaten anything he could find or catch — and he had survived. When the torrential rains had come, marking the beginning of winter, the water had seeped and trickled through the cracks around the beam his chain was fastened to, turning the dirt floor of his prison first into a morass, then into a frozen hell. He had lain, his body and mind immobilised by the numbing cold — but, somehow, he had survived. At the height of summer, when the cellar was like an oven with its intense trapped heat, he had lain, every breath of air burning his lungs like fire, the mud and filth drying and hardening on him, literally baking his body in its own liquids. He had lain in the unspeakable filth, his body attacked, surrounded, ravaged by a multitude of diseases and parasites — again, miraculously, he had survived.

The years of torment and suffering had effaced any resemblance to the virile, young thirty-four-year-old man first imprisoned in the hellhole of a cellar. All hope of escape was gone. He had realised this fact soon after the first rain, when he had noticed that the beam the chain was attached to had become swollen and waterlogged and had begun to rot. With excitement, he had pulled and twisted the rusting chain for two full days and nights, until he finally collapsed from exhaustion, the chain and bolt still holding fast. That had been his last conscious effort to gain his freedom. If escape was truly out of the question, he resolved, then he would concentrate on simply surviving . . .

That had been almost two years ago. Now, as his body and mind had slowly degenerated with repeated submissions to his hopelessness, he had become more and more like an imprisoned animal, docilely living one day after another in his confinement, gradually limiting all rational thought to the basic instinctive rituals of finding food and protecting himself from the cold. No more did he contemplate such things as escape or freedom — such abstract thoughts were well beyond him now.

He scrawled slowly across the filthy dirt floor, heading towards the wall where some drooping, brown weeds had pushed their way up through the ground. As he crawled, his bare knees flattened and moved the piles of excrement in his path, exposing colonies of the writhing white round-worms that almost totally infested his digestive system. Reaching the wall, he pulled up a small clump of the weeds and began eating them. He noticed a small, grey spider crawling up the rock wall; it, too, was added to his meal.

The sound of the trap door being lifted made him turn and crawl quickly towards the steps until he reached the end of the chain. He then sat down and began grinning expectantly — he knew what this meant — food!

Scruggs came down the steps carrying the pail of slop. He stood for a moment, silently staring at the grinning face in front of him, with its wild, staring eyes and chipped and broken teeth. He had given up taunting and threatening Connors, any conversation at all for that matter, a long time ago. Now, he only came down into the cellar when he had to feed his prisoner, then left immediately.

Scruggs emptied the pail containing bits of rotting vegetables floating in a thick brown and green mush on the ground in front of him. He banged the pail a few times to loosen and remove the residue still clinging to the bottom, then went quickly back up the steps, closing the trap door behind him.

Connors hesitated only until he saw the trap door slam closed, then he sprang forward, scooping up the thick concoction with both hands and taking it into his mouth greedily. When it was completely gone and he had licked his fingers clean, he crawled over to the corner of the cellar where he had long ago dug a shallow hole. The hole and its immediately surrounding area were relatively clean in conparison to the rest of the cellar floor. Once there, he flopped over on his side and, sighing contentedly, was asleep within a matter of minutes.

PART 2

5

As the years passed, the unrelenting forces of nature, the world of living, growing things encroached steadily on the small farm, all but wiping out the traces of its fields. What had been cleanly ploughed and furrowed acres were now shaggy, overgrown meadows of thick brush and small trees. Where once the low-slung farmhouse and barn had been visible from the road, now so overgrown was the land that the only evidence of former habitation was the rotting and broken split-rail fence that ran along the all but forgotten wagon trail for some three hundred yards.

A casual memory of Henry Scruggs had been kept alive by the older residents of Pea Ridge. Someone around the stove in the general store might ask, 'What ever happened to that old religious nut, Scruggs? Ain't seen him around for — ten, maybe twelve years.' Everyone would scratch their heads and shrug. No one knew. Gradually, as the small community of Pea Ridge grew, spread out and prospered, and as the population doubled, then tripled, the old-timers died off and were replaced by new young residents to whom the name of Henry Scruggs was entirely unknown.

Henry Scruggs gritted his teeth and rolled on his side in bed as a sharp pain shot through the left side of his chest. What had started only as twinges of discomfort in his chest and left arm a few weeks ago had gradually gotten much stronger. Now, when the severe pains began, they came with crippling effect. He lay now holding his breath, eyes squeezed shut until the pain subsided. He remained still for a few moments longer, his body tensely awaiting another onslaught of the agony. When none came, he slowly let out his breath and sat up in bed.

The passing years had not been kind to Scruggs. As old

age crept up on him, his once powerful body had shrunk and withered to an almost feeble condition. Now, at seventy-one, he had dwindled to a shadow of his former stature; a frail, dried up old man, barely able to get around by himself.

Throwing back the soiled blanket that covered him, he carefully placed his feet on the floor and stood up shakily. He took a deep breath of the stale, fouled air of the bedroom and was immediately gripped with a fit of hacking coughs. The spasms finally subsided but left his throat raw and his lungs burning painfully. The cough had been getting progressively worse in the last few months — or years maybe . . . he hadn't paid much attention until lately. He wiped his tearing eyes with a corner of the blanket, then slowly shuffled out of the bedroom and through the house, nearly tripping over the pile of empty tin cans that covered the floor.

Going out the front door, he made a mental promise to himself about clearing out the empty cans before he fell over them and broke his neck. He thanked God for his huge stock of canned goods; without them, in his sick and weakened condition, he would have starved to death long ago. He stopped on the porch and picked up a canvas sack lying across his chair. Using the wooden porch railing for support, he carefully hobbled down the steps and went out across the overgrown front yard to where he had set out his rat traps.

As his health had diminished and left him increasingly weak, he had limited himself to two activities each day: reading and intimately discussing the Bible with God, and the now nearly exhausting task of feeding his prisoner. He continued the feeding, though the effort strained him terribly, because God had instructed him to do so. God had explained to him on many occasions through the years that Satan would only be imprisoned as long as the body trapping his evil spirit continued to live. If his captive in the cellar were allowed to die, the evilness trapped within the body would again be released upon the world. Scruggs had solemnly sworn to the Lord that he would continue feeding and keeping the body alive until his own dying breath.

Reaching his traps, he noted with satisfaction that he had caught four large rats during the night; more than he

56

actually needed. He emptied each trap in turn into the canvas sack, being extremely careful to keep his fingers away from the small, snapping jaws of the terrified rodents. He tied the mouth of the sack securely with a piece of cord, then turned and trudged slowly back towards the house.

It was strange, he thought. Usually the numbing ache in his left arm that accompanied the pains in his chest would disappear as soon as the pains were gone. This time it persisted — a tingling, prickly sensation in his fingers and arms, as if the circulation had been cut off and his arm was going to sleep. He switched the canvas sack to his right hand, then began opening and closing his left fist rapidly, hoping to relieve the ache a little.

As he climbed the steps to the porch, he felt the now-familiar symptoms begin. Quickly he sat down on the top steps and braced himself for the pain he knew was coming, as first the tingling numbness began throbbing painfully in his arm, then the prickles of pain began around his left breast. He gritted his teeth as the first really crippling bolt of pain sliced across his chest. He almost cried out as a second pain shot from his left shoulder, across his chest and into his stomach. The third excruciating paroxysm was the worse ever, doubling him over with its sheer intensity, and only his tight grip on the porch railing kept him from tumbling down the steps.

As the pains finally subsided, he allowed himself to gently fall backwards onto the porch. His entire body felt drained, completely emptied of strength. The world around him was spinning dizzily, and he found it impossible to focus his eyes. He lay still for a few minutes and breathed deeply through his mouth, hoping to rid himself of the vertigo. His body was drenched with perspiration; the slight breeze blowing across the porch chilled him, but seemed to help somewhat.

This had been the worst attack yet, he thought abstractly as he lay with his eyes closed and listened to his own heartbeats thundering in his ears; it was like something had ripped through his chest and had taken his heart in the grip of some powerful implement of torture.

He finally attempted getting to his feet but found it necessary to lean against the railing until the last of the dizziness had passed. He reached down and picked up the canvas sack, thankful that the rats he had caught had not had time to gnaw their way out. He stumbled into the house and over to the corner of the room that served as the kitchen, where he washed his face with some cold water from a basin. This made him feel somewhat better, in spite of the persistent dull ache in his left arm and shoulder.

What was happening to him? he wondered. He had never been sick, or even felt poorly for a single day of his life that he could remember. He decided that it must have something to do with the malevolent presence trapped in the cellar. As he got older, he reasoned, his body became more susceptible to Satan's evil influence – thus the terrible pains he'd been suffering. He wouldn't have to worry about it, he thought. God had chosen him and had always protected him. He felt sure that God would continue to deliver him from evil.

Picking up the canvas sack, he approached the trap door. Grasping the worn leather thong in his right hand, he pulled hard. The ordeal he had suffered moments before had weakened him more than he had realised – he could only lift the trap door about six inches before it banged shut again from its own weight. He debated whether to attempt it again, but even that slight strain had brought pinpricks of pain back into his chest. He decided that this time he would leave the trap door open, and not have to undergo the exertion of lifting it again.

Gripping the leather thong securely in both hands, he pulled with all his strength, the muscles of his frail arms and chest flexing with the exertion. The trap door rose only waist-high, its rusty hinges squeaking in protest. He held the wooden door for a few seconds; then, taking a deep breath and gritting his teeth from the strain, he reversed his hands so that his palms rested against the underside of the door. With all the power he could muster, he pushed.

As the trap door flew over and hit the floor with a dusty bang, a shattering pain exploded in Scruggs's chest. So utterly crippling was this new pain that his entire body went rigid, hands clutching his chest, eyes bulging. He stood frozen, teetering for uncounted seconds on the brink of the stairway that yawned like a dark eternity below; then his body sagged and he pitched forward, his head striking the top step as he tumbled down.

Scruggs was dead before his body hit the dirt floor of the cellar.

The thing that used to be Connors stirred in the corner of the cellar. He turned his head towards the dull light filtering in through the open trap door, bringing out of the shadows a face so overgrown with snarled hair as to make sight nearly impossible. He had heard the familiar noise of the trap door banging open, then something tumbling and clattering down the steps. This was the usual way of things at feeding time, a routine he recognised. The creature — for he was decidedly more animal than man — licked his scabbed lips in anticipation. The new arrival sounded much bigger than usual.

Imprisoned in the same fetid pit for over fifteen years, the man-creature had degenerated tremendously. His entire world consisted of the concentration and development of basic instincts and the routine of survival — he ate, he slept, he reacted, he existed.

His hand moved up slowly, parting the thick tangle of hair in front of his face. Then he lay completely still, eyes intently watching the body sprawled in the dirt. This immobility was necessary to keep the rusty links of his fetters silent until the inquisitive prey got within the scope of the chain; then a quick lunging grab, a killing bite and the meal was his.

He waited.

Still no movement from the body.

Confusion spread in the creature's brain. He sniffed the air but could detect nothing familiar. He raised his head again and relaxed his taut muscles. From deep in his throat came a low groan. Slowly he crept forward, muscles hairtrigger tense again, ready to pounce at the slightest movement.

At a point only four feet from the body, he hit the end of his chain. When there was no movement even now, it became obvious — even to the creature's simplified mind — that the body was not going to escape.

By lying flat and extending an arm, he brought his groping fingers to within six inches of the body's leg. The creature strained against the chain, trying to shorten the distance.

It had been years since any great strain had been put on the chain, so accustomed had the creature grown to pacing within its limits. The wood around the bolt began to splinter from the long years of dry rot and decay. A colony of termites had long ago infested the rotting beam, which served from time to time as a tasty source of food but also had further weakened the wood. As the pressure on the chain continued, the rotting wood began crumbling in a tiny rain of splinters and moldy powder, and the bolt securing the chain loosened.

Clutching fingers clawed the earth, a bare two inches from the outstretched body, but still could not reach the gigantic prize. In one enormous effort the creature reared up on hands and knees and threw the full weight of his body forward, both hands stretching out desperately.

The sound of the bolt being torn at last out of the rotting wooden beam and the jangle of the chain dropping to the ground was completely lost to the creature as he fell on the body, his teeth ripping into the flesh . . .

After gorging himself on the unaccustomed bounty, the creature raised his head. Fresh blood mixed with saliva oozed from the corners of his mouth and dripped from his tangled beard. He stared up the short stairway through frightened eyes; he cocked his head in confusion and the painful dazzle of daylight coming in from up above. Emitting a low growl, the creature turned and, dragging the loose chain behind him, crawled back across the cellar floor to his familiar place in the corner. He lay on his side with a satisfied grunt and began contentedly scratching at the thick mat of hair that covered his entire body, hair which at one time had been soft and springy but had sprouted more thickly into a shaggy mass of curly fur over the years of resisting the harsh elements in which he had survived. Within a short time, the creature was asleep . . .

In the two weeks that followed, the creature consumed every edible fragment of the body, leaving only a picked-clean skeleton. He then waited docilely for the familiar routine of being fed again.

The creature woke abruptly in the dark as something thumped to the floor and rolled across the wood planking above him. He lay completely still, eyes darting quickly around the cellar, ears straining to hear the slightest sound. Nothing moved: silence. He looked up from under his mane and sniffed the foul air, but his senses could identify nothing. Emitting a low growl of frustration, he began to search the confines of his cellar world for the fourth time in as many nights, hoping to find something — anything — edible.

After being nearly five days without food, the creature's unfamiliar sensation of hunger had intensified into a bewildering, frenzied need. Digging and searching in the cellar had done little good; the tiny, withered fungi and small insects he had found could not come close to quelling his almost ravenous hunger. He had gnawed and sucked all the marrow from the bones of the skeleton, and his attack on the bones themselves succeeded only in breaking two of his already cracked teeth.

Finding nothing to eat during his scavenging of the cellar, the creature was picking again through the scattered pile of bones at the foot of the steps when he heard the sound of a small animal scurrying across the floor above, followed by the rattle of tin cans. The creature froze, eyes staring intently up the steps, ears straining. The sound came again: the unmistakable tapping of tiny claws against the wooden floor as something scrabbled across the room. The creature licked his lips quickly.

The creature crept silently up the steps, slowly, like a large cat stalking its prey — driven by his voracious need past the familiar limits of his world. The only sound that could be heard was the clinking of the chain he dragged behind him. As the creature's eyes came level with the surface of the wooden floor, he froze, body tense and ready, legs bent under him like coiled springs. He strained his senses for another sign of movement.

The darkened interior of the house was as silent as a tomb. Furniture and objects along the floor cast long, mingling shadows, their shapes lost in a general haze of deep greys and blacks.

The creature waited. Only his eyes moved, darting quickly along the floor from one side of the room to the other, searching.

A large grey and brown rat scurried out from the shadows beside the fireplace and across the floor. When it paused momentarily near the mountainous pile of garbage to sniff at an empty tin can, the creature sprang, hands reaching out in front of him, fingers curled like hooks. Slightly off-balance when he leaped, the creature slid along the floor and collided with the mound of garbage, sending it scattering. The rat escaped easily and disappeared into the shadows again.

The creature got slowly to his hands and knees, eyes sweeping the room — nothing moved, silence. The only source of illumination was a stream of pale moonlight coming in through a window. It slanted in a long triangle across the wooden floor, illuminating part of the room. Straightening a bent-legged crouch and supporting his weight in front of him with his arms — looking and moving much like an emaciated gorilla — the creature made his way to the window and looked out at the overgrown, shadowy front yard in amazement.

The bright three-quarter moon hanging just over the trees in the overgrown forest of a front yard gave a shadowy landscape a blue-hazed, almost luminous appearance. Small animals moved about in the underbrush in their nightly foraging for food. As the creature watched wide-eyed, a rabbit scampered out of the thick underbrush and began grazing on a patch of lush, green grass under a tree.

The creature stared at the scene before him in total confusion. In comparison to the cramped confines of the barren, dark cellar from which he had just come, the sight of a forest alive and moving with life was as foreign as the mountains of the moon. He hesitated a moment, stricken with fear of the unknown, but his almost ravenous need for food took over again and he leaped forward, smashing headlong through the unseen glass of the window and landing on his back on the porch amid a shower of broken glass. He scrambled to his feet immediately, then leaped from the porch. With the same crouching, gorilla-like gait he took off across the high grass towards the forest beyond.

As the creature entered the overgrown tangle of trees and bushes, he sucked in a deep breath of the clean, sweet night air, then let it out in a loud growling howl. The creature was now gripped with an exhilaration, a mindless excitement that overshadowed even his ravenous hunger: the incredible feeling of — freedom!

6

The way of life in Benton County had changed dramatically through the last decade and a half. The small squatter's shacks and one-family dirt farms that had dotted the countryside in the 1920s were all but gone now, the land being bought up at low rates in immense tracts by rich cattlemen and farming combines. By June of 1942, large cattle ranches and farming companies, each stretching for miles in any direction, covered the rich, fertile land of the valley and delta. This new breed of landowner — more of them businessmen than ranchers and farmers — prospered through the use of the newest scientific equipment and techniques, and achieved high production ratios unheard of only a few years before.

During a land boom in the 1930s, the Continental-Pacific Lumber Company bought up over 300,000 acres of prime timberland, including a two-mile stretch along the White River where it built its large sawmill complex.

The tiny village of Pea Ridge, located only thirteen miles from the sawmill, grew and prospered almost overnight. Where not so long ago it had been a proverbial one-horse town with only 56 residents and shopkeepers, in just four short years it had grown and spread until it now boasted a population of over 6,700 residents — most of whom drew their livelihood from the sawmill. New businesses flocked to Pea Ridge, buying property and opening shops and stores to accommodate the increase in population. A land development company bought up hundreds of acres of land on the outskirts of town, then erected rows of flimsy, look-alike tract houses with cheap local lumber, selling them to the incoming residents at a huge profit.

The sudden boom in land development and farming, centered as it was on the Pea Ridge sawmill, left vast stretches of overgrown wilderness lying not far out of town to the north. These areas were too densely overgrown, hilly and rocky for cultivation by the farming or ranching companies, and the clearing of them would be too expensive to be practical for land development. These unsold areas were left untouched and in their natural state — exceptionally beautiful forestland, ideal for hunting and fishing.

Although most of the population of Pea Ridge lived within, or just outside the town, there were some people who preferred the unspoiled tranquility of the rural belt around it. People who enjoyed the seclusion of the backwoods along the tributaries of the White River, while still being within driving distance of town via the dirt logging roads. People who enjoyed the fresh, clean air of the forest, yet lived close enough to town to work at the sawmill. People like Eli and Carolyn MacCleary.

Carolyn MacCleary removed her bathrobe, folding it neatly onto a chair in the bathroom. Gingerly, she tested the temperature of the bathwater with the toes of her right foot before stepping into the tub and sinking slowly into the warm, sweet-smelling bubbles. She let out a long sigh as her head reached the back of the tub and the warm, fragrant bubbles swirled around her chin; it felt so relaxing and good after a long, tiring day.

The warm bubble bath towards the end of the evening was one of the few real luxuries she allowed herself in an otherwise plain, rustic existence. She always took it an hour or two before Eli was due home from working late-shift at the sawmill, after the housework and chores for the day were completed and their late dinner was simmering on the stove. By the time Eli got home, all of her tiredness, tension and anxiety had been washed down the bathtub drain with the bubbles. She would be soft and sweet-smelling, and waiting happily to greet him. This, she thought, was the way a man should be greeted after a long, hard day at work.

She could easily admit to herself now that she loved Eli with all her heart, and that the last four years she had spent married to him had been the happiest she had ever known. But, she thought ironically, it had taken her almost the entire first year of their marriage just to get beyond his gruff exterior and discover the wonderfully loving and giving man within. They had seemed like such opposites at

64

first; she, friendly and outgoing; he, withdrawn, blunt and moody. She still could not recall their first meeting without laughing – he had scared the hell out her . . .

She had been working as a waitress at the Pig an' Cluck Diner in Pea Ridge. At a few minutes past midnight, they were in the middle of their second dinner rush as the men on the late shift at the sawmill came off work. She was busy taking food orders and skilfully dodging bawdy suggestions and passes aimed at her by the men sitting at the tables and counter when she happened to glance up and see a new man come in. He was easily a head taller than the other men he came in with and looked to be at least twice as broad. He seated himself alone at the first stool near the cash register and looked sullenly down at his hands. After writing down the order she was taking, she moved down the counter to stop in front of him.

'What'll it be?' she asked.

'Just coffee and – ' he started to say, looking at her for the first time. He didn't complete the order, he just stared at her.

'Come on, what'll it be?' she urged curtly. 'I got a hundred guys waiting.'

'You gotta be the most beautiful gal I ever seen,' he said, a touch of wonder finding a way into his deep baritone voice.

'Yeah, and I got great legs, too,' she answered. It had been a long night. 'Come on, what're you having?'

'Nothing,' he said, shaking his head slowly. 'Just coffee.' He kept staring at her.

'Okay,' she said simply, and turned around to pour him a cup. She set the coffee in front of him, then went on to take care of other customers. Everywhere she went in the diner, she could feel his eyes on her. She found it unnerving.

'No more beer for you, Jeff,' she told one of the lumberjacks. He was a regular in the diner and she knew his limit better than he did. 'You've had enough.'

'Aw, come on, baby. Don't kill my party,' the lumberjack said, his words already slurred from too much beer.

'Sorry, Jeff,' she answered with a shrug. 'You want more beer, you'll have to go somewhere else.'

'Hey, Carolyn,' he said, with a clumsy grab for her that she easily avoided, 'when you-all gonna lemme get into that sweet little pussy of yours?'

She was just turning around again, ready with a stinging remark, when the lumberjack suddenly rose into the air, picked up by the belt and the back of his shirt in the beefy fists of the new man at the counter.

'You talk to this gal, you talk to her right,' he rumbled through clenched teeth, 'or I'm gonna break your head.' He left the lumberjack suspended for another few seconds then lowered him to the floor again. 'Now, I think maybe you should apologise,' he said, and released him.

'Hell,' the lumberjack said, suddenly more sober. 'I'm sorry, Carolyn. I sure didn't mean nothing by it.'

Carolyn barely heard the apology, she hardly heard any sound at all. She was staring transfixed at the towering figure, frightened by his strength but still strangely excited by the power and self-assuredness of the man who had already declared himself to her. She felt drawn to him physically — could, in that brief instant, vividly imagine herself being taken by him, her naked body ravished by his. The thought sent a hot flame of passion through her, a tingle that made her weak in the knees, then the fantasy passed and the sounds of the diner came back to her.

Clyde, the owner, had come rushing out from behind the counter. 'All right, come on fellas, no trouble in here, okay? I don't want to have to call the sheriff.' He put his five-foot-eight-inch body between the two huge men in an effort to keep them separated.

'It's over.' Eli stated simply. 'This boy's just gotta learn to have some respect for a lady.' He turned and walked back to his seat at the counter, picking up his coffee cup again.

He sat there, drinking coffee and watching every move she made, until closing time at 2:00 A.M., when he left grudgingly with a half a dozen other stragglers who had hung around for want of something better to do.

After checking out the cash register and tidying the counter-top, Carolyn was ready to leave for the night. She saw the pickup truck and the shadowy figure seated behind the wheel as soon as she went out the door of the diner. She felt a momentary surge of panic. Who was this man? What did he want from her? Swallowing hard, she tried to pretend she had not noticed him as she turned left and walked quickly down the street. If I can only reach the rooming-house, she thought, then I'll feel better, then I'll be safe. Behind her, the silence was maddening: only the sound of her heels clicking on the pavement as she walked down the dark street. Suddenly, the truck engine roared to life and she followed the sound of the truck idling slowly down the street behind her. Gritting her teeth to keep the fear she she felt from escaping, she kept walking straight ahead.

The truck veered over to her side of the street and pulled up alongside her. 'Carolyn,' she heard the rumbling voice say, 'hold on a minute. I want to talk to you.'

She stopped, figuring whatever was coming, was coming now. She turned and faced him almost fiercely. 'What do you want?' she shouted, hoping someone would hear, or at least that she could scare him off. 'Why are you following me?'

'I don't want nothing,' he answered in that voice that was like an earthquake yet strangely gentle. 'I just want to talk to you, get to know you. I —'

A giggle, then a fit of uncontrollable laughter erupted from her throat with the realisation and relief that this man, whom seconds ago she vividly pictured herself being raped and murdered by — was nothing but a big, lonely pussycat who wanted to be her friend. The laughter continued as her tension and fear drained.

'Don't laugh at me, Carolyn,' he said harshly. 'Don't never laugh at me.'

She took a step closer to the cab of the truck. 'I wasn't laughing at you, big fella,' she said soothingly. 'It's just that — well, you gave me kind of a scare, coming up on me like that.'

'You don't never got to be afraid of me, Carolyn,' he told her gently. 'I'd never do nothing to hurt you.' He reached across the seat and opened the passenger-side door of the truck. 'Get in, I'll drive you home.'

She hesitated an instant, then went around and slid onto the seat next to him.

'You didn't have to do what you done back there in the diner,' she said as they drove slowly down the street. 'Them boys, get a little rowdy sometimes, but they don't mean no harm.'

'Well, they shouldn't be talking to you like you was a

67

whore or something,' he answered with conviction.

'And how do you know I ain't a whore?' she teased. 'How do you know anything about me? I could be the wickedest woman you ever seen.'

'Well, you ain't, I can tell,' he said simply. Then he seemed to reconsider. 'Are you?'

'No, of course not,' she answered, laughing again. 'Oh, I admit I lead the boys on a bit. They love it and it's good for the tips, but the truth is, Carolyn Sanders is a good girl.' She gave him a sly look. 'And I aim to stay that way, so don't go getting no ideas.'

'I, no — never,' he swore, looking a little less innocent than before.

'Well, why the hell not?' she asked, back to teasing him. 'Something the matter with me?'

'No, I didn't mean . . . you're fine . . . ' he mumbled, finally flustered.

'By the way,' she asked, changing the subject, 'what's you name, anyway? I can't keep calling you big fella.'

'Eli — Eli MacCleary,' he answered almost shyly.

'Pleased to meet you, Eli,' she said, taking his hand and shaking it with mock formality. Out of the corner of her eye, she studied him. He had to be at least six-five or six-six, broad shoulders, well built. Brown hair and eyes — rugged yet kind of a handsome face, she decided. He struck her as being more man than any three she knew combined.

He suddenly pulled the truck to a stop in the middle of the street. He turned to her, dead seriousness on his face. 'If I tell you something, Carolyn, you promise not to laugh at me?'

'Sure,' she said, eyeing him carefully. 'What?'

'I met a lot of gals in my time,' he said slowly. 'Ain't none of them come anywhere close to you.' He took a deep breath, as if he were trying to boost his courage. 'Carolyn,' he went on, serious as before, 'no matter what I gotta do, and no matter how long it takes me — I'm gonna marry you.'

She looked at him in shock. They had known each other barely ten minutes. He looks serious, she thought, but he can't possibly *be* serious . . .

Carolyn and Eli were married a little less than three months later.

Carolyn reluctantly left the warmth of her bath and, taking a large Turkish towel from its rack by the side of the tub, briskly towelled herself dry. She found the towelling ritual as invigorating as the bath itself; she loved it. She looked at her nude body in the full-length mirror that was mounted on the back of the bathroom door. Not bad for thirty years old, she thought to herself, at least nothing's sagging or getting flabby yet. She ran her finger lightly over her narrow waist and firm belly and thought uneasily about what having children was going to do to her. The inevitable little paunch of fat, those terribly ugly stretch-marks . . .

They had been trying to have a child for the last two years now, but so far with no success. She knew that having a child was very important to Eli, but as far as she was concerned, it was something she would happily put off for as long as possible. To her, having a baby meant more work and more responsibility — two things she could easily do without. Not to mention the devastating effect it would have on her figure . . .

Slipping into her terry-cloth bathrobe, she looked critically at her face in the mirror. Little lines and creases were beginning to appear around her eyes and the corners of her mouth; she looked at them with genuine loathing. She was sure that she would have crow's-feet within the year. She ran her fingers through her long, chestnut-brown hair, which hung nearly to her buttocks and shone with silky brilliance from its hundred-strokes-a-night brushing. She knew that her long hair and pale-green eyes were her most attractive features, and she wanted to keep them beautiful for as long as possible. The world could be coming to an end and her hair would still not miss its nightly brushing.

Leaving the bathroom and heading towards the kitchen, she nearly tripped over Charlie, the golden retriever who lay spread-eagled and snoring quietly on the floor. Eli, an avid hunter, had insisted they get Charlie, not only as a companion for him when he went on his frequent hunting jaunts, but also as company and protection for her when she was alone at night. Although she didn't show it as much as Eli did, she loved the dog dearly.

Cussing the dog silently, she went into the kitchen to check dinner. Tonight they were having spare ribs, corn-on-the-cob and mashed potatoes — all Eli's favourites — and everything was done. Turning the flame off under the boiling corn, she glanced at the wall clock. Eleven forty-five — good, she thought. I'll have almost an hour to get into that book I've been trying to read, before Eli gets home . . .

She looked around the tidy living room for her book and found it on a table in the corner under some magazines. Taking the book, she settled in her favourite easy chair and marvelled again at how quickly she had adapted to living outside of town.

She had made it clear to Eli right from the start that she had no pioneer blood in her and could not live with just the bare necessities, as he had done. In order to make her happy, he had single-handedly added another room to the house, modernised the kitchen and bathroom, and had either made by hand or bought any and all the furniture she needed. The one and only luxury she was still without was a telephone, but the telephone company in town had told them that it would be far too expensive to string wire all the way out to their house just for one family.

She had been reading for about twenty minutes when Charlie suddenly sat bolt upright on the floor, eyes staring intently at the front door, ears alert and tuned to some unfamiliar sound heard only by him. She was startled by the dog's sudden movement and mildly alarmed by the tense way his body shook.

'What's the matter, Charlie?' she asked, making light of it in her own mind. 'You hear something?'

In answer, the dog emitted a low, throaty growl, and was immediately on his feet and moving towards the front door, where he alternated between staring at the door and staring at her.

She got to her feet and went to open the front door, almost being knocked over by the dog as he jumped around in whining anticipation. As soon as the door was opened, the dog took off with a barking growl and disappeared within seconds into the thick foliage that bordered the front yard of the house. Moving out onto the wooden porch, she could hear him in the distance, barking wildly at whatever it was he was pursuing.

She sat down on the top step of the porch and took a deep

breath of the clean, sweet night air. In the distance, she could hear Charlie, still yapping at whatever he was chasing. His aggressive bark suddenly turned to a high-pitched yelp of pain. She laughed to herself. Sounds like poor old Charlie done bit off more'n he could chew, she thought. Probably cornered hisself a raccoon or a skunk and it bit him on the nose. Poor, brave old doggie, she thought, shaking her head. My hero.

She looked up into the clear night sky at what seemed like a million stars, all blinking back at her. A huge, orange-tinged full moon hung in the sky just above the treetops. She loved to sit out on the porch on nights like this with Eli . . . the starry sky always filled her with such wonder . . . it was all so big, so beautiful . . .

She realised abruptly that she had not heard the dog bark for — how long had it been? Five minutes? Fifteen minutes? She had lost track of the time while lost in stargazing.

'Charlie,' she called, getting to her feet and walking down the path in the direction the dog had gone.

There was no answering bark, no response whatsoever. He was probably playing possum to get more attention.

'*Charlie,*' she shouted sharply. 'Here, Charlie! Where the hell are you, dog?' She reached the line of underbrush he had disappeared into. Pulling her bathrobe tighter around her, she carefully parted the thickly tangled bushes and stepped through. 'Charlie,' she called again. There were no sounds at all now, except the sound of her own voice. She wanted to go back to the house, but would feel better if the dog was with her.

The atmosphere of the forest at night soon unsettled and unnerved her. The same lush, green foliage and stately, picturesque trees that during the day portrayed such a beautifully tranquil scene, by night seemed to take on a hideous, shadowy life of their own. The always moving shadows seemed to be closing in on her; the tree branches, like long, skinny talons, scratched and clawed at her. Behind every tree and clump of bushes a shadow demon seemed to lurk, waiting for her to pass. Once, she almost cried out in terror as something scurried out of the bushes and across her bare feet, then disappeared again into the underbrush. The intense fright made her dizzy for a moment, but she mastered it and began walking again.

She stopped momentarily as she came to a small, shadowy clearing. She strained her ears to listen for a sound, any sound. She heard nothing; no birds, no familiar chirping of the crickets — nothing but the sound of the wind gently rustling the boughs of the trees above her, and her own heartbeat banging in her ears. She debated for the hundredth time in the past five minutes whether or not she should turn and run away, back to the safety of the house. No, she decided. It was all her imagination. If she would only calm down and stop imagining a lot of scary things that weren't really there, then there was nothing out here in the forest that could hurt her. She took a deep breath in an effort to calm her nerves. She had to keep looking for Charlie. He might be scratched up and probably needed her. Admittedly, the forest at night was an eerie place to be, but if she could only keep her wits about her, she'd be all right.

She started walking again, searching the underbrush for any sign of the dog. She was sure that he couldn't have gone far; he had to be around there somewhere. 'Charlie,' she whispered, somehow not feeling brave enough to call him out loud.

As she reached the other side of the clearing, she heard some sounds; a series of sharp, cracking noises. She stopped again to listen. Although she couldn't readily identify the sounds; they seemed vaguely familiar; like something she'd heard many times in the past, but had never taken particular notice of. The sounds came again, and at once she knew what they were. They were the sounds of splintering bone. She had heard it enough times when she gave Charlie steak or chicken scraps and he would crunch through the bones like they were nothing. She had found him!

The sounds had come from off to her left, and she moved quietly in that direction, hoping to surprise the dog with whatever he had caught so she could not only scold him for running off and worrying her so, but also for catching and killing some unfortunate animal. Reaching the place from where the sounds seemed to emanate, she quietly parted the thick bushes and stepped through.

After leaving the relative brightness of the moonlit clearing, the deeply shadowed underbrush and densely over-hanging tree limbs cast her adrift in an inky blackness. 'Charlie,' she whispered, trying desperately to accustom her eyes to the dark. She took two more steps forward and tripped over something soft and yielding in her path, going down hard onto her knees. She felt around frantically and her hand touched the soft fur of her dog, sticky-wet with what she knew in her heart was blood. She backed quickly away from the dog's body, an involuntary gasp escaping her lips, then she froze in blind terror and for one split second it felt as if her heart had stopped beating. Something was crouched in the bushes, not ten feet in front of her. She remained motionless for what seemed like an eternity, too petrified to breathe. Then she heard a low, growling snarl and whatever it was began moving slowly towards her. With a soul-wrenching scream that went far beyond simple terror, she bolted to her feet and began running blindly through the thick undergrowth. From the corner of her eye she caught only the briefest glimpse of a shadowy form springing at her and a split second later there was a hard tug on the back of her bathrobe. She kicked out frantically with her foot, at the same time her fingers clawed at the sash around her waist. The sash came loose and the bathrobe billowed out behind her, giving her two more feet of room as she bolted from the bushes and into the clearing. There was another growl just behind her, and a second and more violent tug sent her spinning completely around as the material was torn from her back. She lost her balance as she fell; first her flailing right arm, then the side of her head collided with the trunk of a tree. She bounced off the side of a tree from the impact, her limp body tumbling over the bank of and into a small ravine; a drop of about ten feet. Her body hit the ground below hard, then rolled over once and was still . . .

The man-creature had wandered aimlessly through the forest and countryside after escaping from the root cellar, his degenerated, animal-like brain giving him no other purpose or direction. As he had done for years, he now survived solely by his newly acquired instincts. Food, in the form of game, had not been a problem for the creature because small animals were plentiful and he had long ago acquired the skills of stealth, patience and fast reflexes. In a mere three weeks since his escape he had gained almost forty pounds.

The creature had adapted easily to his new environment, changing rapidly from a thing, confused and cringing from the slightest sound or movement, to a crafty, aggressive hunter, hiding and sleeping during the day and prowling the forest in search of food after dark.

On this particular night, the creature had just caught and killed a rabbit and had settled down to eat it in the patch of underbrush he had made his temporary home when he had heard threatening animal sounds approaching. Within seconds, another beast had come hurtling through the bushes to attack him with savagely snapping jaws. Being of superior size and strength and accustomed to the dark, the creature had quickly killed his attacker, then had returned to his meal.

The creature had almost finished eating the rabbit when again he heard the sounds of something approaching. He froze, listening intently for any clue of possible danger. He sniffed the air. This was different from the other, there was something familiar about this one, but his disused, repressed thought processes could not tell him what.

Then it came through the underbrush and the creature saw it. The creature remained motionless, waiting for any sign of aggression or danger. Then it seemed to leap towards the creature, while making a low sound. The creature growled a warning; this was his home and his food. A high, shrill sound that thoroughly terrorised the creature made him immediately spring to the attack, grabbing at the fleeing figure with his fingernails. He succeeded in tearing off a piece of it . . .

The creature now huddled in the safety of the dense underbrush, watching the prone figure on the ground intently. It seemed no longer to represent a danger. After a few moments of feeling relatively secure, the creature's curiosity returned. Slowly, he crept forward, ready at the slightest provocation to leap back into the safety of the tangled underbrush. He sniffed tentatively at a foot of the prone body, then sniffed the leg. Still the body didn't move. Feeling safer now and all the more curious, the creature continued his inspection. Still watching the body closely, he lightly ran his hand across the left thigh and between the wide-spread legs. His fingers came away damp. The creature smelled his fingers, then tasted them.

A spark of something, a long-forgotten craving ignited within the creature's brain and travelled like an electrical charge through his body, awakening primitive desire. He moved quickly forward, first sniffing, then hungrily licking the damp area. Rearing back, he fell on the prone body like a stud dog after a bitch in heat, driving his hard penis deep into the warmth of her. The creature had an orgasm almost at once, the entire process taking only less than a minute in the uncounted moments of the forest night.

The creature withdrew and looked curiously at the prone body. Since the body represented no danger and the creature was no longer interested in food, he quickly lost interest in it. He backed slowly away and returned to the underbrush, where he quickly decided that this temporary home would no longer be good; it had been discovered by other creatures. Picking up in his teeth what was left of the rabbit, he loped slowly away, hoping to find a better sanctuary deeper in the forest.

7

Eli MacCleary was dead tired. Production at the sawmill had more than doubled in the last few weeks, and as assistant yard foreman that made his job nearly impossible. Now, because of being short-handed due to the unbelievable work load, he not only had to supervise every operation, but also had to pitch in and work right alongside the men in his crew, lifting and stacking the heavy lumber. In the last two nights alone his shift had moved, cut and stacked for delivery almost half a million board feet of lumber. He knew that it was a rewarding job with a good future, but he had to admit that lately he was beat before the end of his shift.

He pulled the pickup truck onto the short access road leading to the house, a road he had personally cleared some years back, and parked the truck in the carport at the side of the house. He got out of the cab of the truck and stretched, trying to relieve some of the tiredness in his muscles. He wondered what kind of a mood he would find Carolyn in tonight; he hoped a receptive one. They had not made love for the last five nights because she had gotten her period; tonight, tired or not, he was ready. They would have made love, period or not if it were up to him. Things like that didn't bother him particularly. But it did bother Carolyn, and of course he respected her wishes.

Entering the front door, the delicious aroma of broiled spare-ribs made his mouth water. He saw the bathroom door ajar and the light on inside. Smiling knowingly, he tiptoed quietly across the living room and slowly pushed open the bathroom door.

The last time he had come home and found her still in her bath, he had burst into the bathroom and jumped into the bathtub with her, clothes and all, playfully attacking her breasts with his lips; scaring her, momentarily, and soaking both himself and the bathroom floor. She had soundly scolded him for the next two hours, but he knew for a fact that she really enjoyed surprises like that, so he did things like that at every opportunity.

He looked with astonishment into the empty bathroom. If she wasn't in there, where was she? He looked in the bedroom. Empty. He went into the kitchen and looked with growing alarm at their dinner, drying up and growing cold on the stove. This was definitely not like her; she would never leave the house, even for a few minutes, at the price of a ruined dinner. And Charlie, he suddenly realised. Where the hell was Charlie? That damn dog could hear him coming a mile away and was always right there to greet him. Something was terribly wrong, or they *both* would have been there . . .

He went quickly out onto the front porch. 'Carolyn? Charlie!' he shouted, cupping his hands around his mouth.

He got no response of any kind. He called again. Still no answering shout or responding bark.

He ran quickly out to his truck and jerked his powerful flashlight from its clip under the dash. Turning it on, he quickly returned to the front of the house and played the strong beam in a wide sweep across the front yard, looking for any signs of where they might have gone. Finding the bent-over grass of Carolyn's footprints, he quickly took off in the direction in which she must have travelled.

Being an expert hunter, with the light he had no trouble in tracking Carolyn's path through the dense underbrush. As he went through the forest, deftly sidestepping twisted roots and thick, clawing bushes and moving under and around the low-hanging tree limbs, his mind kept the thought that he would find her safe.

Breaking through the tangled underbrush and into the clearing, he played the beam of his flashlight around the area, then rushed quickly to where a patch of dirt was freshly scuffed and gouged. Shining his light down into the ravine he saw her in the wavering beam, lying prone in the high grass below him. An agony of fear clutched at his heart, holding him motionless where he stood. He stood for a few seconds, staring down at her twisted body in shock, convinced beyond doubt that she was dead. He slowly slid down the embankment until he was standing over her, his body and mind feeling numb and useless. He could do nothing more than simply stare down at the beloved body at his feet.

She was lying on her back in the wet grass, a few torn shreds of her bathrobe bunched around her back. As he slowly played the flashlight beam over her, he could see that the entire lower half of her naked body was covered with grimy filth. Her body was covered with cuts and bruises of varying sizes, the worst of which was a large, purplish lump on the right side of her forehead. Her arms and legs were splayed out from her torso at curious angles, her thighs spread obscenely.

Fighting back the tears, he knelt down beside her and gently cradled her head in his hands. 'Carolyn — darling . . . ' As he bent forward to kiss her bruised fore-head, he noticed for the first time her shallow respiration, the slight flutter of her eyelids. She was alive!

With the realisation that Carolyn was badly injured but obviously still alive, Eli's mind was immediately filled with a thousand unanswerable questions, all occurring to him at the same time. What had happened to her, who or what, if anything, had done this to her? How badly was she actually hurt? His brain spun for a moment and he felt a deep anxiety building up. He had to think, think rationally, before he did anything – before he did the wrong thing . . .

He looked around the moonlit clearing in confusion, not knowing exactly what he was looking for . . . some trace, some clue perhaps, of what terrible thing had happened out here. *The dog*, he thought suddenly, *where was the dog*? The dog must have accompanied her out here, or perhaps she had come looking for him. He shook his head, the dog would have to wait. The most important thing at the moment was to get her out of these goddamn woods and safely home.

Slipping his hands gently under her limp body, he carefully began lifting her into his arms. Her right arm, which dangled loosely, bumped against his thigh, and even in her unconsciousness her face contorted into a grimace and she groaned in pain. Balancing carefully on one knee so as not to drop her he gingerly inspected her arm. It was immediately obvious by the queer angle of the forearm that it was broken.

Picking her up in his arms, he looked at her. She seemed so small, so vulnerable – and precious. He silently swore to himself that nothing like this would ever happen to her again, he'd see to it. But, first things first, he thought. There was no doubt now that he would have to get her some sort of medical treatment; her broken arm and the injury to her head were far too severe for anything less. The nearest hospital where she could get the emergency treatment she required was in Bentonville, a sixty-mile drive. He had learned that the hard way, after injuring his hand at work some time back; the only medical facility Pea Ridge had to offer was a senile old doctor living behind the local pharmacy. By the looks of her battered body, he knew she'd need better treatment than that old codger could offer.

Lifting her to a more cradled position in his arms, he gently kissed her bruised forehead, then, being careful not to shake or jar her as he walked, he began picking his way back through the tangled overgrowth, towards the house.

8

Eli sat slumped and dozing in the waiting room at the Bentonville Community Hospital in a chair three sizes too small for his large frame. Fatigue from working an almost twelve-hour shift at the sawmill, coupled with the acute mental anguish he had experienced over the last few hours, had drained him completely, leaving his body and mind feeling as though they were made of lead. After the nurse showed him into the waiting room, he had begun pacing the floor, thinking, wondering, fearing the worst. Within a short time, though, utter exhaustion had betrayed his body and his tired brain went numb on the onslaught of thoughts, each seemingly more terrifying than the last. He had finally collapsed into a chair, his mind blank of all thought except one — that his Carolyn would be all right.

After carrying Carolyn back to the house, he had quickly fashioned a splint for her right arm out of strips of kindling wood, to keep the broken bones from shifting. Then, after wrapping her in a blanket, he had carried her out to the cab of his truck, where he placed her carefully against the locked door in a sitting position next to him, and took off. Even though he drove as fast as he could when he hit the asphalt country road, the sixty-mile drive to Bentonville was without a doubt the longest he had ever taken.

Squealing to a stop outside the Bentonville Community Hospital, he carried her quickly through the double doors marked EMERGENCY and into a small reception area.

'My wife's been hurt real bad,' he bellowed to a startled nurse seated behind the desk. 'Get a doctor!'

'In here,' the nurse said, coming quickly around the desk and going through a large doorway. 'Lay her over here,' she instructed, indicating a metal bed surrounded by a draw-curtain. He laid Carolyn gently on the bed, and the nurse expertly swung the metal sides up and locked them into place, then drew the curtain all the way around the bed.

'If you'll just follow me,' the nurse said, returning to the reception room, 'there's some information I'll need from you. The doctor will be with your wife shortly.'

'Shortly ain't good enough!' Eli bellowed. 'I want a doctor in there *now!*'

'Sir,' the nurse said with practised calm, 'you have to be patient. Yours is not the only emergency and at the moment we're terribly understaffed because of the war.'

Eli suspected that what the nurse said was true because, glancing back into the emergency room, he saw at least twelve patients, a couple of them bleeding badly, with apparently only one doctor in attendance.

When he looked back, the nurse had rolled a printed form into her typewriter. 'Name?' she asked.

'Eli MacCleary.'

'Wife's name?'

'Carolyn.'

'Mailing address?'

'Post office box sixteen, Pea Ridge.'

'Now, as to your insurance — '

By the time the nine separate forms were completely filled out, Eli saw the doctor finally part the curtain around Carolyn and go in.

'The doctor is with your wife now,' the nurse said, clipping all the paperwork together and putting it into a folder. 'He will be out to talk with you in just a few minutes.'

That had been four hours ago.

'Mr MacCleary,' the voice said, and there was a gentle nudge at Eli's shoulder. Eli came awake with a start and, shaking his head in an effort to remove the fog of sleep from his brain, saw the doctor standing beside him, scowling.

'How is she, doc?' he asked, jumping to his feet and towering over the doctor, now fully awake.

'Your wife is in no danger, she'll be fine,' the doctor answered curtly. 'But, I would think your concern for her wellbeing is coming a trifle late.'

'What?' Eli said, confused by the doctor's attitude.

'It is not my place to go into that sort of thing with you, sir,' the doctor answered, still in a curt manner, but obviously cowed by Eli's size. 'Suffice it to say, your wife has suffered some serious injuries, the worst of which was a mild brain concussion, due to a hairline skull fracture between the frontal and parietal sections of her cranium. We've already done a series of cranial X-rays and a spinal tap, and can safely rule out any serious brain damage. With rest, the injured tissues should heal rather quickly.'

'Then she'll be fine, doc?' Eli asked, not understanding most of what the doctor had said.

'Yes,' the doctor answered, but still with a look of disapproval. 'Her right arm will take somewhat longer, though. The right radius was not only broken but splintered. Her arm has already been set and cast, and it will probably be necessary for her to wear the cast for at least six weeks. After that, she will still have to be careful not to put any strain or pressure on it for some time.'

'That's great, doc. Long as she'll be okay.'

The doctor took a deep breath. 'Mr. MacCleary, you do realise that I will have to report this to the authorities. Your wife has taken quite a beating there, and I feel it is my duty to – '

'What're you talking about,' Eli interrupted. 'Report what?'

'Well,' the doctor said, looking uncomfortable, 'as I said, your wife has taken quite a severe beating. I don't know what sort of an argument the two of you had but – '

'Are you nuts?' Eli bellowed. 'I never laid a hand on her in my life! I never would. You can just get them ideas out of your head – '

'I'm not . . . suggesting that. I have no reason to, at this point. But one must ask, then, exactly how did her injuries occur?' The doctor was looking at him suspiciously.

'I' . . . I don't know,' Eli admitted. 'She wasn't at the house when I got home, and I went out looking for her. I found her laying in the woods – like that.'

The suspicion in the doctor's eyes deepened. 'Are you saying that your wife was beaten and injured that severely – by person or persons unknown? I find it hard to believe – '

'I don't give a damn what you believe!' Eli shouted, glaring down at the doctor. 'I wanna see my wife – *now!*'

'She's probably still unconscious. We've moved her to

the last room at the end of the hall,' the doctor explained. 'I would suggest that she remain in the hospital for at least four more days, in order to get the proper treatment and medication.'

Eli, calming down a bit and thinking more rationally, agreed.

'I'm sorry, Mr. MacCleary, but I will still have to report this,' the doctor said, after seeming to deliberate the point.

Eli's face flushed with anger and he seemed ready to say something more. Instead, he walked down the hall towards his wife's room.

Conciousness was slow in coming for Carolyn. Her first wakening impressions were simply lighter swirls of grey in the abyss of nothingness. Gradually the swirls took on shape and colour, light and shadow, and everything took on a clearer hue. It was like surfacing from the depths of a deep black pool to the sparkling sunlight.

Her first physical sensations were that of warmth and comfort. She could feel the soft pillow beneath her head and the bedsheet tucked tightly around her. It all felt so pleasant, like floating, being cradled in a sea of white clouds. She got a contented little sigh past her lips.

'Carolyn, sweetheart. Are you awake?' A soft, rumbling voice. 'Can you hear me?'

Hearing the deep voice close beside her, the first thought that ebbed through her drug-fogged mind was that God was speaking to her, calling her name. Slowly, she opened her eyes. Everything looked blurred and unclear to her, but still she couldn't mistake the silhouette of her husband, sitting by her side.

'Eli — why — you — doing here,' she mumbled. Her tongue felt thick and dry and her lips wouldn't work properly. She closed her eyes and let the warm, comfortable feeling drift over her again. Taking his hand, she held it lightly, drawing comfort from his presence.

Suddenly the horror and pain of her ordeal flooded back into her memory in vivid, grotesque detail. She clutched Eli's hand with surprising strength, a single sob escaping her; then, as if a dam had broken, she let out a string of disconnected, hysterical words and phrases.

Eli did his best to calm her, holding her close and letting

82

her choke out the pain against her shoulder. He tried to listen attentively to her tear-streaked mumbling, but could not piece together enough of it to understand what had happened.

A nurse hurried into the room carrying a syringe. 'I'm giving your wife a tranquilliser,' she informed Eli, and expertly injected it into Carolyn's arm. 'She'll be asleep in a few minutes.' She smiled understandingly at him, then left.

Carolyn seemed to calm down almost immediately and her words came clearer and more distinct.

'Charlie gone . . . looked for Charlie . . . dark . . . horrible hairy thing . . . growl and jump at me . . . grabbed for me. Ran scared . . . horrible thing . . . ' She continued mumbling the same phrases over and over until her words became slurred and trailed off.

She was asleep again.

Eli sat for a long time while she rested, continuing to speak soothingly to her.

'Don't be afraid, darling. Whatever it was is over. It can't hurt you anymore. Don't be afraid, I won't let anything hurt you ever again . . . '

The creature was hungry again. The rabbit he had eaten earlier that night had not been enough, he needed more food to hold him through the day of sleep that lay ahead.

The creature had wandered into the swampland that bordered the forest to the west, and had begun hunting again. He had discovered a deep, narrow cave, almost completely hidden by the overgrowth of brush around it, and had made it his home.

Dawn was just breaking in the east as the creature moved carefully through the high grass bordering a riverbank, his eyes alert, senses keen for any movement.

The creature had hunted in the swampland before and knew from experience that the area abounded with small animals, easy prey. So far, though, his efforts had gone unrewarded.

The creature suddenly froze. Ahead of him, in the tall grass that grew along the riverbank, something moved. Slowly, the creature settled back, legs tucked under him and ready to spring, not taking his eyes off the place where he had seen the movement.

A water moccasin's greenish-brown head was first to appear through the parting grass, followed by the four-foot length of scaly body. The snake paused, tongue darting quickly in and out of its mouth, sensing the area ahead of it.

The creature waited, tensed and ready.

When the snake moved to within five feet of the creature he sprang, hands held out like claws, ready to grasp the head and twist. There was a blur of movement as the snake struck, sinking its fangs deep into the fleshy part of the creature's left forearm. With a howl of pain, the creature made another grab for his elusive prey, and was struck again on the palm of his outstretched hand. The two snake-bites began immediately to burn and swell painfully, and the creature, letting his prey slither off into the grass, began to shake his injured hand wildly in an effort to throw off the burning agony.

All thoughts of food were forgotten as pain moved up the creature's arm and into his shoulder. An instinct told him to seek refuge and nurse his wounds, but as he moved through the underbrush, towards the cave, pain invaded his chest, restricting, then strangling his breathing. As an aching numbness settled into his limbs his movements became jerky and spasmodic.

He reached the hidden mouth of the cave, but his legs would no longer support him and he toppled forward into the grassy dirt, where he lay for a few moments, gasping. Intense dizziness clouded his vision and it was becoming increasingly difficult to breathe. His lips and teeth were stained with droplets of his own blood as something within him ruptured. Finally, with his last bit of strength, the creature dragged himself into the safety of his den, the thick bushes closing behind him, completely covering the entrance.

Death stood guard at the mouth of the cave.

Carolyn lay in a fitful, drug-induced sleep. The heavy cast on her right arm had been strapped down to the metal bed railing to prevent her from rolling over on it in her sleep, and on her left an IV tube was inserted at the fleshy portion of her inner elbow. Her head was bandaged tightly and held immobile by a metal retainer.

At the moment of the creature's death, a sharp, burning

pain lanced across her lower abdomen, making her groan and toss in her sleep. The strange pain passed quickly and soon she had fallen back into dreamless unconsciousness.

9

Carolyn examined herself closely in the full-length bathroom mirror. There could no longer be any doubt in her mind. She shivered as she ran her fingertips lightly over and around the telltale swelling of her breasts and what she thought was a round puffiness of her abdomen. She was definitely pregnant. She had suspected the possibility when she missed her menstrual cycle the last two months and realised she was almost three weeks late with it this month, but there was still the possibility that her horrible ordeal in the forest and her injuries could account for a temporary change in her monthly cycle and the recurring nausea she had been experiencing lately, especially in the morning. But now, she thought dismally as she gingerly pressed her fingers into the slight roundness of her belly, this makes the fact undeniable. 'Just look at me,' she said to herself. 'I'm pregnant.'

The doctor had warned her, upon her release from the hospital, to expect some side effects from the concussion, but he in no way prepared her for the almost three weeks of dizziness, nausea and severe, blinding headaches that had made her recuperation a living hell. The simple act of getting up and walking to the bathroom was made virtually impossible by an immediate attack of vertigo that would send her staggering on rubbery legs back to bed. At first, even just sitting up in bed had made her head spin dizzily and sent the sensation of nausea spreading through the pit of her stomach, sending her into fits of dry heaving.

Eli, full of guilt and concern, had taken a month-long leave without pay from his job and had devoted himself to her care and well-being. He had fed her meals with a spoon, carried her in his arms to and from the bathroom — anything he could to make things easier and more comfortable for her. He blamed himself completely for what had happened to her, reasoning that he should never have left her alone and unprotected at night, especially in the secluded and — as he now saw it — potentially dangerous area they lived in. He had been too full of remorse to make love to her. Instead, throughout her long convalescence he had apoligised repeatedly for allowing the accident to happen, promising over and over to see to it that she was protected and safe from that moment.

Eli kept his promise some weeks later after discussing the matter with his chief of security at the sawmill. He purchased a large, two-year-old German shepherd named Otto. The dog had been involved in a number of attacks on the men and on other dogs and had been found unsuitable, even for night guard duty at the sawmill, due to his overly aggressive, vicious behaviour. Eli had brought the dog home, drugged and tightly muzzled in the back of his truck, and had released him into the forest surrounding the house. From that moment on, they almost never saw the dog, and were reminded of his presence only by the empty dog food bowl they found on the porch every morning and the dwindling number of birds and small animals left in the area. Personally, Carolyn feared the new dog, but she had to admit she did feel much safer knowing he was around . . .

Still nude, she turned slightly to the right, checking her profile in the mirror. She experienced a momentary pang of anxiety at the sight of her pasty-white, skinny right arm. The arm looked so ugly and deformed — it had no right hanging from her otherwise healthy body. She had had to wear the cast, stretching from her armpit to the palm of her hand, for almost a full three months. It had been cumbersome and clumsy, and had made the arm itch maddeningly. She had hated it.

The cast had been removed two days ago, leaving her arm withered-looking and pale, the skin and muscle tone gone due to lack of use. The doctor had told her that after just a few weeks of normal exercise the arm would be as good as new, but seeing how skinny and misshapen it looked now, she found it hard to believe she could get things back to normal that soon.

As she slipped into the new bathrobe Eli had bought her, the incredible thought kept running through her mind — she was, without a doubt, pregnant. She knew that Eli would be pleased beyond words when she finally told him and, thinking about it seriously now, she had to admit that she was kind of happy, too.

An old thought occurred to her; she stared at her reflection in the mirror, no longer able to avoid it. 'How?' she asked herself out loud. 'How could I be pregnant?' She saw her reflection shrug its shoulders. It seems impossible, she thought, running over the facts in her mind for what seemed like the hundredth time. 'I just got done having my period when that horrible thing happened to me in the woods, so I know I wasn't pregnant *then*. 'Or maybe I was,' she said out loud suddenly, startling herself. 'Maybe I was and didn't *know* it . . . ' She watched the image of her slowly nodding head in the mirror. 'Sure,' she said as the new idea — or could she have thought about all of this before? — took shape in her mind. 'I heard about things like that happening — a girl getting pregnant just before her time of the month but getting her period anyway. Sure,' she repeated to her image, 'that's *gotta* be the way it happened. Eli got me pregnant before my last period, and before my horrible ordeal in the woods.

'What, in God's name, is Eli gonna say when I tell him?'

She stopped, momentarily holding her breath as a new, frightening realisation came to her. 'If I *was* pregnant when that horrible thing happened to me in the woods,' she thought, her hands unconsciously going back to her stomach, 'could what happened to me have . . . hurt the baby?'

All she got in response to her question was a shudder of dread from her reflection.

Carolyn forced herself to concentrate on the dinner cooking on the stove. It was another one of Eli's favourites: lamb chops, sweet potatoes and corn. It did smell delicious.

After taking her usual bath she had put the dinner on and then worked to fix her hair into an attractive pulled-back style. She had put on the dress she knew Eli found most attractive. She hoped it would all make the mood, her husband's disposition, as favourable as possible when she told him of the news of her pregnancy. She had to admit that the clinging dress now bulged a little in the wrong places, but not enough to spoil its effectiveness.

As she stirred the corn, she glanced nervously at the clock — for the third time in the last ten minutes — and noted, with a mixture of excitement and apprehension, that Eli would be home in a matter of minutes.

What's he gonna think when I tell him? she wondered as she turned the flame out under the saucepan on the stove. What's he gonna think? She loved Eli very much, and because of that, she didn't want any doubts between them — doubts that could very well eat at and destroy an otherwise happy marriage. But, how could she explain this to him so that he'd best understand, when in all honesty, she didn't completely understand it herself?'

The sounds of Eli's truck pulling into the driveway sent her running into the bathroom to check her appearance one last time. Her hair was still in place, the dress fitted smoothly enough and looked good . . . On an impulse, she snatched up a small bottle of perfume — one of Eli's favourites — and dabbed a drop behind each ear and one between her breasts. I'll need all the help I can get tonight, she thought as she left the bathroom and stood nervously waiting for him to come in the house.

He came in through the kitchen door with a large bag of what looked like groceries. He looked tired and dirty from work, his clothes and hair rumpled, and at that moment Carolyn felt such an intense love for him, it was almost like a physical ache inside her.

'Payday today,' he explained, setting the package next to the sink. 'I figured I'd pick up a couple of extras — things we ain't had for a while, to kind of celebrate you getting better.' He turned and looked at her. 'You look terrific,' he said, his eyes widening slightly. 'What're you all dolled up for?'

'For you, you dope,' she said, giving him a kiss. 'Can't a girl dress up pretty for her man once in a while?'

'Mmmmm, and you smell good, too,' he said, playfully biting her on the neck.

'Well, you sure don't,' she scolded, gently pushing him away and wrinkling up her nose. 'Go take a shower while I get dinner on the table.'

Dinner was a constrained affair for Carolyn, pre-occupied as she was with thoughts of the conversation that would have to follow. Forcing a pleasant, though nervous smile and babbling irrelevant small talk, she picked at her food, moving and mixing it around in her plate with her fork in a show of at least consuming something.

Eli, on the other hand, ate zestily, smacking his lips with pleasure with each mouthful. If he was at all aware of her tense mood, he didn't show it.

'That was mighty good,' he said, shovelling the last of his third helping into his mouth and pushing his empty plate away. 'You sure know how to feed me, sweetheart.'

Carolyn nodded silently in answer and cleared the dinner dishes off the table, carrying them into the kitchen, where she placed them in the sink.

Eli pushed his chair back from the table and stood up, then followed her into the kitchen.

'Uh, sweetheart,' he said hesitantly, 'can you leave the dishes for now? I'll help with that later. Right now, there's something I want to talk to you about — something important.'

Carolyn shot him a quick look. Did he somehow already know? He had a nose for things like this. Could he only just suspect? Silently, she allowed herself to be led out onto the moonlit front porch.

'I talked to a real estate guy in town,' Eli began as they sat down on the top step. 'I got a chance to buy a deserted farm about three miles from here, real cheap.'

Carolyn breathed deeply in relief, but before she could say anything he continued with real excitement in his voice.

'County records says it used to belong to a man named Scruggs, but he seems to have up and abandoned it years ago. From what I was told, the farmhouse is overgrown with weeds and about ready to fall down, but it's sitting on about fifteen acres of good, rich land. Because nobody's claimed the place, it kinda reverted back to the county, and I can pick it up for two thousand dollars in back taxes.' He watched her reaction closely, obviously hoping she would be all for it.

'I don't think we better,' she said, shaking her head. 'There's . . . something you don't know — '

'I know all I got to know about this,' he went on en-

89

thusiastically, 'I know it's worth the two thousand, even run down like it is. And I got a feeling land around these parts is gonna be worth a fortune someday.'

Carolyn took a deep breath to steady herself. 'Eli, we can't be spending the money. We're gonna need it for something else.'

'Something else? What else could be more important than buying land for our future?'

She reached out and took his hand, then placed it gently on her stomach. 'Saving it for our son or daughter, whichever it's gonna be,' she answered softly.

He stared at her for a few seconds, then broke into a wide grin. 'Are you sure?'

'I'm sure,' she answered, still waiting for the inevitable. 'No doubt about it. I figure I'm pregnant about three months.'

'Sweetheart, that's wonderful,' he exclaimed, picking her up as if she were light as a feather and swinging her around at arm's length. 'Just great!' He hugged her to him with almost bone-crushing force.

'Well, put me down, damn it,' she grunted, 'before you squash both of us.'

He set her down gently, then opened his mouth to say something. His mouth suddenly closed again and his brow knitted in uncertainty.

Carolyn waited. She could almost see the doubts forming in his brain.

He stared at her for a second in total confusion. Finally he managed, 'How's three months possible? I ain't come from the time you got hurt until the last couple of weeks,' he said, looking at her intently. 'And before that — well, you know.' His expression changed to a look of sympathetic understanding. 'That just ain't possible, sweetheart; you can see that, can't you? You gotta be making a mistake.'

'I'm not making no mistake,' she said firmly. 'I've been feeling the symptoms for over a month now, but I thought I was just feeling that way because I got hit on the head and knocked around so bad. But now I'm sure.' She poked herself in the belly with a finger. 'Just look at me, I'm blowing up like a balloon.'

'But how?' Eli asked, still totally confused. 'When do

you figure you got pregnant?'

'Just before my last period,' she answered simply, as if it all made perfect sense to her. 'You just think about it,' she encouraged. 'Lord knows we were trying often enough to have one back then, and one time I guess it worked and I conceived. But all this must've happened so close to my normal cycle that, well, I guess the natural juices still had to flow. But, that little bugger must've been strong, like its daddy, and it just held on through everything.' She paused a moment, allowing his mind to absorb the new facts.

'If that's true,' Eli said slowly, slipping back into his feelings of guilt again, 'couldn't you've lost it when, you know, you was hurt out there in the woods?'

'Oh, I could have — and probably should have — but the important thing is *I didn't*. I was thinking about that earlier and I figure if I was ever gonna lose it because of what happened to me, I would of lost it already.' She patted her belly again. 'This kid in here is strong, and I guess it was just — meant to be.' She leaned close and kissed him on the cheek. 'I love you so much,' she whispered.

They sat gazing up into the starry sky for a long time, each lost in a world of private thoughts.

'Carolyn, do you believe in God?' Eli asked suddenly.

'What?' she asked, surprised by the question.

'Well, we ain't never talked much about religion — ain't never been a reason, until now. Though I ain't been to church for as far back as I can remember, thinking about it now I guess I believe in God.' He turned and looked at her. 'Do you?'

'Yeah, I reckon I do,' she admitted. 'Why're you thinking about that now?'

'Well,' he began hesitantly, 'we both been wanting a baby for a long time now, but ain't been able to have one.' He said it slowly forming the idea as he spoke. 'Could it be, like the old saying goes, that the Lord kinda moved in some strange way and, well, kinda made it possible for us to be having this one?'

'That must be the answer,' Carolyn agreed solemnly, stirred by Eli's reverence for the life within her.

'Well, whatever the reason or answer is,' he said, hugging her close and smiling happily, 'the important thing is, we're gonna have us a baby.'

10

Carolyn lay wide-awake on the bed, her body tense with expectation. When the awaited kick finally came, it was in the form of a dull push from within her left side, just below her rib cage. It was immediately followed by two more powerful jabs. Every one seemed more intense than the last lately. The kicking and other movements within her weren't painful, really, but were more like series of intense little pressures, the squirming and moving about of a living thing already impatient with having the walls of his dark and tiny world so close around him.

She had enjoyed the feeling of movement within her from the moment in her fifth month whe she had thrilled to the first wriggle of life deep inside her. She had been awed by the wonder of it; a living being, growing and developing inside her body — she was creating another human being, feeding it just as regularly as she fed herself, keeping it safe down below.

There had been numerous times in the last few months when her baby would stretch or kick and she would see the near-perfect outline of a hand or a foot pressing against the skin of her already stretched belly. It was all part of the total wonder she felt.

Her baby had been extremely active in the last few months, its movement growing steadily until, in the last few days, the squirming and kicking had become outright powerful. Also, tonight something new seemed to have been added: a cramping pressure in her lower back and pelvis that made her buttocks throb uncomfortably.

She had tried her best, all through her pregnancy, to ignore her discomforts as best she could and had firmly resolved not to complain to Eli about them. Although he was more than sympathetic, he still could not help finding humour in the fact that once she sat in a chair she needed help getting up again; none of her clothes fit her any longer and she had been doomed for the last three months to wear one of his old bathrobes instead of her own; and she seemed to be in the bathroom peeing about every ten minutes. She had decided not to complain to him about the morning sickness that had stayed with her almost to her sixth month, the constant backache she always had from carrying around all the extra weight in the front, or the baby's constant kicking that now tended to keep her up most of the night.

She turned over on her left side and tucked her left arm under herself to support her belly — her favourite and most comfortable position — and looked lovingly at her husband snoring contentedly beside her.

Needing to go to the bathroom for the third time in the last hour, she hoisted herself out of bed, being careful not to wake Eli, and waddled into the bathroom to sit on the toilet. Barely a trickle came, but it was enough to relieve the pressure on her bladder for a while. She grunted to herself as the slight pushing pressure needed to urinate brought on another of the sharp pains in her lower pelvic area.

At her last monthly visit to her obstetrician at the Bentonville Community Hospital, the doctor had explained to her that since she had entered her ninth month and was close to full term she could go into labour at any time. He had briefly explained to her about labour pains and contractions in the uterus and had cautioned her that although the contractions meant that the baby had moved into the birth canal and labour had begun there would probably be no need to rush or worry. Considering this was her first child, labour would probably take time. Just have her husband get her to the hospital as soon as was conveniently possible, he told her. She wondered now if *these* were the labour pains he had referred to . . .

The downward pressure in her lower back and buttocks seemed to be intensifying, growing much stronger, making it nearly impossible for her to sit on the toilet without a great deal of pain. She slowly got to her feet and carefully went back into the bedroom, hoping that if she lay down on the bed again it would relieve these new, extremely uncomfortable twinges.

The baby's activity had completely stopped; it now seemed to be resting. Good, she thought. If baby sleeps, mommy sleeps. She didn't know if the very sleepy feeling that had suddenly come over her was part of going into labour. All she did know was that it was becoming harder to keep her eyes open. She debated for a moment whether or not to wake Eli and tell him what was happening. But she wasn't sure herself what *was* happening, and she decided against it; the doctor had said that if she went into labour there would be no rush, and, after working an entire day, Eli needed his rest. She'd wait a little while longer before waking him and see what happened.

She rolled over on her left side, tucking her arm under her again and bringing her knees up until they rested against her stomach. This seemed to be the most comfortable position at the moment; she closed her eyes. The intense, aching throb in her lower back and pelvis did not subside, but she found that if she remained in that position and relaxed her body, they at least didn't get any worse.

Slowly, she drifted off into a needed sleep.

Carolyn woke with a grunt, her abdomen gripped in the light pressure of the contraction. She lay still, holding her breath for a moment as the tight knot of contracting muscles flexed and bulged, moving slowly downward from just below her breast-bone, across her abdomen and ending in her lower pelvis; the entire contraction causing intense and unfamiliar downward pressure. This had been the strongest contraction yet; for a moment she couldn't help thinking it was like being gripped with severe constipation and her body was pushing, straining with all its pressure to eject something from her system. Perspiration stood out on her forehead and upper lip from her body's exertion. She took a long, calming breath, held it for a few seconds, then let it out slowly through her teeth. She moved her legs to a more relaxed position and noticed for the first time the cold, damp feeling between her legs. Her first frightened thought was that she was bleeding; that something had happened, gone wrong. She quickly switched on the small table lamp by her side of the bed, then drew back the covers and looked down at herself. The hem of her nightgown and the bed beneath her buttocks were soaked with water. She got carefully out of bed, the wet nightgown clinging to her legs, and went into the bathroom, the dribbling water that was still flowing from her leaving a trail behind her across the floor.

In the bathroom she took off her wet nightgown, then seeing that it was useless to try drying herself, carefully stuffed a towel between her thighs to catch the continuing trickle. She leaned for a moment against the sink, bracing herself, as she felt the onset of another contraction; they seemed to be coming about five minutes apart now.

When the contraction ended, she slipped on Eli's bathrobe, then went back into the bedroom to wake her husband up. The clock on the dresser told her it was 4:10 in the morning; as good a time as any for my baby to come, she thought to herself.

'Eli, darling — wake up,' she whispered, shaking his shoulder gently, then more firmly.

Eli grunted, mumbled something unintelligible, then rolled over on his side and was asleep again.

'Come on, Eli,' she said louder, pushing him with all her strength, which was just enough to roll him over on his back again. 'Come on, get up. It's time.'

'Huh? What . . . what time?' he mumbled, his mind fogged with sleep.

'You gotta get up,' she said, 'I'm getting some real bad pains. I think the baby's coming.' She quickly lay down on the bed as she felt the beginning of another strong contraction.

Eli was instantly awake and out of bed, tension and excitement on his face.

'Well, get up — come on,' he almost shouted. 'We gotta get you to the hospital.' He looked frantically around the bedroom. 'Where's your bag? I'll stick everything in the truck while you get dressed. You gonna get dressed? Naw, you don't have to — you can go just like that.' His mind seemed to be travelling in five different directions at the same time. Finally, his attention centred on her, still lying on the bed. 'Well, come on — let's get *going*.'

'In a minute,' she managed to say. 'Soon as the pain quits.'

Eli quickly pulled on his pants and a shirt, then his boots. 'How long you been getting the pains?' he asked, coming

95

around to her side of the bed. 'How bad are they? Why the hell didn't you wake me up?'

'They wasn't so bad — until now,' she answered, as the contraction passed. 'Wasn't no need to wake you until I was sure.'

As he leaned across the bed to help her up, his hand went to the wet spot. 'What the hell's *that*?' he asked, throwing the covers back.

'My water broke,' she explained. 'Doctor told me it would happen. Ain't nothing to worry about.' With Eli's help, she slowly got out of bed.

'I'm okay now,' she said, shrugging off his helping hand. 'I can walk out to the truck myself — if I take it nice and easy. You get the bags.' She started moving slowly out of the bedroom and towards the front door.

After making Carolyn as comfortable as possible on the front seat of the truck, Eli moved quickly around to the driver's side. In his haste to slide behind the wheel, he forgot his height for the split second that counted and banged his head into the top of the doorjamb.

'You okay?' Carolyn asked, concerned at seeing a trickle of blood oozing from the small cut over his right eyebrow.

'Yeah, great,' he answered between gritted teeth as he slid onto the seat and slammed the door hard. 'Just in too much of a goddamn hurry.'

'Well, you just take it easy,' she soothed, trying her best to calm his obvious tension and nervousness. 'We'll get there in plenty of time.'

'You told me them pains of yours are coming every three minutes,' he snapped. 'We ain't got time to take it easy. We gotta get there *now*.' He jammed the key into the ignition and pumped the accelerator hard. The engine turned over briskly, then popped a few times, then continued to turn over cold, the starter grinding.

'Shit!' Eli bellowed, smacking his fist down on the steering wheel and making a dent. 'I flooded the goddamn carburetor!'

He forced himself to wait a few minutes before trying it again; in which time Carolyn had two more strong contractions. The carburetor was still flooded; the engine wouldn't start.

Eli waited.

He tried the engine again with no luck, then a fourth and a fifth time, until they finally heard the horrible sound — at least to them — of the starter dwindling down to a low growl. The battery was dead.

'What the *hell* do we do now?' Eli asked in utter desolation. The look in his eyes was the closest thing Carolyn had ever seen to pure panic.

'It'll be all right, Eli. Don't you worry,' Carolyn said, summoning up all of her self-control and speaking with a calmness she definitely did not feel. 'Help me back in the house.'

'But, we can't — '

'We gotta,' she answered, managing to keep her voice even. 'We got us no choice.' She opened the truck door and stepped down onto the gravel walk, then began waddling as best she could towards the front door. After a few seconds of hesitation, Eli caught up with her, and taking her arm, helped her the rest of the way into the house.

'I can't do it,' Eli said, shaking his head with finality. 'I don't know nothing in this world about birthing a baby.' He looked at her almost pleadingly. 'Carolyn, if I do something wrong — '

'You ain't gonna do nothing wrong,' Carolyn said, as confidently as she could. She shared his feelings of hopelessness and fear, but she couldn't let him know it for fear he would go completely to pieces. 'Why, people been — ,' she started to explain, but was gripped by another contraction, causing her to hold her breath tensely. When it had passed, she continued, she hoped, as confidently as before.

'People been bringing babies into the world theirselves for a lot of years — and so can we. Now don't you worry; we'll do just fine.'

'I'll go for some help, get someone who knows — '

'How you gonna do that?' she snapped, his continued negativeness making her nervous and adding to her own fright. 'Your truck don't start, we ain't got no telephone — where the hell you gonna go on foot?' She took a deep breath as another contraction began. 'You can't be leaving me now, Eli. The pains're coming about every minute and I'm gonna need you here — it's gonna be any time now.'

She parted her thighs as wide as she could in the hope of relieving some of the pain and terrific pressure she now felt.

'The pains are coming . . . harder and quicker than . . . they was before,' she said between grunts of exertion, 'but I think I'll be okay for right now. You go check on the water, and I'll call you if I need you.'

He had helped her into bed again and, at her direction, had propped two pillows under her buttocks, raising the lower half of her body and making it more accessible. Now he covered the lower half of the bed with clean towels. After starting a large pot of water boiling on the stove, he had assembled an array of things they might need near the bed: more towels and sheets, a small pair of scissors, a spool of thread and a bottle of rubbing alcohol.

The baby had been extremely quiet for the last hour or so. This had caused Carolyn to wonder, considering how active it had been the last few weeks. She had remembered the doctor explaining that once the baby entered the birth canal it would relax, allowing the contracting uterus to push and manoeuvre it in the proper direction.

The contractions were coming more frequently now, and were much stronger and lasted longer than before. It was taking all of her willpower not to scream for the intensity of them. She writhed and rolled on the bed, her body glistening with perspiration. Now, as a contraction ended, a new one began immediately; this last one seizing her with such force, such pressure, that it felt as if the flesh of the inner vagina was being torn. She gritted her teeth against the unexpected intensity of it.

'Eli!' she called between gulps of air as the contraction finally passed.

Eli came rushing into the bedroom, a look of alarm on his face. 'What? What's the matter? What happened?'

'Ohhhh,' she hissed between gritted teeth. She gripped the bedpost above her head and squeezed, her knuckles turning white. 'Ohhh, it'll be any time now. I can feel it pushing — pushing real hard.' Another contraction began and she lapsed into silently biting her lower lip, her face contorted.

'Just try to hang on another minute,' Eli almost pleaded. 'I got water boiling on the stove.' He was struck by how ridiculous his last statement seemed to be. He could think of no useful purpose for the water now that he had it boiling.

'Well, hurry up,' she managed between clenched teeth. 'Another minute's all I got.'

After returning to the kitchen, Eli pulled the pot off the stove and was carrying it over to the sink when he heard a muffled bark, followed immediately by a sharp bang on the back door. Shielding his eyes from the reflected inside light, he looked out the kitchen window and saw two pin-points of light staring back at him. Otto? he thought in surprise. They had not seen the German shepherd in weeks, maybe longer, and had assumed he had taken up running with a pack of wolves, occasionally seen prowling the forest.

Switching on the porch light, he opened the back door. 'Hey, boy. Where you been keeping – ' he began. Then he got a good look at the dog as it backed slowly away: the wide, glaring eyes filled with fear, ears pressed back against the sides of its large head, hackles standing high. The dog was obviously terrified by something, but what? To Eli's knowledge, the dog had never shown fear of *anything*. As Otto reached the darkness, just outside the ring of illumination cast by the porch light, he stopped, staring fixedly at Eli, then emitted another growling bark – like some kind of warning.

'What's got into you, dog?' Eli asked gently, taking a tentative step out onto the porch.

'*Eli.*' Carolyn's urgent cry suddenly commanded Eli's full attention. Slamming the back door, he ran back through the house, towards the bedroom.

'Eli, now! Hurry!' Carolyn pleaded, her eyes glazed with pain. More perspiration stood out on her face and body, soaking the pillow and sheet beneath her.

Moving to the end of the bed, Eli could see that the lips of her vagina were puffed out slightly, the opening being pushed apart from within by what looked like a round, pink ball of flesh. A mucous discharge oozed slowly from the opening and ran down her buttocks onto the towel.

'I can see it – the head!' he shouted excitedly, seeing the pink dome slowly push farther out of the opening. 'What – what do you want me to do?'

'The — alcohol,' Carolyn managed, between grunts. 'Clean around real good — with alcohol.' Remembering the doctor's instructions on what she would have to do when the time came, she raised her knees and spread her thighs, then pushed, bearing down as hard as she could.

'The head's coming!' Eli shouted excitedly. There was no mistaking the awe in his voice. 'It's out — the head's out! Push! Keep pushing — the shoulders're coming!'

Carolyn took a deep breath and waited a few seconds for the beginning of another contraction, then bore down hard. There was a second or two of terrific pressure and pain, then a flood of relative relief as the shoulders were forced through the opening and the tiny body squirted forth into Eli's waiting hands.

They both flinched, startled, as a long, baleful howl sounded from outside, directly beneath their bedroom window. It was followed almost immediately by a series of more distant howls from the woods beyond, yet both of them were too excited to pay it much mind.

'It's a boy!' Eli rumbled in pure delight, cradling the baby's body easily in his large hands. 'We got a son — and he's just beautiful!'

Carolyn was still trying to catch her breath. 'The — thread,' she instructed. 'Take the thread and tie it tight around the cord — near his belly. She relaxed her body and got her breathing under control while Eli tied the thread as he was told.

'Now what?' he asked a moment later.

'Tie it again, about an inch away — then cut the cord with the scissors.'

He did as she instructed, then picked his son up by the heels — the only way he'd ever heard to do it — and gave the baby a slap on the buttocks.

The bedroom was filled with a wailing cry of their child's first breath.

Eli carried the baby into the bathroom, where he carefully wiped the blood and discharge from the tiny body with a warm, wet cloth. He wrapped his son in a towel and brought him back into the bedroom. 'Now, will you show me how to shut him up?' he asked, laying the still screaming newborn next to Carolyn.

Taking the baby in her arms, she began slowly rocking

him back and forth. Within a matter of minutes, the baby was quiet and seemed to be sleeping.

'Well, you got your wish,' Carolyn said, placing the baby gently on the pillow beside her. 'And you said if it was a boy, you wanted to name him after your father.' She reached into the towel and, taking out the tiny right hand, placed it into Eli's, in the manner of a handshake. 'Eli,' she said, with mock formality, 'say hello to your new son, Michael MacCleary.'

Eli was beaming with happiness, unable to say anything.

'I only hope,' Carolyn said, taking Eli's other hand and looking up at him with happiness and love, 'that this boy turns out to be exactly like his father.'

PART 3

11

Carolyn sat contentedly in her rocking chair. She put one foot up on the porch railing in front of the house and took a long, satisfied breath of the cool afternoon air. This was her favourite time of day, after the daily housecleaning was done and just before she had to start dinner. She looked forward, at this time of day, to relaxing for an hour or two on the front porch and quietly watching as little Michael played in the front yard.

She found her son to be a constant source of amazement to her, and sometimes downright spooky in his seeming ability to concentrate fully on whatever held his attention at the time. Like now: as she watched, Michael, on his hands and knees, was moving slowly towards a bird pecking at the grass a few yards away. His movements were almost imperceptible, as he moved, every so slowly, towards the bird — stalking it. She was sure beyond a doubt that he would catch the bird, as he had caught so many other small animals while he played what seemed to be his favourite game. He would then proudly bring whatever he had caught to show her and, after a suitable amount of praise, would release it unharmed to scamper or fly off again. She saw no harm in what he did, as long as he wasn't cruel to whatever he caught, and she was fascinated and amazed by the acute concentration, the stealth and cunning he displayed.

Almost from the day of birth, Michael's physical appearance had been a source of confusion and mystery to both her and Eli. Gazing down at his new son, Eli had been puzzled by the baby's pale-blue eyes and fringe of reddish, peach-fuzz hair. She had explained that most babies were born with lighter colour hair and eyes and that in time they would change and darken to match his.

But they had not changed. If anything, the colour of the

105

boy's hair and eyes had become more pronounced, more intense in the last four years; the hair growing into a thick mop of rusty-red curls; the eyes, pale-blue and piercing.

She had then told Eli an out-and-out lie; the first time she could recall ever doing so. She had told him that she remembered her grandfather as having the same colour hair and eyes as Michael, and that this must be one of those twists of heridity that jump a generation or two. Surprisingly, he had seemed satisfied with her explanation.

'Mommy! Mommy, look!' Michael shouted happily, scampering up onto the porch with the fluttering bird held gently in his fingers. 'I caught the birdie!'

'Oh, that's just wonderful,' she praised, clapping her hands together. 'But, remember what mommy told you about little living creatures. We don't want to hurt it.'

Michael looked thoughtfully at the bird for a moment, then up at her. He had a way of looking at you, she admitted to herself, that gave you the definite feeling that those unblinking blue eyes of his were boring into yours, able to reach your very soul.

'I'll let the birdie go?' he asked, taking a moment to reach the desired conclusion.

She nodded yes and he opened his hands. The bird fluttered once against his palms, surprised by its sudden freedom, then flew away. He then ran back to play in the grass again.

There had been many times in the past when she had caught Eli staring fixedly at the child, his face a picture of some unsettled doubt. But he never once verbalised any of his thoughts, and Carolyn knew that he loved and cherished the child as much as she.

Eli had recently gotten the promotion to yard foreman on the day shift, which meant that along with extra pay, which they could certainly use, he was now home early in the evenings and they could finally be a real family. Now hardly an evening went by that Eli was not either playing catch with his son or taking him for two-hour walks through the outskirts of the forest. Their walks usually ended with Michael coming home with some sort of new pet, and the carport on the side of the house was now stacked floor to ceiling with wire cages of gopher snakes, turtles, frogs and the like. Also, she thought happily, the change in Eli's working hours had not done their sex life one bit of harm. Eli had always been ready and eager for sex — but now! She couldn't help smiling when she thought about it.

Her musings were interrupted by a rustling sound coming from the bushes that fringed the front yard off to her right. Suddenly frightened, she got to her feet, ready to order Michael out of the yard and into the house, away from whatever might be out there. She immediately breathed a sigh of relief as the brown and tan head of the German shepherd poked cautiously out of the bushes, his eyes watching them intently. Otto? she thought in surprise. What the hell's he still doing around here?

For years, the dog had only come around to eat, and the rest of the time they had literally seen neither hide nor hair of him. Finally, a year ago, after finding the dog's food bowl untouched on four consecutive days, they assumed he had wandered off and they had stopped putting out food for him. Now, it seemed, he was back.

'Mommy, look — doggie!' Michael squealed happily, getting up from where he was playing on the grass and running towards the dog. The dog froze halfway out of the bushes and watched the child intently.

Carolyn was filled with alarm again; she didn't like the wild, untrusting look in the dog's eyes; the way he held his body stiff, as if he were ready to spring. 'Michael!' she ordered sharply. 'Don't go near that dog! He'll bite you!'

Michael stopped immediately at her harsh tone. 'No, mommy, he's a nice doggie,' he said, clapping his hands, together and making little kissing sounds. 'Here, doggie,' he called. 'Nice doggie.'

The dog advanced slowly into the front yard, responding to the boy's encouragement. When he was within a few feet of Michael, he stopped, body still held tensely, eyeing the boy's outstretched hand. A low, threatening growl emanated from his throat.

Carolyn stood frozen at the porch railing, terror now gripping at her heart. She knew there was no way she could reach her son in time, and any sudden movement — ! Forced to stand where she was, she held her breath and said a silent prayer to God.

'Nice doggie, don't be afraid,' Michael cooed, taking a step closer to the dog, then another. The growl turned to a baretoothed snarl, the dog's hackles standing high.

'No, doggie. You be nice!' Michael scolded him as if he was without fear of the aggressive animal. He moved his hand forward to pet the dog. As his hand got close, the dog snapped at it with bared teeth.

As swift as the dog's movements had been the boy's reactions were quicker, and the teeth snapped empty air, a quarter of an inch from his arm. A flash of anger crossed the boy's face. 'No, doggie!' he shouted, slapping the dog hard across his muzzle. 'You be nice, or I'll hit you again!'

The dog stared intently at the boy for a few seconds, then his body seemed to relax, his ears went back in submission and he began wagging his tail. He then licked the boy's face.

'Good doggie,' Michael praised, stroking and petting the dog's head and back. Grinning happily he turned towards the house. 'See, mommy, the doggie's being nice.'

Carolyn rushed from the porch and, being leery of the dog, swept Michael up into her arms and hugged him to her.

'Why're you crying, mommy?' Michael asked.

'Mommy was scared the doggie was going to bite you,' she said, carrying him into the house. Still holding him, she watched through the window and saw the dog stare at the house for a few more minutes, then go trotting off into the bushes again — never, she hoped to God, to return.

She continued holding her son close and watching out the window until she was confident the dog had really gone and would not be returning. Only then did she set the boy down and collapsed into a chair near him.

'Sweetheart,' she began, struggling to find words he'd understand, 'you mustn't do that. You about scared mommy to death.'

'Do what, mommy?'

'Don't never go near a strange animal like that again. You never know what an animal's thinking, or what he'll do. That doggie might have hurt you.'

'No, mommy. The doggie wasn't mad at me,' Michael explained simply. 'I know what the doggie was thinking, and he was just very, very scared of me . . .'

'Now, how do you know what a doggie's thinking or feeling?' she asked, looking at him disapprovingly. 'That

108

doggie looked to me like he was all ready to bite you.'

'I could feel the doggie being scared of me, like I can feel the hot when I go near the stove. The doggie was scared I would hurt him. I showed the doggie I was nice, so he stopped being scared and now we're friends.'

Carolyn was amazed at how simply her son had stated an obviously impossible notion. She watched him closely for a few seconds, trying to detect telltale signs that he was making up a story in order to get out of being scolded. There were none. He simply returned her stare with those guileless blue eyes of his, eyes that harboured no falsehood. It gave her a strangely creepy feeling as she finally realised that — as far as he was concerned — he was telling her the truth.

'Are you telling mommy that you could *feel* that doggie's fear?' she asked, still looking at him sceptically.

'When he got real close to me I could.'

'And you wasn't scared of the doggie, even when he made teeth at you?'

Michael shook his head. 'The doggie was the one scared of *me*.'

Carolyn suddenly got another strange impression. 'Sweetheart,' she said slowly, watching her son carefully, 'can you tell what mommy's thinking or feeling right now?'

'No, mommy — that's silly,' Michael answered, laughing. Then his face turned serious. 'Mommy, why was the doggie so scared of me?'

'I don't know why,' she answered, leaning back in her chair thoughtfully. 'I really don't know . . .'

When Eli arrived home that evening, he could tell immediately that something had happened. It was nothing tangible, just the obviously subtle break from routine; usually when dinner wasn't quite ready when he got home they would have time to have a beer together and talk, but tonight dinner was done and on the table and they ate almost immediately; usually, Carolyn bubbled and talked incessantly about trivia, tonight she was nervous and preoccupied. Knowing her as well as he did, he understood that when she had something important to tell him she liked to pick her moment. He waited.

When dinner was finished, the dishes washed and

Michael bathed and put to sleep for the night, they went outside, as they usually did on early summer evenings, to sit on the front porch and enjoy the cool night air. This, Eli knew, was Carolyn's favourite setting when she had something she thought important to tell him.

'Something the matter, honey?' he asked, giving her an opening.

She hesitated for another minute, as if collecting her thoughts, then: 'Remember that dog, Otto? Well he was back today — walked right into the front yard — right up to Michael, growling and snapping. I'll tell you, it about scared the hell outa me.'

'Otto?' Eli said in surprise. 'I thought that dog either run off or was dead by now. Never expected to ever see him again. Dog didn't hurt the boy, did he?'

'Oh, he tried — tried to take a piece out of his arm, but that ain't the thing. It's Michael. It's the way he acted; just stood there staring at the dog in that kind of strange way he does — but he wasn't scared or nothing. And when the dog snaps at him and tries to take a piece out of him, Michael just smacks him across the nose and tells him to be a good doggie. I'm telling you, Eli, it ain't natural. Any other kid woulda come running to momma, scared and crying, but he just stood there, calm as could be.'

'Good,' Eli said, and shrugged. 'I'm glad the kid ain't scared.'

'But he shoulda been scared when a dog bigger'n him acts mean and tries to bite him,' Carolyn insisted. 'And it ain't just that, it's a lot of things — little things that ain't quite right. Like when I asked him about it, he says he could feel the dog was scared of him — he could *feel* it, Eli. And how about the way he catches birds and things — just creeps right up on them. And that way he got of staring at you with the blue eyes of his — like he can look right into your head and see what you're thinking.'

Eli sat, seemingly deep in thought, and said nothing.

'I know you think I'm silly for what I'm saying,' Carolyn said. 'It's just that I'm with him every day and I see things, things I just can't figure out — and they give me the creeps, sometimes.' She took a long breath. 'I was sitting and thinking about it before you come home, and I can't remember one single time that he was crying or scared.

There's just something about him — he just ain't like other little kids.'

'I seen him scared once,' Eli said in a low voice, as if what Carolyn had told him triggered a memory. 'Didn't think nothing about it at the time, but it was, well, kinda strange.' Prompted by Carolyn's concerned look, he went on. 'It was that time, maybe a month or so ago, when I took him fishing over at White Water Creek. We was coming back 'long that old wagon road when he stops real sudden like and goes staring off into the bushes — right at where that old deserted farmhouse is standing — the place I wanted to buy five, six years back — excepting you couldn't see it from the road. He asks what's over there, and I kind of felt like joking with him so I says it's an old haunted house and does he want to take a look. He says yeah, and we got through the bushes and up towards the house. Well, we get about fifty yards from the house and he stops, real sudden like, and he starts saying no, no, and shaking his head like he's real scared of something. Then he comes running to me, crying and begging me to take him home, saying that he's scared and he don't never want to go in that house ever again.'

'Well, no wonder he was scared,' Carolyn said disapprovingly. 'You scared him bad by telling him it was a haunted house.'

'No, that ain't it,' Eli said, shaking his head. 'He was saying he didn't want to go in there — *again*. Carolyn, he ain't never in his life been there before.'

They looked at each other, puzzled, then lapsed into silence, each in a world of confused thoughts, private thoughts. Also scarey, and about their *own* precious son . . .

12

Michael sat slouched behind the desk the nice lady had assigned to him, feeling bored and miserable. The seats and rows all around him were filled with dozens of other children, but he felt alone and abandoned. The nice lady — the teacher — was standing in front of the class, saying something about welcoming them all to Pea Ridge Elementary School, but so deep was he in his own thoughts and unhappiness that he caught only a few isolated words and phrases.

He had cried and carried on a lot that morning, begging momma and daddy not to make him go, not to leave him there, saying that he didn't want to go to school, that he wanted to stay home like he'd always done, playing on the grass with his animals or playing hide-and-seek with momma . . .

'I understand how you feel, boy,' his daddy had said, sitting him down on the front steps of the porch, then sitting beside him, 'but you're seven years old now — gonna be eight real soon, and you gotta be starting school. Should have started last year, matter of fact.'

'I don't wanna go.'

'Sure you do. Don't you wanna grow up to be smarter than your daddy?'

'No, I don't,' Michael had answered emphatically. 'You're smart enough, daddy. You're one of the bosses down at the sawmill, ain't you? That's smart enough for me.'

'Naw, it ain't. I got far as I did by using what I got up here,' he explained, tapping his forehead. 'I just learned to work real hard and keep my mouth shut and wait for the right chance to prove myself, that's all. Yeah, I went to school when I was your age, but I only went up to the fourth grade. If I woulda kept going, I probably could have been

112

about anything I wanted to be today, instead of having to near work myself to death at that sawmill.' He took Michael's hand and looked at him with concern. 'I want it to be different for you. I want you to really be able to make something of yourself.' He waved his hand in a dismissing gesture. 'School ain't gonna be so bad. You're a smart boy and you'll take real good to book learning.'

'I don't care,' Michael had wailed. 'I don't wanna go. Please, daddy, don't make me go.'

'You gotta go — ain't no choice about it,' Eli had said with finality. then he softened and even looked a little sad. 'Ain't gonna be so bad. I'll drive you there on my way to work in the morning, then you stay a couple of hours and learn what they got to teach you, then momma'll pick you up in the car later. It won't hurt you none and it'll probably be a lot of fun.'

'But, daddy — ' Michael had pleaded.

'Ain't no more to say about it. Now go get the lunch momma fixed for you and let's get going. You don't wanna be late your first day.' . . .

They had arrived at the school and his daddy had introduced him to the woman in charge of the class. She seemed to be a nice lady who smiled a lot.

'So your name is Michael,' she said, beaming down at him. 'My name is Miss Platt, and I'll be your teacher. It's a pleasure to meet you, Michael.'

Michael stood silently, staring up at her.

'My, but you're a handsome young man,' she said, still smiling. 'And you have such pretty blue eyes.'

Michael continued staring at her.

'You have to excuse him, ma'am,' Eli said apologetically. 'He's just kind of shy around strangers.'

'Well, we'll fix that soon enough, won't we, Michael?' she said, still trying to draw him out. Seeing that she was getting no response, she turned to Eli. 'You can leave now if you like, Mr MacCleary. I'm sure Michael and I will get along very nicely together.'

Michael looked up at his father, his eyes filled with a last silent plea.

'You behave yourself now and make me proud of you,' Eli said, bending down and kissing Michael on the cheek. Then he turned and left the classroom.

'This will be your place when the class begins,' the teacher said, pointing to the third desk back on the left side of the classroom. She took his hand. 'Now, come with me and we'll meet some of the other children in your class.'

Until that day, Michael's entire world had consisted of his mother and father, their house and front yard and the forest immediately surrounding it. His contact and experience with other people, especially other children, had been severely limited; occurring only on rare occasions when his mother needed to do some shopping in Pea Ridge. On trips like these, except for perhaps a polite remark from a housewife telling his mother what a darling child he was, adults usually had ignored him completely. At times when he did see another child in town, he would stand mutely and stare, the other child staring back, neither of them making the first overture of friendliness. This had never seemed to bother Michael; to him, people were to be watched from a distance, not to be gotten close to.

Now, suddenly, he was surrounded by them, laughing and talking at him, asking him a lot of silly questions — invading his life. Children, carrying on loudly about every little thing, asking him a thousand annoying questions, punching and poking, fighting and giggling; boys, standing in little groups, talking and acting tough and mean — for some reason always either making fun of him or trying to exclude him from the group; girls, batting their eyes at him, though if he happened to glance in their direction they would quickly lapse into fits of giggling and whispering among themselves.

Feeling the intense pressure of strangeness in this new and unfamiliar situation. Michael had withdrawn into himself, quietly moving away from groups to stand by himself in the school-yard, and now, sitting behind his desk, locking himself away with thoughts and fantasies of exploring the woods near his home, catching and playing with the animals he found there; doing all the things he liked to do the most. School, he decided, with all of its don't-do-this, don't-do-that, sit-down-and-be-quiet rules would never be for him. He longed to be out —

He was suddenly aware of the undercurrent of laughter in the class and that all eyes were on him. He looked up quickly to see the imposing figure of Miss Platt standing in front of him. This time, she was not smiling.

'I asked you a question, young man,' she said sternly. 'You answer me now.'

'What? Huh?' Michael mumbled.

'Young man,' she said, her tone growing even more severe, 'there will be no daydreaming in this class. I expect you to be paying attention at all times. Do you understand?'

'Yes, ma'am.'

'Now, I asked you if you've ever had tutoring.'

'No, ma'am,' Michael answered, looking up, 'I ain't never been sick a day in my life.'

The class erupted with laughter.

Miss Platt's expression turned positively ominous. Michael found himself wondering what had happened to the nice, smiling lady his mother had left him with.

'Young man, there is no room in this class for a smart aleck. If you continue with these antics, you will be punished. You understand what I'm telling you?'

'Yes, ma'am,' Michael answered, looking sheepish and embarrassed.

Miss Platt turned and walked up the row. When she reached the front of the class, she turned and the smile returned to her face.

'I know some of you were in Mrs Curley's class last year and others have transferred in from other schools. I must get an idea of what you've already learned before I can organise your study groups.' She picked up the attendance folder and a pencil. 'Now, how many of you have already studied reading?'

Half the class raised their hands.

'Mathematics?' she said, counting.

The majority raised their hands.

'Spelling?'

Half the class.

'Michael,' she said, looking at him, 'you seem to be the only one not to raise your hand.

'Yes, ma'am,' Michael said with a shrug, 'I guess I just don't know nothing.'

Again, the class roared with laughter.

Picking up a wooden yardstick from the top of her desk, Miss Platt walked slowly down the row towards Michael, holding the ruler in her right hand and tapping its edge lightly into her left palm as she got closer.

'I've warned you about being a smart aleck and disrupting the class,' she said, looking at him severely. 'Stand up, young man, and hold out your hand.'

Michael reluctantly stood up and extended his palm towards the teacher.

Miss Platt stood for a few seconds, savouring the shocked hush that had swept over the class, her complete command of the situation. The best way to handle a cutup or disrupter, she believed, was to deal with him harshly and immediately, thereby not only gaining his obedience, but also the respect of the entire class. With a quick movement, she brought the ruler down hard across the extended fingers.

Michael gasped and closed his fist tightly against the stinging pain, then stood staring fixedly into the teacher's eyes.

'Well, young man, what have you got to say for yourself now?' she asked, expecting the eminent victory of his submission.

'Don't you never hit me like that again,' Michael said slowly between gritted teeth, his eyes continuing to bore into hers. 'If I do something wrong, you just tell me about it and I'll try not to do it again. But don't you never *hit* me.'

'What . . . did you say?' she demanded. Looking into those piercing blue eyes, she felt some of her confidence slipping for the first time she could recall. He looked so menacing, young and small as he was, it scared her.

'I don't mean no disrespect, ma'am,' Michael amended. 'I just don't wanna be hit.'

Feeling suddenly this unsure of herself, she found it hard to keep eye contact with him. She had, at first, thought him to be so quiet and submissive — more easily dominated than most of the other children. But now, there seemed to be a fierceness, a defiance in him; she could see it in his eyes. It was the look of a trapped jungle animal, ready to spring at her. Involuntarily, she took a step backward, then wished she had not.

She was suddenly aware of the thick, tension-filled silence that had fallen over the classroom, the shocked, staring faces around her. She sensed that, for the moment, it was just as well not to take the chance of striking this boy again, but she also realised that something needed to be done in order to impress upon the class that she was not tolerating this kind of disruption or lack of respect.

'Come with me, young man,' she ordered sharply, grasping Michael's arm and propelling him as roughly as she dared towards the front of the classroom. 'You'll stay in there until lunchtime,' she commanded, pointing to a small broom closet near the front door. 'Do not think this incident will be forgotten,' she said loudly for the benefit of his classmates as she put him in the closet. 'I am going to discuss this with your parents.' She closed and locked the door.

'And now, class,' she said, turning back to the other children, 'I will seat you in groups, according to how advanced in your studies you are.'

As she rearranged her students into new groups and assigned them their new seats, her eyes kept returning to the locked closet door, and, abstractedly, she wondered about Michael MacCleary.

Michael, unable to stand upright in the crowded closet, sat himself on a bundle of paper towels and leaned back against the wall. He wrinkled his nose against the strong smell of dust and disinfectant that kept threatening to make him sneeze. He looked nervously around him. The interior of the closet, illuminated only by what small amount of light could creep in under the heavy oak door, seemed so small and overcrowded with brooms, mops and other cleaning paraphernalia that there seemed to be no room to breathe. His nervousness grew quickly and he was suddenly very frightened; the closet seemed to be getting smaller and smaller, closing in on him, threatening to suffocate him.

He put his hands against the opposite wall and pushed; the wall was solid enough and was not actually moving towards him, it only seemed to him that it was. He repeated this to himself. He took a deep breath and swallowed hard in an effort to calm down. He realised that the terrible, closed-in feeling was all his — imagination is what his daddy had called it. He could recall daddy telling him many, many times that, 'If something scares you, but you know whatever it is ain't real then it's just your imagination and there ain't no *reason* to be scared . . . ' He had never fully understood what daddy had meant, but he was sure it must be true.

What was making him so scared? he wondered. What was giving him this terrible feeling of being closed in, trapped? It had to be the closet itself; so dark and cramped, there wasn't even room for him to stand up or turn around. It must be getting to his imagination.

Leaning back against the wall again, he closed his eyes and pictured himself at home, lying on the grass in his front yard. This helped to dispel his fear and made him feel better — for a few minutes.

The image was slowly dimming, getting darker in his mind's eye, as if the sun were setting on his dream. Try as he might to concentrate, to sharpen and brighten the mental picture, a hazy nightfall still descended on it, until he could make out only dark, shadowy outlines.

Something flashed quickly across his mind; a fleeting impression of something dark . . . cold . . . filthy. He opened his eyes with a start, fear rising within him again. Before he could assemble one rational, calming thought, the horrific mental images were back; glimpses, impressions flashing instantaneously through his mind, assailing all his senses at once with their vividness. An odour seemed to invade his nostrils, sickening him; his mouth seemed filled with the taste of dry, foul dust; his body gripped with the physical sensation of intense cold and, even more acutely, the overpowering pain of starvation; starvation like nothing he had ever experienced or could even have imagined. He had the brief impression — startlingly visual but more than that — of lying in dark, gritty filth, his entire body shivering from bone-chilling cold and starvation that numbed him to everything but its own excruciating pain . . .

The mindless panic building within him erupted like a volcano. He sprang to his feet, banging his head on an overhanging shelf, and began beating on the closed door with both clenched fists. The thick wood of the door panel began splintering and cracking.

'Lemme out a here,' he screamed in terror. 'Please, lemme *outa* here . . . '

Once more a hush fell over the classroom; all eyes turning in the direction of the broom closet. The teacher stared with them.

Michael had driven both of his fists through the door panel.

Miss Platt sat back in her chair and regarded Carolyn MacCleary's angry face across the desk. Being the teacher, and this being her class, she felt justified in applying any disciplinary action or punishment she deemed necessary, whenever she felt it to be necessary, without having to explain her actions to irate parents. In this case, though, she felt she might have gone a little too far — or too soon, maybe — with the MacCleary boy; the entire incident had turned out badly. Still, she felt, the justification had been there.

'Mrs MacCleary, you've got to understand,' she began slowly, as if she were talking to one of her students, 'your son disrupted the class, not once but a number of times. He has destroyed that door over there. I must keep order in the classroom, so he had to be punished for it, not only to teach him a lesson but also to show the other students that I will not tolerate outbursts of silliness or disrespect in my classroom. I assure you, I was not singling him out or picking on him in any way. His punishment was called for and needed to be done.'

'My son's a good boy,' Carolyn said angrily, 'and he knows his manners and respect. He'd never purposely cause no trouble in the class without a reason.'

'The fact is, he did. And of course he was punished for it.'

'That your idea of punishment? Rapping his knuckles with a ruler and locking him in a closet?' Carolyn stood abruptly and glared down at the teacher. 'For whatever reason you had, how'd you like it if someone did that to you?'

'I suppose I wouldn't like it,' Miss Platt answered in a placating voice. 'That might make me think about paying more attention to my teacher. Anyway, that's not the issue here — '

'The issue here is I don't never want to hear that you hit my boy again,' Carolyn said hotly. 'Any punishment he needs will be took care of by my husband and me. And let

119

me tell you, my husband would be madder than hell if he heard about this.'

'Mrs MacCleary, there is no need for profanity. Suffice it to say, if your son will only behave himself, there will no longer be any *need* for punishment. Now, please sit down and calm yourself, there is another, more important matter to be discussed.'

Warily, Carolyn took her seat again.

'First of all, are you aware of the fact that your son has developed a rather bad case of claustrophobia?' Miss Platt, seeing the blank look on Carolyn's face, elaborated. 'He seems to have a terrible fear of closed-in places.'

'Well, I wouldn't like it, neither,' Carolyn said, her anger rising again. 'What the hell did you lock him in the closet for?'

'Why he was punished is not the issue I'm trying to discuss,' Miss Platt said, trying to put aside her annoyance at Carolyn's seemingly one-track mind. 'What I'm referring to is that, along with an obvious case of claustrophobia, your son also has quite a temper − abnormally so, if I'm any judge. Why, for a moment there, during the − incident, I actually thought he was going to attack me.'

'I wouldn't have blamed him if he did − hitting him and locking him up like that.'

'I think once again you're missing the point. I have had years of experience with children, and a normal child − '

'You saying my kid ain't *normal*?'

'No, of course I'm not. Really, Mrs MacCleary, you misunderstand me. I used the word normal as meaning . . . average. The average child your son's age, when confronted with a stiff or perhaps painful punishment, will usually turn subservient − cry, perhaps, or want to be forgiven. Your son, on the other hand, displayed traits that disturb me greatly.'

'So he ain't afraid of you − so what?' Carolyn shrugged. 'He ain't afraid of nothing − except maybe being locked in closets.'

'Mrs MacCleary, what I'm trying to say is − '

'I know what you're trying to say. You had my kid in your class for one day, and now you're going to tell me there's something different about him. Well, I've known there was something different about him. Right from the day he was

born. I prefer to think of him as somebody special.'
Carolyn drew a long breath. 'I know he's got one hell of a
temper for a little kid and he don't get scared by most things
easy, but down under it all he's just a quiet little boy that
don't want no trouble and don't like to be messed with. If
you don't give him trouble, I'm sure he'll mind his
manners.'

'Mrs MacCleary, I think we both know that his
problems go a lot deeper than that — '

'Well, even if they do,' Carolyn said with finality, 'you
just worry yourself about teaching his reading and writing,
and let his dad and me worry about the rest of it.'

Michael sat on the lunch bench in the schoolyard, waiting
apprehensively for his mother to finish her conference with
the teacher. He could guess what they must be talking
about. Him, of course; the trouble he'd caused; his embarrassing outburst in the closet. He groaned inwardly at the
thought of it; the entire class laughing at him; the strange
look on the teacher's face when she opened the shattered
door; returning to his seat with the eyes of the class
strangely on him. An uncontrollable shudder ran through
him; it had been terrible, something he wanted never to
experience again.

What would daddy think? he wondered. Daddy never
spanked him or even raised his voice; at times of displeasure, he would just look at him with a frown on his face.
To Michael, that frown of disapproval said enough. It said
everything.

'Hey, Mike, remember me? Jerry Wilson — I sit right
behind you in class.'

Michael turned to see a short, blonde boy walking towards
him, a grin on his face. 'Yeah. Hi, Jerry,' he said tonelessly.

'Man, you sure told old fat Platt,' Jerry said, clapping
Michael good-naturedly on the back. 'Ain't nobody ever
talked to old stoneface like that.'

'I didn't mean any harm,' Michael said defensively. 'I
just don't like to get hit — and that really hurt.'

'That's okay,' Jerry said with a dismissing wave of his
hand. 'It was great. Most guys ain't got the guts to talk up
like that.'

'Yeah, except now I'm really gonna get it from my folks,'

Michael said, his black mood undispelled.

'Well, she still had it coming — your first day and all.'

'Is she always mean like that?' Michael was visualising a very dim future at school.

'Naw. I had her last term. She always pulls that kind of stuff on somebody the first day — to show the kids how tough she is. It lasts a couple of days and after that, she's kinda nice.'

'I sure hope so,' Michael said, shaking his head.

'I'm gonna have to go pretty soon — my mom's coming to pick me up,' Jerry said. 'What do you say to us eating lunch together tomorrow, so we can — '

'*Hey, chicken shit!* You with the red hair!'

Jerry turned to see who was shouting, then groaned. 'Here comes Eddie the ape,' he whispered. 'He bullies everyone. Just stay clear of him, you don't wanna be his next victim.'

Michael turned and saw a tall, heavyset boy, perhaps a year or two older than him stomping towards them, a sneer on his face. 'What's he want?' Michael whispered. 'I don't even know him.'

'Wants to fight you, probably. He fights with all the new kids. He thinks he owns the schoolyard.'

'I don't wanna fight him,' Michael admitted nervously. 'I ain't never fought no one before.'

'Then don't start with him — he'll murder you.'

'Hey, chicken shit, I heard you got scared and pissed in your pants today because the teacher put you in the closet!' Eddie was beside them now, towering over Michael.

'Come on, Eddie, leave him alone. He didn't do nothing to you,' Jerry said in defence of his newfound friend. He got an elbow in the stomach for his trouble.

'Come on, chicken shit, I'm talking to you,' Eddie persisted 'You should be sitting over there with the girls — you squat to piss, don't you?'

Michael stared at Eddie through large, frightened eyes, but said nothing.

'Get on your feet, chicken shit. We gonna settle this right now.'

'Settle what?' Michael managed to stutter, his mouth feeling dry as cotton. 'I don't even know you -- and I got no reason to fight.'

'You don't, huh?' Eddie suddenly jumped forward and wrapped an arm around Michael's neck. He pulled Michael roughly from the bench and down to the ground, then fell on Michael's back hard, his arm tightening.

Michael let out a grunt as the larger boy's full weight came down on his back, forcing the air from his lungs. His throat made strangling noises as the arm tightened even more around his neck, pressing painfully on his windpipe. Bright spots began dancing before his eyes and he could feel his face redden as the strangling pressure around his neck increased. His vision blurred and darkened as his consciousness began slipping away. His heart began banging heavily in his chest; he struggled feebly but could not break the vicelike grip around his throat.

Then a feeling began slowly seeping through his body, a strange sensation like blood returning to numbed limbs. It spread through his arms and legs, stomach and chest, and finally into his brain. It was a sensation of strength, power — and something more, much more. In place of approaching unconsciousness, a wondrous suffusion of power came to claim him, and he willingly gave himself to it.

The choking pain in his throat was now unfelt; all pain was gone. His breath began hissing noisily through his gritted teeth as the feeling, the power within him, intensified.

Drawing his knees under him, he sat up, seemingly unhindered by the weight on his back. Gripping the strangling arm around his neck in both hands, he pried it away with seeming ease. He held the arm tightly for a few seconds, examining it almost critically. He could see the muscles and tendons of the captive limb flexing with tension, the bluish-grey veins crisscrossing below the skin's surface, could feel the blood pulsing where his fingers dug into the flesh. He was suddenly seized by an impulse; an impulse so overpowering it was not within his power to resist it. Bringing the arm quickly towards him again, he bit down hard, sinking his teeth into the flesh of the forearm. As warm blood flowed into his mouth, his taste buds seemed to explode with intense sensation, his lips, his entire mouth tingling with the deliciousness of it. Ignoring the high-pitched screams of pain, the frantic wrenching and twisting of the trapped arm, the fist beating frenziedly on his back, he bit again, then sucked and licked at the sticky-sweet blood that welled from the wound.

He was oblivious to the shouts and commotion going on around him until a hand gripped his hair and his head was pulled roughly back, and he was slapped smartly in the face. Another pair of arms pulled him roughly to his feet, but he sank quickly to the ground on his hands and knees again. He hunched quietly now, still breathing noisily through blood-stained teeth and lips, trying to concentrate on the strange buzz of human voices around him. His mind seemed to be coming back from somewhere a long way off; he was slowly waking from a dream. The strength seemed to ebb from his body, leaving him feeling drained and disoriented. Slowly, his mother's voice filtered through the haze that sill clouded his mind.

' . . . the hell did you expect him to do when that big kid started choking him?' Carolyn was shouting at Miss Platt. 'I know my boy, and he wouldn't start up like that with *nobody*.'

'That's true, Miss Platt,' Jerry spoke up. 'We was just sitting and talking when Eddie just jumped on Mike for no reason at all.'

Faced with such corroboration, Miss Platt had no choice but to abandon her argument that Michael was mentally ill and had brutally attacked the other boy. She quickly left for the school infirmary to check on Eddie Mathews's condition.

For Michael, whatever it was that had happened seemed now to have subsided completely. He sat up slowly, still feeling shaky, and rubbed the soreness at his throat. He had a foul, sticky taste in his mouth, but could not recall what it was.

Carolyn knelt down beside her son and, taking a handkerchief, wiped the blood from around his mouth and the sides of his face. 'How you feel?' she asked, looking with concern at the large, purple bruise forming on his neck. 'You ain't hurt bad, are you?'

'No, I'm okay, momma,' Michael managed to answer, holding his stomach, 'but my belly feels kind of sick. I want to go home.' . . .

When they were in the car and heading towards home, Carolyn asked, 'What the hell started all that back there?

124

Did you really have to bite into that kid like you did?'

'I don't know, momma,' Michael answered truthfully. 'He just jumped me and started choking, and I got real dizzy, then — I don't know what all happened. I don't really remember.'

'Well, your teacher says you got a real bad temper, and I think I'm beginning to agree with her.' She shook her head. 'You sure got yourself into a peck of trouble today.'

'You gonna tell daddy about it?' Michael asked a little hesitantly.

'Of course I am. Your daddy and me, we discuss everything together. We'll all talk about it later — and try to understand what happened.'

'He's gonna be real mad, ain't he?' Michael could imagine the look of disapproval on his father's face.

'I don't think so. At least not when I tell him the whole story.'

As they drove along, Michael thought about all that had happened to him that day. 'You know, momma,' he said finally, looking at his mother soulfully, 'I don't think I'm gonna like school too much.'

13

Carolyn stirred the pot of beef stew bubbling on the stove, then reduced the flame beneath it. Dinner was all ready; now she could relax for a few minutes before Eli got home from work. She debated again whether to tell him the events of today as soon as he got home or to wait, as she usually did, until dinner was over and they could relax on the front porch and discuss matters in a calmer atmosphere . . .

She looked up in surprise as she heard Eli's truck crunching down the access road, then come to a squealing stop in front of the house. She glanced at the clock; it was only 5:15. He must have flown home . . .

Eli burst through the front door, his agitation evident on his face. 'What the hell *happened* today?' he demanded. 'Where's the boy? He okay?'

'He's just fine — nothing to worry about. He's in taking his bath.' She looked at Eli questioningly. 'How'd you find out about it so fast?'

'Sam Mathews, one of the guys in my crew, he got a phone call from the school this afternoon, then he come at me, bitching and shouting how his kid and Michael got into some kinda beef and Michael damn near chewed his kid's arm off. I tried calling the school to find out what the hell happened, but by that time there was nobody there. Now, what happened?'

'Oh, they got into a fight all right,' Carolyn said, smiling ironically, 'but I bet he forgot to mention that his kid is bigger and about two years older than Michael, and that his kid started it by grabbing Michael around the neck and damn near choking him to death. I guess Michael just fought back the only way he could.'

'But *he's* okay? Michael didn't get hurt or nothing?'

'Oh, he got a couple of scratches and bruises, but nothing real serious.' She looked thoughtful for a moment. 'Lots of things happened to him today — things that got him upset. I'll tell you all about them later. The point is, I don't think you should get after him for any of it right now. Give him a little time until he feels better.'

Feeling he needed some time to think it over himself, Eli agreed.

All through dinner, Michael stole apprehensive looks at his father, expecting him, at any moment, to put down his fork in that precise way he had when he was about to say something important and scold him for all the trouble.

Eli, of course, could not miss noticing his son's nervousness. He decided to put an end to it. 'Heard you got into a tussle today,' he said, putting his fork down on the table. 'Want to tell me about it?'

'It wasn't my fault, daddy,' Michael answered, his words coming in a rush. 'I didn't mean to cause no trouble.'

'Take it easy, boy,' Eli said, holding up a comforting hand. 'I know you ain't to blame if a bigger boy starts to pick on you. I just want to know what started it.'

Michael breathed a sigh of relief. 'I thought you was gonna be mad about me getting in so much trouble with the teacher.'

'Oh, yeah,' Eli said, shooting a quick look at Carolyn. 'Well, I guess your momma just didn't get 'round to telling me about that.' He frowned at Michael. 'What kind of trouble you get into with the teacher, son?'

'I didn't do nothing,' Michael answered with a shrug, 'least I didn't mean to. She ask me a bunch of questions I didn't understand, and when I answered her, she said I was talking sassy.'

'I had a long talk with his teacher,' Carolyn explained, 'and I think we got the whole thing straightened out. Long as he behaves himself from now on, he won't have no more trouble. Now, leave that be for now. I can tell you about it later.'

'Okay,' Eli said with a shrug. 'Seems like I'm always the last to know things around here.' He eyed the bruise on Michael's neck. 'That kid hurt you bad?'

'Yeah,' Michael admitted, 'guess he did. But momma says I hurt him even more.'

'Why'd you want to bite him, of all things?' Eli asked, uneasy with the idea. 'Couldn't you just hit him back?'

'I don't know why. I don't even remember doing it. He was on me and choking me — then momma says I bit him.' Michael shrugged again.

'Well, I'll be off from work this Saturday, what do you say I teach you a little about fighting? That way, if anybody starts up with you again, you'll be able to take care of yourself.'

Michael's face brightened. 'Gee, daddy — yeah. That'll be great.'

Carolyn looked meaningfully at the clock. 'Right now, I think you should go get your teeth brushed. I want you in bed early tonight. Daddy and me got something to talk about.'

'Aw, momma,' Michael pleaded, 'couldn't I just stay up 'til — ?'

Carolyn cut him off with a stern look. 'Go,' was all she said. Eli nodded in agreement.

'I had a long talk with his teacher,' Carolyn began, after Michael was tucked into bed and they had taken their usual positions on the front porch, 'and she thinks that Michael . . . '

Michael had been in bed and asleep for nearly an hour before the dream began. It was one of those uniquely strange dreams in which, although deep in sleep, the conscious mind is completely aware of the dream and one had no choice but to watch the sequences unfold as if watching a singularly personal tableau.

The scene all around him, viewed through his eyes, was that of a greyish nothingness; a slowly revolving vortex of randomly changing hues. There was solidness beneath his feet, and movement was possible, but only in extremely slow motion. He looked out at the calming shades of grey, swirling and eddying all around him. He felt frightened; frightened of what, he didn't know — there was nothing *there* . . . He took a step forward, then another; it was like trying to move under deep water, his movements were awkward and exaggerated. He looked around him again, behind him — nothingness; nothing could be seen, heard or felt. Why the growing apprehension he felt? The horrible feeling of foreboding? There was certainly nothing around to hurt him.

Something began taking shape in front of him, off in the distance. At first it seemed to be nothing more than a slightly darkening mass, moving slowly towards him, then, as it grew closer, its shape took on form, became more distinct. It was a human shape, but it was no human. It had arms and legs, a torso and a head, and as it drew silently closer it towered above him — and he knew with every fibre of his being, it was not human, and, somehow, not yet entirely frightening. Unable to move in the colourless void, he watched it.

It stopped suddenly, its features obscured by a filmy grey curtain that separated it from Michael. It raised a hand and pushed soundlessly against the filmy barrier; the insubstantial membrane, seemingly nothing more than a wisp of greyish smoke, yielded to its touch but would not part. It raised both hands and began beating its fists against the dream-scene, and as absolute silence still prevailed he saw the thing's jaws open and he did not hear but *knew* it had emitted a startling, horrible bellow of rage. He could feel a total evilness emanating from the loathsome thing; a malevolence beyond anything imaginable — and it was trying to . . . pass through the barrier that separated them — get to *him*.

He took a step backward, then another, away from the presence that clawed furiously at the barrier between them; all the time bellowing and growling in rage and frustration. He turned to run from it but could not. He was being drawn backward, pulled towards the evil on the other side of the barrier. He cried out in horror now, and with every ounce of his strength he tried to run from it . . . run from it . . . run from it . . .

On the porch, Eli and Carolyn jumped to their feet and hurried into the house as the scream sounded from Michael's bedroom. Pushing open the bedroom door, they rushed to the bed, then stood for a moment staring down at the thrashing, crying boy tangled in the sheets.

'He's having a nightmare — a bad one,' Eli asked urgently. 'Should we wake him up?'

'Let me do it,' Carolyn said, sitting down on the edge of the bed. She took her son's head and shoulders gently in her arms and eased him towards her.. 'Michael . . . ' she whispered. 'Darling, wake up.' She shook him gently.'

His body relaxed against her, then he stirred; his eyes fluttered a few times, then opened. 'Momma,' he cried, his face between her breasts, 'I was *scared* — it was chasing me . . .'

'Shh,' Carolyn said, rocking him in her arms. 'It's okay now, darling. Nothing's gonna hurt you. It was just a bad dream.' She turned to Eli. 'Get me a towel or something — he's wringing wet with sweat.'

'It was so terrible, momma,' Michael sobbed. 'It wanted to get me.'

'Ain't nothing gonna get you.' She took the towel from Eli and gently wiped his damp face.

After a few moments, she laid him back on his pillow and sat on his side of the bed. 'Whatever it was is all gone now,' she said, her head on his shoulder. 'Now close your eyes and go on back to sleep. I'll sit here with you and hold your hand until you do.'

Michael relaxed and closed his eyes. Within a matter of

minutes, he was asleep again.

If, during the night, he dreamt again, he did it without waking them . . .

14

'He seems to be sleeping quietly enough tonight,' Carolyn said, returning exhausted from Michael's room and feeling her way back into bed for the third time that night. Three weeks has passed since Michael's first nightmare.

Eli turned over in the dark and propped himself up on his left elbow. 'I'm really worried about him − having that same dream off and on most every night, about something big and ugly chasing after him and trying to get him.' He shook his head slowly. 'Maybe we ought to take him to a doctor or something. The poor kid's afraid to go to sleep. He's dog tired all day from it.'

'When I was in town shopping a few days ago, I stopped by the library and looked at a book the lady working there told me to read. It said that dreams over and over like this means there's something in his sub − un − the back of his brain that's really pestering him.'

'How about school?' Eli said. 'How's he doing in school now?'

'Oh, he's doing okay now. I talked to his teacher again, and she says he's acting kind of quiet and keeps to himself a lot. Still, he's been behaving okay and ain't having no more trouble. Seems since he got into that ruckus with the other kid and bit him, the other kids're staying away from him.'

'Well, you say he's sleeping peaceable tonight. Maybe whatever it was quit bothering him.'

'I sure do hope so,' Carolyn said. 'I been worried about him.'

'Yeah, I know.' Eli slid over beneath the blankets and brought his lips to her ear. 'And I been getting kinda jealous about it.'

'Jealous about what?' she asked, arleady knowing the answer.

'Well, you been giving whatever ails the kid all your attention,' he said, putting a ridiculous-sounding pout in his voice. 'You know, the old man needs attention too, healthy as he is.' He slipped his hand under her nightgown and began easing it up over her thighs.

'Eli MacCleary, you ain't nothing but a sex-hungry animal,' she said, protesting weakly, but allowing her nightgown to be pulled up over her head and thrown off into the dark.

When the dream came to Michael later that night, it began as it always had: the grey void; him moving in slow motion; the appearance of the great, howling thing and its inability to break through to him. Everything seemed the same to his mind's eye — but, no — it was different somehow. The thing's frustration and rage seemed much more desperate this time, as if clawed and threw its weight furiously against the yielding barrier. Gradually, as he watched, wide-eyed, small indentations formed, indentations that began stretching and cracking, the small cracks splitting and getting wider. For an instant he recalled his own desperate hands smashing through the door of the broom closet at school, remembered the terror he had felt then — and knew that the thing, like him, was going to burst through. He screamed the silent scream of his terrible dream world and turned to run — run from the thing finally coming to claim him.

Something touched his shoulder. He screamed and tried to pull away, but he couldn't. Arms enfolded him and drew him backward; not roughly or savagely as he had feared but gently, almost lovingly. As the arms encircled him, drawing him in close, he was aware of pressure but not the expected pain. The pressure seemed to intensify around him, drawing him in deeper and deeper until, for an instant, it disappeared completely, only to resume. Now the pressure seemed to be *within* him, at the very beginning of him, and it was pushing outwards. The pressure flowed through him, expanding within him as it moved; as if he were being infused with an irresistible flow of gas. The skin all over his body felt tight with the outward pressure of it, and his head felt ready to explode. The pressure intensified until his head *did* seem to burst . . . in a great eruption of bright, shimmering lights and swirling sparks.

His head cleared quickly, the bright flashes lasting only an instant. His dream now seemed to have taken on a new dimension; things around him now seemed more real, more acutely defined in the dream than they ever had been in the waking world. There was a moment of shadowy blur, then he was jumping to the grassy ground outside his bedroom window. The soft, damp grass seemed to move with a life of its own beneath his bare feet, the leafy bushes stroked his arms and legs gently as he moved quickly through them in the moonlight. His senses seemed more acute and alive than ever before; hearing, smell, touch — all sharpened to new clarity, all greedily absorbing a world of stimuli; his body and mind revelling in the bombardment of heightened sensation and feeling. And overshadowing it all was an all-consuming drive, a total compulsion deep within him; a desperate need, a hunger for something undefined that pushed him on. Time and distance no longer seemed to have meaning for him as he bounded swiftly across the grassy field and into the thick foliage beyond.

Reaching a fence made of heavy wire and wood, he vaulted easily over it, then froze in his tracks and dropped quickly to his haunches as the unmistakable odour of sheep assailed his nostrils. His conscious mind would always identify sheep as what they were, but now they seemed to him as something else — something more. As he crept slowly forwards, eyes keenly watching the herd grazing a dozen yards in front of him, the sight and smell of them awakening instincts and emotions never before felt, making his mouth salivate with a strange anticipation, he realised that the sheep were no longer merely sheep — now they were living food!

As he bolted forward, the herd scattered in fright. One little lamb, separated from its mother, stood frozen with fear, bleating pitifully. He was on the lamb within seconds, hands gripping it tightly around the neck and pulling it to the ground, bared teeth lustily seeking its soft throat. As his teeth sunk in, he pulled and twisted his head violently, ripping and tearing at the flesh. Warm blood spurted into his mouth, nearly driving his senses wild with sensation and causing an orgasmic shock to course through his body. He dug his teeth in again, tearing the throat open, then savagely licked and chewed at the shredded flesh.

Minutes or perhaps hours later — it was impossible for him to tell which — he stood up slowly. The driving need within him had been satisfied, and now replacing it was a bone-tired weariness that threatened to make him collapse where he stood. Slowly, on legs that felt as if they were made of lead, he crossed the pasture and scrambled back over the fence, then made his way through the woods again, towards home. At the creekbed he slipped in the slick mud of the shallows, falling once faceforward in the boggy black water.

Reaching the house, he clambered clumsily up and through his bedroom window, then fell, exhausted, onto the bed. He lay languishing on the bed for a long time, revelling in the feel of the soft mattress against his tired body. In his dream, flashbacks of the earlier part began returning; springing on the lamb; teeth ripping and slashing the throat; blood bubbling hotly into his mouth — the exhilarating feel and taste of the kill. Only then, reliving these sequences again in vivid detail, was he frightened. His fright built quickly into an unreasoning panic. A part of his mind told him that it had only been a dream, another part screamed in horror.

Carolyn sat up in bed, listening. In her sleep, she thought she had heard her son cry out, but now she wasn't sure. She sat for another moment, listening to the silence of the house and debating whether or not to check on him. She finally decided that, as long as she was awake anyway, a little peek wouldn't hurt. Being careful not to wake Eli, she got out of bed and slipped on her bathrobe, then tiptoed down the short hall to Michael's room.

Entering his room, she could see her son's silhouetted form twisting and turning fitfully on the bed. The poor child, she thought sadly to herself as she sat down quietly on the side of the bed. He's having another one of them nightmares. She reached out in the darkness and took his hand. 'Michael, wake up, darling,' she said in a hushed voice, shaking his shoulder gently.

Michael stirred, a low, sobbing moan escaping his lips, then he was suddenly fully awake. He sat up abruptly, and throwing his arms around her waist, snuggled against her. 'Momma,' he wailed, 'I was so scared — it was terrible — '

'Shh,' she comforted. 'It was just another one of them nightmares. There ain't nothing to be scared of — momma's with you now.'

'This one was really awful,' he whined, burying his face deeper between her breasts and trembling. As he trembled against her, she could feel the cold wetness of his pyjamas through her housecoat.

'You poor thing,' she said sympathetically, 'you're dripping wet with sweat.' She gently ran her hand across his forehead and down the side of his face. Her hand came away wet, but the wetness seemed to have a strange sticky feel to it. Fumbling for the nightstand, she switched on the bedlamp.

'Eeelliii!' she screamed, looking down at her son in horror.

Eli, waking instantly, was out of bed and down the hall. 'What the — ?' he began, entering the bedroom. Then he stopped, stunned by the scene before him. 'What the hell happened?'

Michael sat trembling on the bed, his face, hands, and the entire front of his pyjamas soaked and smeared with a thick, gritty mixture of muddy filth and blood. The bedsheet was streaked with wet smears of crimson and greyish black, as was Carolyn's bathrobe. Eli could only stand, looking dumbfoundedly from one of them to the other.

'I — I don't know,' Carolyn wailed helplessly, still staring with horrified eyes at her son. 'I came in here, because he was crying and having another of them nightmares, and — ' She gestured desolately at the scene around her.

'Is he hurt anywhere?' Eli demanded, rushing to the bed and quickly unbuttoning Michael's pyjama top to inspect him for injury. It was hard to tell whether the blood was from him.

Eli got to his feet, eyes sweeping the bedroom, looking for any clue to the strange mystery. Noticing a series of dark streaks on and around the windowsill, he hurried over to take a closer look.

Two reddish-brown smears glistened wetly on the

windowsill, each ending in a small, perfectly defined hand-print. Another set of handprints discoloured the floor, just below the window. After seeing this evidence close up, Eli knew that his son had, for whatever his reason, climbed in through that window from the outside, then had placed his hands on the floor to balance his weight while he pulled his legs in after him. The only question was — why?

Turning to face Carolyn, Eli realised that she had not moved a muscle since he had entered the bedroom. She was still standing by the bed, hand pressed to her mouth, eyes staring fixedly at her son. 'Carolyn!' he said loudly, hoping to snap her out of her trancelike state.

Carolyn's eyes blinked a few times, then she slowly turned to look at him. Still, she said nothing.

'You okay, honey?' he asked, troubled by her now pasty-white complexion and wide, staring eyes.

Silently, she nodded.

'Well, get him cleaned up and see if you can find out what the hell happened,' he said, hurrying past her. 'I'm going to have a look around outside.'

Eli dressed quickly, then pulled on his boots and heavy overcoat. 'Be back soon,' he called over his shoulder, as he reached for his 30-06 rifle sitting in its groove in the rack over the couch. Leaving through the front door, he went around to the side of the house to inspect the area beneath his son's window.

Hearing Eli leave the house and the front door slam, Carolyn felt herself to begin functioning again. Picking Michael up under the arms and holding him as far away from her as possible, she carried him out of the bedroom and down the hall to the bathroom.

'Momma, is daddy mad at me?' Michael asked, fear in his voice.

'No, sweetheart, he — uh, ain't mad at you,' Carolyn answered, trying to choose her words carefully. 'He's just, well, upset about all that . . . icky stuff all over you. Where's it come from?'

'I don't know,' he said helplessly. 'I started off having the same bad dream again, but this time it was different — this time it got out and grabbed me, and there was a lot of blood and — ' He stopped talking in order to stifle a shudder. New tears filled his eyes.

'Well, don't you go thinking about none of it now,' she said, seeing that he was getting upset again. She turned the shower on and tested the temperature. 'Let me get you cleaned up a little, then we'll sit and talk . . . about your dream.' She picked Michael up and, pyjamas and all, placed him under the warm spray. As she removed his now sodden pyjamas, she watched the gritty reddish-black slime, now diluted by the shower, run in long rivulets down his body, puddle around his feet, then form a long stream leading to the drain.

The only disturbance in the area around the bedroom window was two sets of small, distinctly marked footprints leading both to and away from the house. Eli decided to follow them.

There was a full moon. Being a skilled hunter, he had little trouble in following his son's trail through the bushes of the forest and across the open field. As he travelled, eyes alertly watching the ground, one thought kept running through his mind. What could his son have been doing out here in the middle of the night? Sleepwalking? — or more accurately, going by the telltale signs he was finding on the ground — sleep-running?

As he came to the wire fence marking the boundary line of the Cavcart sheep ranch, their nearest neighbours to the south, he saw a large herd of sheep grazing off in the darkened distance. One sheep, standing off by itself near the fence, was pawing at something lying on the ground. Hopping the fence, he went over to investigate.

Leaning on the butt of his rifle, he kneeled down and stared in disbelief at the slaughtered lamb in front of him. Something had not only killed it but also had mauled it badly; its throat had been torn out. His first thought was that perhaps wolves had done it, knowing that small packs of them did exist in the forest . . . God, he thought, Michael could have been killed, like that lamb. But, no; wolves or any other predator he could think of would have preferred, after the kill, to feed on the soft under-belly. Except for the jagged, gaping neck-wound, the rest of the lamb's body was unmarked and intact.

He anxiously searched the ground for any evidence of paw prints. His son's small footprints were the only clear ones he could make out.

He tried desperately to think of an explanation for everything that had happened, for everything he had seen. There was none. As he stared down at the small mass of blood-stained wool, as the beginning of a realisation was banished within his brain. Gradually, the truth became undeniable, even to himself, and the realisation sickened him. Michael had been out here, probably only a few minutes after wolves that could have torn the child to pieces. Michael had almost stumbled over this viciously torn carcass, had probably looked down at it as Eli had to force himself to do now. Then Michael must have knelt down and . . .

Picking the lamb's carcass up easily in one hand, Eli returned to the fence; the sheep, still reluctant to leave her baby, followed after him, then stood and bleating pitifully as he hoisted himself and the dead lamb over the fence.

Entering the thick woods again, he dropped the carcass to the ground, knowing that the forest predators would soon find it and dispose of it. It would be better, he felt, for the lamb's body not to be discovered or even missed until he could find out exactly what had actually happened. If what he feared were true, his son's fits and sleepwalking had put the child in terrible danger.

Carolyn stopped her nervous pacing as Eli came in and dropped heavily into his chair. Going over to him, she sat down in the chair next to his.

'Where is he?' Eli asked in a tired monotone.

'I cleaned him up, put him in clean pyjamas and put him back to bed. Took me a while to get him calmed down. That nightmare he had got him pretty scared. Worst one yet. In this dream, he says he saw himself — '

' — kill a lamb by tearing its throat out,' Eli said, finishing her sentence for her.

She looked at him in surprise. 'How'd you know that?'

'I just saw the lamb,' he answered, his eyes meeting hers.

It took a moment, but finally his meaning dawned on her. 'Oh, Eli, no,' she said, shaking her head. 'You can't mean you think he actually — '

'I don't know what the hell to think,' he answered truthfully. 'But I can tell you one thing,' he added with dead seriousness, 'I sure aim to find out.'

15

Eli felt his eyelids droop and his head nod forward as the comforting mist of needed sleep began seeping into his consciousness, relaxing his exhausted brain. Yawning, he rubbed his eyes and sat up a little straighter on the seat in the truck. He shook his head in an effort to clear the grogginess that still clouded his mind, then unscrewed the top to the thermos lying on the seat beside him and poured himself a cup of hot, black coffee. He took a long swallow of the strong, bitter coffee and immediately felt its reviving effects as it burned its way down his throat and into his stomach. He poured himself another cup and downed it also. Sleep was something he definitely didn't want right now; he had to stay awake and keep watching — until he was sure.

For the last three nights, he had sat up all night in his truck, parked on the access road, facing the rear of the house. From this location, he had a clear view of not only his son's bedroom window, but also the forest beyond. If, for any reason, anything happened near that window, he could not help but see it — if he could only stay awake.

After the shocking incident of a few nights ago, Eli had been sure that what he suspected was true; that Michael had, for whatever unexplained reason, actually gone out into the night and come upon the slaughtered lamb, danced around the damn thing in his sleep for all he knew. But now, after three long and sleepless nights of sitting and waiting and watching, he was no longer sure what to believe.

On a few occasions, as he would sit, brain dazed from the lack of sleep, his mind would idly drift and wander, and brief, fuzzy remembrances would come to him; traces and impressions of things he had heard about long ago, in the past; stories he had heard as a child, perhaps. Although he could not remember it in any detail, still there was some-thing about the nighttime setting all around him, the things that had happened recently that seemed to vaguely remind him of something, but he had no idea of exactly what.

Setting his coffee cup on the seat beside him, he again began mulling over everything that had happened recently. Could it have all been nothing more than a unique series of coincidence? he wondered. No, there was still that blood smeared all over Michael's face and hands to explain — it had to have been him.

Carolyn, of course, had been overly defensive and pro-tective of Michael. But he had been there and had seen the remnants of the bloody slaughter that could just as well have been the death of his son as that of the lamb.

Thinking about it, he was again besieged by familiar fragments of old information, events he dimly remembered hearing about. Still, he couldn't see any relationship to them, but a glimmer of something seemed to be taking form in the back of his mind.

On the one hand, he prayed with all his heart that such a thing was not true, but at the same time, he found himself almost hoping to catch his son during one of these midnight escapades, wake him up out there in the woods and explain things to him, and in so doing, put an end, once and for all, to the doubt and mystery — for both of them.

He looked at his watch in the bright moonlight. Four-fifteen, he thought sullenly. Another night shot to hell. Have to give it another hour, then —

He first caught the movement out of the corner of his eye as something sprang from the bedroom window and darted across the grass, then disappeared into the thick foliage of the forest. Eli was out of his truck and moving towards the spot where the small form had disappeared into the bushes even before he had fully comprehended what he had seen. Had that been Michael? he thought incredulously as he tried to close the distance between himself and whatever he had seen. It had moved so incredibly fast, and it had not been running upright, but rather in some kind of a crouch . . .

Reaching the outskirts of the woods, Eli plunged in through the thick bushes and crowded trees, then came to an almost skidding halt. Which way had he gone? he wondered as his eyes desperately swept the shadows in search of footprints, broken twigs — anything that might give him a clue as to direction.

Giving out a sigh of frustration, he checked the area again, more closely; all the while regretting his stupidity for not thinking to bring a flashlight. Still, he found no trace of anything passing over the ground or through the bushes. He stood for a moment, confused. It seemed impossible for Michael — if it had *been* Michael — to have moved so swiftly through the tangled underbrush yet leave no trace of his passing. Especially when he had so easily followed his son's trail a few nights ago . . .

On a hunch, he decided to go in the direction of the Cavcart sheep ranch — which he had now begun to think of as the location of his son's last killing. Maybe, just maybe, Michael had gone back again.

He abandoned the idea with relief as soon as he came within sight of the fence and saw the flock of sheep grazing peaceably and undisturbed. He stopped, slowly rubbing the back of his head in confusion as, again, traces of a subconscious remembrance flickered teasingly through his brain; the moonlit forest; the mental picture of something prowling the night . . . it all seemed to remind him of something long forgotten, but he couldn't remember what, and now it was gone . . .

Eli turned and began trudging back towards the house, wondering as he went what the hell he could tell Carolyn that would not send her into a fit of hysterics.

When Eli entered the house, he was surprised to find his wife awake and pacing the floor nervously. One look at her distraught features and the way she was wringing her hands gave him a good idea of her mental state. He had seen her like this only once before: four nights earlier, when they had discovered their son, covered with blood. He shuddered inwardly; now he would have to give her some kind of an explanation, an explanation he didn't as yet have, an explanation he knew she wouldn't accept.

'Eli, where have you been? Michael's gone!' She rushed to him. 'I got up to check on him and he ain't in his bed.'

'I know,' he said, slumping into a chair. 'I was sitting out in the truck and I seen him go running like a rabbit into the woods.' He made a helpless gesture. 'I tried following him, but he must have been moving like a cat. I couldn't pick up his trail or nothing.'

'Eli, what's *happening* to him?' She was half-shouting, confusion and worry on her face. 'He's just a little kid — supposed to be sleeping peaceable in his bed. What's he doing out there in the woods in the middle of the night?'

'Come on and sit down beside me, darlin',' Eli said slowly, keeping his voice as calm as he could. 'We got us some real serious talking to do.'

His last statement seemed to scare her more than whatever she had been thinking. She silently took the chair next to his, and sat staring at him intently, waiting.

'There's something going on with Michael — I don't know rightly what, but I think it's something real bad.'

'You mean with his dreams, and everything? That don't mean nothing. It's just — '

'Now, just hear me out,' he said, holding up a hand to silence her, 'and after I'm done saying my piece, then we'll set and we'll both talk about it. You hear?'

She fell silent but let him talk, her face drawing even tighter with worry.

'Now,' he began, trying to choose his words carefully, 'we've known since he was born that there's — well, something different about him — that he didn't seem to think or act like other children. Well, we was right — he *is* different, but in ways you can't begin to imagine. I ain't got all the answers yet, but you just think on it — the strange way he always had with animals . . . the way he was never scared of nothing, until just lately . . . the way he bit that boy at school instead of just hitting him.' He paused to take a deep breath against the tension that was coming back to his chest. 'It was all leading to something, I don't know rightly what, but . . . well, that *something* has happened to him.'

'What're you talking about, Eli?' Carolyn was looking at him as if she thought he was out of his mind. 'Ain't nothing happened to him. But these terrible dreams and — '

'Use your head, woman,' Eli shouted, in spite of himself. 'That wasn't no goddamn dream a couple of nights ago — he really went out there and like to tore out that lamb's throat with his teeth. I seen it. He's out there somewhere now, doing — God knows what!' He almost sobbed with the effort of saying it aloud to her — and to himself.

Carolyn stared at him, her mouth agape.

Eli regained his composure and his face softened sympathetically. 'You're right, it is terrible. God help me, it's no dream — not no more.'

'Eli, you're talking crazy,' Carolyn said, looking at him strangely, as if he suddenly grown another head. 'That's your son you're talking about — your own flesh and blood — and you're talking about him like he was some kind of — *monster*.'

'No I ain't, I mean, he ain't — ' Eli began. Suddenly it came back to him, flooding into his memory; the stories he had heard, the legends — everything. It was his own son who was the legend. The realisation of what he knew to be true struck him like a sharp blow to the stomach, momentarily sickening him. He stared at Carolyn for a few seconds before speaking again.

'I don't know — maybe he is,' he said, feeling defeated by the possibilities around him.

'I don't want to hear no more of this!' Carolyn, nearly hysterical, jumped to her feet and covered her ears with her hands.

'How do you think I feel — praying to God there ain't nothing wrong, but knowing in my heart that something *is*!' Eli's words ended in a sob.

Carolyn turned around and saw the tortured look on his face, the tears glistening in his eyes — something she had never seen from him before. She felt a rush of sympathy that for a moment overcame her own anguish; how much it must have taken for him to have said what he had. Going to him, she cradled his head in her arms and soothingly stroked his back.

'He's . . . possessed by something,' Eli mumbled between deep sobs, the tears rolling down his face. 'Possessed by a demon of some kind — making him do the things he's doing.'

'I know you must believe all the things you're saying, Eli,' she told him softly, 'but it just ain't true — it can't be.'

'It *is* true — believe me, it is,' he said emphatically, 'and we got to do something to stop him — to help him — before it's too late.'

She looked at him, puzzled. 'Too late how? Too late for

what?' she asked, the fear creeping back into her voice.

Eli was silent for a long moment, his face pressed against her stomach, seemingly collecting his thoughts. Finally, he raised his head and blinked to look deeply into her eyes.

'When I was a little kid, not much older than Michael,' he said slowly, 'my grandma used to sit me down with her in front of the fire at night and tell me stories, stories she'd heard way back when *she* was a little girl up country, about the cursed ones — the ones that stalked the forest in the dead of night by the light of the full moon, attacking travellers on the road, killing livestock, sometimes even stealing little children right out of their beds and luring them off to be raised with the wolves, to be *like* them. Horrible, tortured souls, possessed by the spirit of a demon wolf. Stories that used to scare the bejesus outta me, but stories I naturally never really believed — until this started up.'

Carolyn drew back from him involuntarily and looked down at him in shock. 'Oh, Eli — no! You can't honestly mean what you're saying — '

'I do believe it — now,' he answered, looking away from her towards the window. 'Michael's possessed, like with the spirit of a werewolf.'

'Why, that's just stupid superstition,' she declared, looking at him as if he were the one possessed. 'Them things are just old grandmother's scarey fairy tales. You can't believe that stuff — and you sure ain't gonna convince me.'

Now it was Eli's turn to look at her strangely. 'What *will* it take to convince you?' he asked seriously. 'Think of everything that's happened until now — could be happening right now, out there, for all we know. What more do you need — for him to come prancing in here on all fours, growling and snapping?' He drew a long, tired breath. 'Whatever he seen out there, it's like he wants to become part of it. Can't you see that?'

'What — what do you say we should do?' she asked, fearing the answer she would hear.

'I don't know,' he admitted, spreading his hands in a hopeless gesture. 'I don't even know where my boy is. We have to help him somehow — keep him from doing this . . . ' His voice trailed off.

'How can we, Eli?' she asked gently.

She was interrupted as a muffled thump sounded on the porch at the front door. Their eyes met for only an instant to exchange the unspeakable terror they both felt, then they were both on their feet, rushing to the front door.

Michael lay in a tight, shivering ball on the porch. His pyjama top had been almost completely torn from his body and hung in tattered shreds at the cuffs and neck, and he seemed to be bleeding heavily from his mouth. Sticking to the congealing blood smears on his face and hands were a multitude of tiny, brown feathers. Blood flowed from two jagged wounds on his left arm and wrist, spreading on the porch in an ever-widening pool. He was exhausted and weak, barely able to cry.

Eli quickly stooped and picked his son up in his arms, then carried him through the house and into the bedroom. While Carolyn went to get bandages, he stripped Michael naked and inspected him carefully for further injury. The bleeding around Michael's mouth and the wounds on his left arm, although ugly, proved not to be severe and were the only damage he found.

'Looks like some kind of animal bite,' he said as Carolyn returned to clean the wounds and apply dressing. Neither of them could find where the blood around his mouth had come from. 'Must've bit his lip or something,' Eli said, wringing out the washcloth for Carolyn. 'If I didn't know better I'd say he got set on by a hawk, from the looks of these feathers. But these here holes in his arm is from teeth.'

Michael was asleep before he was finally cleaned up. His parents put him in fresh pyjamas and tucked him into bed again, then left the bedroom, closing the door behind them.

'He's just sleeping,' Carolyn said to Eli in amazement. 'After whatever all he must have just gone through — he's just sleeping. I wonder if he was ever awake.

Eli was holding one of the small, brown feathers under the lamp, examining it closely. 'Hawk or a eagle, I would have figured,' he said, more to himself than to Carolyn. 'But . . . them's chicken feathers he's got all over him.'

16

Eli shrugged into his coat, then straightened his tie. He hated wearing a suit and tie, but Carolyn had insisted, saying that if they were going into a church he would have to look presentable. After being up until dawn, he was too tired to argue. Anyhow, he thought as he looked at his blooshot, red-rimmed eyes in the bathroom mirror, he had more important things to worry about.

After getting Michael back to bed and to sleep, he and Carolyn had sat up for the rest of the night, trying to decide what they should do next . . .

'I think we ought to take him to a doctor,' Carolyn had said. 'We have to get them bites on his arm took care of, anyway — and maybe if we let on a little of what's been happening with Michael, a doctor could tell us what we could do.'

'What the hell would a doctor know about a kid being possessed like a werewolf?' Eli said bitterly, the sleepless hours of tension leaving him on edge. 'Unless maybe you want to take him to a veterinarian.'

'You got a better idea?'

'Well, you could say the problem we got here is kind of supernatural,' Eli said after thinking for a minute. 'Maybe if we took him to a minister or a priest or someone like that — maybe *he* might know something about it.'

Carolyn thought it over. 'We could take him to the Congregation of God in Pea Ridge. We was married in that church, I'm sure Reverend Simmons will be willing to see us. He once told me that if we ever needed his advice — '

'You nuts?' Eli snapped. 'We have to *live* in this town. We can't go telling anybody in Pea Ridge about it. It would be all over town in a matter of hours.'

'But the reverend's a man of God; anything we told him has got to be confidential.'

Eli gave her a dubious look. 'You must be joking. You ever tell anyone around here, including the reverend, that your kid's running around the countryside at night, sniffing around animals what's had their throats tore out — it would be like putting it on the front page of the Sunday newspaper. Our friends and neighbours'll come storming over here in a mob to lynch us.' He shook his head emphatically. 'No, we can't go telling no one around here about it — we gotta protect the boy until we get to the bottom of this.'

'I still want to take him to a doctor and get his arm looked after. We can't take no chances with infection or nothing.'

'Okay,' Eli agreed, 'but not around here. First thing in the morning we get ourselves dressed and take a drive over to Bentonville or Rogers — someplace we ain't known — find us a doctor to look after Michael and then hunt up a church. We ain't even gonna give out our right names.'

Eli ran the comb through his hair again in an effort to get the cowlick that was standing up in the back to stay down. He threw the comb into the sink as the cowlick popped up again and walked out of the bathroom to find Carolyn helping Michael into his coat by the front door.

'We're all ready to go,' she said, glancing up at him appraisingly. 'You look real nice,' she said, smiling at him.

'Ain't it kind of too warm for a coat?' he asked, too upset to hear the compliment.

'Probably is,' she agreed, 'but I wanted to keep his arm covered up tight. Don't want to give no one a reason for asking a bunch of questions.'

'I just got to stop by work,' Eli said, 'let people know I won't be in today. Then we'll be on our way.'

'Daddy,' Michael asked, 'where we going?'

'We gotta take a drive over to Bentonville to get your arm fixed up by a doctor, then we're gonna talk to a man that can . . . maybe . . . help you to stop having them dreams that're scaring you so bad.'

'Momma says I'm having dreams because I'm sick — that true?'

'Well — sorta true,' Eli answered, giving Carolyn an annoyed look. 'It's not the kind of sick like you had a cold or nothing. It's like there was something bothering you in your head — something special. We're hoping the man we're gonna talk to can help you with it so you'll stop

146

having scarey dreams and be okay again.'

'I don't feel sick — except maybe that my arm hurts so. Do we got to go?'

'Yeah, we got to. It's very important we do.'

'Why?'

'Because I say it is,' Eli answered with finality, annoyed with himself that he had tried to give Michael an explanation he didn't have. 'Now go with your momma and sit in the truck. I'll be out in a minute.'

Eli waited until he saw Carolyn, leading Michael by the hand, pass the window and walked towards the truck before he went into the kitchen. From the top shelf of a cabinet, he took down a bottle of bourbon left over from their wedding and still unopened. Although as a rule he almost never drank and knew Carolyn disapproved, the tension-filled night he had just spent and the kind of a day he saw ahead of him convinced him that, morning or not, he needed one. Breaking the seal on the bottle, he poured three fingers of whiskey into a small glass, then, taking a deep breath, downed it in one long gulp. It had the desired effect as he felt the whiskey warm away at the knot of tension that had formed in the pit of his stomach, relaxing him somewhat. Returning the bottle to its hiding place on the top shelf, he went to the front door, feeling ready to face whatever the day might bring.

'Eli,' Carolyn called from outside, concern in her voice, 'there's someone coming down the road, heading this way.'

Stepping out on the front porch and locking the door, Eli turned to see Ned Grissom, his neighbour, in the familiar battered pickup truck coming up the access road leading to the house. 'Damn,' Eli muttered to himself, 'what the hell does *he* want?'

Ned Grissom owned a small farm bordering their property, and by no stretch of the imagination could he and Eli be termed friends. They had only spoken to each other twice in their lives that Eli could recall, both occasions ending in an argument. The first time was when the dog Otto was still around, and Grissom had come over to complain that the dog was coming over onto his property at night, scaring his livestock. When Grissom threatened to shoot the dog on sight, the argument began. The other time they had had dealings was over a deer Eli had shot while hunting. Grissom had come over, half drunk as usual, saying that the deer was shot on his property and that he was entitled to half the meat. Eli had told him to go to hell, and they had not spoken since.

Eli walked slowly down from the porch as Grissom pulled his truck to a squealing stop right in front of him, a good distance from where Carolyn and Michael were waiting. 'Howdy, Grissom,' he said politely, anxious to be off. 'What brings you over here?'

Grissom sat regading Eli silently for a moment, then went right to the point. 'Something – or someone – got into my coop last night – killed most of my chickens,' he said, eying Eli closely.

'Oh, yeah?' Eli said, forcing the grin that Grissom's ill-fortune would under normal circumstance have caused. 'Sorry to hear that.'

Grissom's face flushed slightly. 'Yeah. Well, I heard the ruckus and sent Holly, my sheep dog, out to take a look. Whatever it was killed her, too.'

'That's a real shame,' Eli sympathised, putting as much mock sadness as he could into his voice. 'Why tell me about it?'

'Figured you might *know* something about it,' Grissom said, his face darkening with repressed anger.

Eli merely shook his head negatively. 'Fox or wolf, most likely.'

'Look, MacCleary!' Grissom shouted suddenly, 'whatever it was fighting with my dog and running away afterwards, it didn't run like no animal, but up on two legs,' He cast a long, meaningful look over at Michael. 'Where was *he* last night? I mean, maybe he *seen* something.'

'You saying my kid has something to do with your chickens?' Eli asked, his voice turning hard. He could feel the knot of tension returing to the pit of his stomach. This was trouble.

'Two tenant fellers what live on my land *seen* somebody running upright on two legs and weren't no bigger'n your kid there. You got the only kid living right in these immediate parts. Ask him.'

Eli leaned in close to Grissom's face, as much to see if Grissom had a shotgun in the truck with him as to put force behind his words. 'You saying my boy killed your chickens.'

Grissom, who had no gun that Eli could see, made an effort to control his anger. 'I ain't accusing nobody of nothing,' he replied, backing down instinctively from the imposing figure of Eli, 'but that's 'cause I ain't got no proof — yet.'

'Then we ain't got no more to say, do we?' Eli rumbled through clenched teeth. 'So now you can just get the hell out of here, and don't come back. You ain't welcome.'

Grissom started his truck and began to move, then he glanced curiously at Michael, then back to Eli, 'What's the matter with your boy's arm? He's holding it kinda funny.'

'He fell out of a tree and hurt it,' Eli answered lamely. 'Ain't none of your concern.'

The shrewd look that crossed Grissom's face turned again to one of anger.

'Just a fair warning to you and yourn, MacCleary,' he shouted, pointing his finger at Eli's face. 'Right now I got me about a dozen chickens and with their heads either hacked or torn off and a dog with her neck broke — and I don't like it, I don't like it one damn bit! From now on, anybody trespassing on my land gets shot — and shot dead. *Anybody*.' Grissom floored the accelerator of his truck and sped away, turning the road into a tunnel of dust behind him.

'What was all that shouting about?' Carolyn asked, as Eli slid behind the wheel of the truck. 'I couldn't hear what you was saying.'

'He knows,' Eli said, pounding his fist down on the seat between them. 'That son-of-a-bitch knows.'

'Knows what?' she asked, surprised to hear him swear in front of Michael.

'He knows what must have happened last night.' Eli explained, carefully watching his words now. 'I should have just let him talk, but I got so damn mad at him looking at Michael thataway . . .'

Carolyn, looking stricken, said nothing.

'Carolyn,' Eli said, trying his best to keep the emotion he felt out of his voice, 'if Grissom knows what happened, or even just guesses — then others are going to know. We got to do something to end this . . . nightmare, before it's too late.'

Eli parked their truck at the curb in front of the church, the only one he could find of their denomination in Benton County. Going up the stone steps, they entered the church through a pair of arched wooden doors, Carolyn holding Michael tightly by the hand. They stood in the vestibule, looking around selfconsciously.

'Boy,' Carolyn said, looking in wonder at the stained glass windows, the carved decorations and statues on the walls and the ornate filigree of the altar, 'I never been in a church this nice. Ain't it just beautiful? Makes the one back in Pea Ridge look like a wooden schoolhouse.'

'Yeah — sure is pretty,' Eli said distractedly. 'I wonder where everybody is.' He started walking down the centre aisle, lined on both sides with deserted pews. When he was halfway down the aisle, a door to the left of the altar opened and a grey-haired man who Eli guessed to be in his late fifties came out.

'Good morning,' the man said with a wide smile. 'May I be of service to you?'

'Howdy,' Eli said, a little uneasily, 'we're — uh, looking for the minister. Want to talk to him about something.'

'That would be me,' the man said, his smile broadening. 'Please pardon the business suit, I've just returned from the bank. If this is for confession, please give me a moment to — '

'No, no, nothing like that,' Eli said quickly. 'Just a personal problem the family has. We don't know who else to talk to.'

'I see. Well, I would be happy to discuss whatever it is with you and see if I can be of help. My name is Benjamin Thomas.' He extended his hand.

'Mine's Martin,' Eli said, saying the first name that came to mind, 'Eli Martin. This is my wife, Carolyn and our son, Michael.' He shook the priest's hand.

'Pleased to meet you folks,' Father Thomas said, smiling benevolently. 'If you'd like to come in here,' he suggested, indicating the small office from which he had come, 'we can talk without being disturbed.'

'You just set right here and read your comic book while we talk with the father,' Carolyn said, turning to Michael. 'We won't be long.'

150

'The boy is more than welcome to join us,' Father Thomas suggested.

Eli shot a quick glance at Carolyn, who shook her head slightly. 'Naw, I think it'd better he didn't,' Eli answered, dropping his voice. 'This – uh, problem, has to do with him.'

'As you wish,' Father Thomas said, leading the way into his office. After seating them in chairs beside his desk, he went to a small stove where a teapot had just begun whistling.

'May I offer you some tea?' he asked, pouring himself a cup.

They both refused the tea and sat glancing nervously at each other as Father Thomas fixed the tea to his liking, then sat down behind his desk.

'Are you from around here, Mr. Martin?' Father Thomas asked, taking a sip of tea.

'Huh?' Eli faltered, momentarily forgetting the name he had just given. 'Uh – no, we're from up north. Just in town for the day.'

'I see,' Father Thomas said thoughtfully. 'I must say, I find this a little unusual. Most of my consultations are with members of the community and of the church. But, of course, I'm here to help whenever I can. Now, what seems to be troubling you?' He leaned back in his chair and took another sip.

'It's our son, father,' Carolyn said, mastering her fear for the first time. 'We think he's possessed by some kind of demon. He thinks he's like a werewolf.'

Father Thomas sputtered and coughed as the tea he was drinking went down the wrong pipe. 'I – I don't believe I heard you correctly,' he said, when his coughing finally subsided. 'You believe your son is a – *what?*'

'Possessed, like a werewolf,' Eli said, repeating Carolyn's statement. 'I think it all started back when he was a – '

'If this is your idea of a joke.' Father Thomas said, looking at Eli indignantly, 'I assure you, I do not find it the least bit amusing.'

'Never more serious in my life,' Eli said, spreading his hands in a helpless gesture. 'How do you think *we* feel – thinking it's true?'

'What you're saying makes no sense,' Father Thomas said, looking at them in disbelief. 'The werewolf is nothing more than a myth, a superstition — a fairy tale. You can't possibly believe that such creatures exist — much less that your son is actually *possessed* by one, or any such nonsense.'

Eli shrugged again. 'We think it's true,' he said simply. 'Our son *is* like he's a werewolf. Ain't no doubt about it in my mind.'

'But — ,' Father Thomas began again, then he reconsidered what Eli had just told him. 'What, exactly, makes you believe this so strongly?'

Eli then spent the next forty-five minutes giving Father Thomas the best account he could of everything that had occurred, from Michael's birth, up to and including the strange events of the night that had just passed. When he had finished his story, he sat back in his chair, and in the heavy silence that followed the three of them just sat staring at one another.

Father Thomas finally cleared his throat. 'Mr Martin, I can not dispute what you've just told me, only your interpretation of it. I do not believe this is a question of a supernatural being possessing your son, but more a gross lack of moral and spiritual training, causing him to imagine the things you've described.' He took a deep breath, as if still considering his thoughts. 'If you'll just call your son in now, there are a few questions I'd like to ask him.'

'But he don't know nothing about none of this,' Carolyn explained. 'He still thinks it's all just a bunch of bad dreams.'

'I have no intention of saying differently,' Father Thomas assured them. In fact, he thought to himself, the child is probably right.

After Michael had come in and was sitting on his mother's lap, Father Thomas asked him, 'Tell me, Michael, do you believe in God?'

'I believe in Jesus,' Michael answered. 'Momma reads the Bible to me and says Jesus is the Son of God. Is that the same thing?'

'Yes, it is. Tell me, do you understand what she reads to you?'

'Yeah, I guess so — some of it.'

Father Thomas turned his attention to Carolyn. 'And do *you* understand what you're reading to him.?'

'Most of it,' she answered, nodding. 'Some of the begetting and begots get me a little confused.'

He turned back to Michael. 'Tell me about these frightening dreams you've been having.'

Michael told him about the woods, and the moon — but not about the thing beyond the veil.

'What do you suppose is causing you to have such terrible dreams?'

'I don't know,' Michael answered. 'Momma says it's because when I go to sleep, my imagination wakes up and is scaring me.'

'Tell me, do you ever dream about God or Jesus?'

'Naw, never,' Michael answered, confused. 'Should I?'

Father Thomas put the palms of his hands on his desk top, a look of confidence on his face. He turned to Eli. 'As I stated earlier,' he said, ignoring Michael's question, 'the boy is clearly suffering from a lack of proper moral and religious training. Now, our church offers an excellent programme for young people. The classes meet every Tuesday and Thursday afternoon.'

Now it was Eli's turn to wear the disbelieving look. 'You mean to say, after everything we told you before — you want to put him in Sunday school? What we told you before was the gospel truth — it got nothing to do with him not knowing the disciples' names backwards and frontwards — he really is hexed like I said. Ain't there some kind of ritual or something you can do to him to rid him of the — bad thing that's plaguing him?'

'No, of course not,' Father Thomas said with a dismissing wave of his hand. 'What you were suggesting before was nothing more than superstitious fantasy. There is nothing the church can do for you if you hang tight to such notions.'

'Then I guess we'll just have to take care of it ourselves,' Eli said, getting to his feet. 'Thank you kindly for giving us so much of your time and talking to us. Now I think we better get going.'

Father Thomas was taken aback. 'I assure you, Mr. Martin, after a strict religious programme — '

'Thank you again,' Eli said, as he ushered Carolyn and Michael out of the office and closed the door behind him.

'You go in the house and make us some lunch,' Eli told Carolyn as he pulled the truck into the carport beside their house and cut the engine. 'Me and Michael are going to take us a little walk down by the creek.'

'You gonna talk about his sleepwalking, ain't you?' Carolyn asked, a look of concern on her face.

Eli nodded.

'You sure that's the best thing to do? You're gonna scare him terrible.'

'It's the only thing I *can* do. Now, we ain't got no choice — he's gotta know. He'll handle it,' Eli forced a grin. 'He's my son, ain't he?'

Eli walked with Michael for a long time in silence. Michael, knowing that something was wrong but not what it was, continually glanced up at his father, a look of worry on his face. When they finally reached the spot that Eli had had in mind, he stopped and motioned for his son to sit down on an overturned log by the creek bank.

Michael could stand the suspense no longer. 'Daddy,' he asked, 'am I in trouble for something? Did I do something wrong?'

'Naw, it's nothing like that,' Eli said, stalling against the inevitable. 'There's just some things I got to tell you — about yourself, and I want you to listen up real careful and try to understand what I'm saying.'

'Okay, daddy, I'll try,' Michael promised bravely, the worry on his face deepening. 'What is it?'

'Well, this ain't easy for me, but I guess the only way to say it is to come right out with it,' Eli began. Kneeling down, he took Michael's hand in his and looked the boy squarely in the eyes, the sorrow he was feeling a tangible ache inside him. 'Like it or not, son, the fact of the matter is — uh, them bad dreams you've been having — they ain't just dreams.' He took another deep breath, then continued. 'You're possessed by some kind of a — something, and come nightfall . . . '

17

Eli carefully backed his truck up to the rear of the house, out of sight of the road and just outside Michael's bedroom window, and began unloading pieces of lumber and hardware. One of the advantages of having worked his way up at the sawmill was that he could get as much lumber as he needed, whenever he needed it; today he had taken advantage of that fringe benefit. After the materials were stacked beside the house, he went inside to let Carolyn know he was home and to see how Michael was feeling.

'Did you get everything you needed?' Carolyn asked, her tone still showing traces of the fight they had had hours before.

'Yeah, I think so,' Eli answered, trying to ignore the sarcasm in her voice. He looked around for Michael, then saw the closed bedroom door. 'He still as upset as before?' he asked, opening the refrigerator to get a beer.

'Sure he is — what do you expect?' Her earlier anger was now rekindled. 'Honestly, Eli,' she said, looking at him, 'you could've tried to be a little gentler about telling him what you're going to do. He was crying and upset, and asking me a million questions almost the whole time you were gone. I finally had to lay him down in bed, he got so bad.'

'I *was* gentle — gentle as I could be,' Eli said defensively. 'But, the way things are now, I had to tell him something — wasn't no other way of doing it.' He looked at her challengingly. 'Considering the kind of things we had to try and explain to him — things we hardly understand ourselves — could *you've* done different?'

'I guess not, but you could've at least told *me* what happened; you left me here, worried sick while you was out there talking to him. Then you bring him home, damn near hysterical, and go racing off to town to get whatever it was you needed so bad — and left me to answer all his questions.'

'You're right — I'm sorry. It's just that I had to get that stuff, so I could get the damn thing built and put up before nightfall.' He took a deep breath. 'Well, you know what I told him, so I don't got to go into that. After I finished, he must've thought I was just joking with him, because he started laughing. Then he must've . . . all of a sudden realised I was dead serious because he got like a shocked look on his face for a long time, then he started crying and asking me if it meant he was some kinda monster or something. I told him no — it just meant he had a special kind of trouble, and that we'd help him with it — protect him, keep him out of trouble and, above all, keep it a secret until we could find a way to rid him of it. He was real upset, but I think he understood. He's a smart boy.'

'I wish I understood,' Carolyn said, on the verge of tears.

Eli nodded, then looked at his watch. 'It's getting late. I better get to it if I want to get done before night,' he said, getting up and walking towards Michael's bedroom.

'Do you have to bother him now?' Carolyn said. 'He was so upset, and I just got him quieted down . . . '

'I figure if I can get him to help with the building of it, it'll help him to accept it — to understand how it's got to be from now on.' He knocked lightly on Michael's door and went in.

Michael lay awake on his bed, staring fixedly at the ceiling as Eli entered the bedroom. Fresh tears streaked his face, and as he turned his head slowly towards his father, his eyes showed a mixture of sorrow and fear.

'How you doing, boy?' Eli asked softly, sitting down on the edge of the bed.

'Oh, daddy,' Michael wailed, sitting up and putting his arms around Eli's neck, clutching at him tightly. 'I'm so scared. What's going to happen to me?' He began crying again.

'I ain't going to let nothing happen to you,' Eli promised solemnly, hugging his son to him. 'Yeah, it's a terrible, terrible thing that's got hold of you, but it's something we can fight together — just the three of us. We can't let anybody else find out about it, because if they did, they wouldn't understand and they'd make trouble — trouble I couldn't do nothing about.' He held is son at arm's length and looked seriously into his eyes. 'You got to promise not to tell nobody — not even your closest friend — about it; that way, we can try to fight this thing that's — cursing you without worrying about somebody messing in our business.'

'I promise, daddy.'

'Good,' Eli said simply, putting on a smile he didn't feel; the sheer tragedy he felt inside threatened to bring tears to his own eyes. He knew he could not let that happen; he knew *he* had to be the one with the strength. Without him to rely on, to lean on, Carolyn, and certainly Michael, would not be able to handle this horrible situation and his worst fears would definitely come to pass.

'There's a couple of things we need to do right away, to make sure you don't get in more trouble,' Eli explained, as lightly as he could.

'What do we have to do?' Michael asked, worry returning to his face.

'Well, if you take to it again,' Eli said, 'we can't be having you running all over the countryside any more. Whatever it is what happens, we have to make real sure you're kept safe in your room here at home and out of trouble. I told you about old man Grissom and what he said. Well, you can bet he's gonna be watching for something to shoot at, so we just have to make sure you don't wander over there, or anywhere else for that matter. Do you understand?'

Michael shook his head no; the tears beginning to glisten in his eyes again.

Eli took a deep breath and finally forced himself to say it plainly to his son. 'We have to put bars on your windows, Michael. And a bolt on the bedroom door. That way if you do get caught up by — whatever, you'll be kept right in here.'

Michael began crying again.

'Oh, it won't be so bad,' Eli said, wiping a tear from Michael's face with his thumb. 'It'll just mean that, while you're sleeping, the door will be locked — that's all.'

'I don't wanna be locked in my room at night,' Michael subbed. 'It'll scare me terrible. What if I have to go to the bathroom or something?'

'Now, don't go worrying about that kinda stuff. You can

take care of that before you hit the sack, and you'll have the little chamber pot in there too. If you need anything else in the middle of the night, you just give a holler and me or momma'll come right in.'

'I don't care,' Michael insisted, the suffocating memory of the dark closet at school almost making him gasp. 'I'm scared to be locked up like that.'

'Now, boy,' Eli said, his voice becoming stern. 'I explained everything to you — you can see we don't got a choice. You say yourself when this . . . this thing comes over you, it's like you was in a dream and you got no control over what you do.' He paused, groping for the right words. 'When this thing happens to you, we gotta be able to control it — else you're likely to get into a lot of trouble, either by hurting somebody or something, or maybe getting hurt yourself. Grissom says if he sees anybody on his land again he's gonna shoot to kill — and the way that man drinks I believe him.' He paused again and his voice softened. 'Anyhow, you don't want to be going out and killing animals like that, do you?'

'No, daddy, 'course not.'

'Well then, I guess you can see the point of it — until we can find a way to rid you of whatever's cursing you like this. You can see we got us no choice, can't you?'

Michael agreed, looking anything but convinced.

'Right now, we got us some building to do,' Eli said, getting up from the bed and smiling as cheerfully as he could. 'Want to help me?'

Michael put his feet on the floor beside the bed, then sat still and looked up at his father. 'I guess so, daddy,' he said after a moment. 'but it makes me feel funny — helping you build my own cage.'

While Michael held a short length of four-by-four lumber against the outside of the house just below the window, Eli fastened it in place by driving long wood bolts completely through holes he had drilled in the beam, and into the frame of the house. He then drilled a series of larger holes, spaced six inches apart, into the top of the four-by-four. Into the holes he had drilled, he then inserted lengths of wooden dowelling, each an inch and a half thick and three feet long. After drilling corresponding holes in another piece of four-by-four, he fitted it over the top ends of the dowelling and bolted it securely to the house, just above the top of the window frame. The result was a crude set of sturdy bars covering Michael's bedroom window. To this he added a border of thick, scalloped moulding to the top and sides. The finished product looked picture-framed and decorative; Eli hoped the extra touches would hide its actual purpose if anyone ever wandered around to the back of their house. As an added precaution, he painted the bars and moulding the same colour as the trim of the house.

'I can't look at it,' Carolyn said, turning away in disgust after seeing Eli's handiwork. 'Every time I look at it, it'll remind me of . . . what he is.'

'Every time we look at *him*, we're going to be reminded of what he is,' Eli said, more curtly than he had meant to. His voice softened. 'I know how you feel, sweetheart, but this is necessary. So is the sliding bolt I put on his bedroom door. We need it all.' He took her hand and led her around towards the front of the house.

'But, to keep him a prisoner in his own bedroom . . . '

'We have to. We got to keep him confined and under some kind of control. When it happens to him again — and it *will*, God help us — we can't be letting him run all over the countryside, maybe killing someone or getting his ass shot off by somebody like Grissom. Can't you see that?'

She stopped and looked at him. 'Eli, are you sure?'

'Sure about what?'

'Sure that all this is the right way.' She looked at him steadily, hopefully. 'Maybe you're wrong — maybe it's just — '

'I ain't wrong,' he shouted, again without meaning to, the tension of the situation getting to him. 'I ain't wrong,' he repeated quietly, almost sadly. 'And if you can't see that — especially after everything that's happened until now — ' He gave a long, meaningful look at the barred window. 'I got a feeling we're going to see it for ourselves. And soon enough.'

They both lay awake in bed that night, each hoping the other was asleep.

Eli lay on his back, staring vacantly up at the dark ceiling.

He had known it would be impossible for him to sleep when he had gotten into bed; he had made the pretence for Carolyn's sake, hoping that if she thought he was asleep, she would drop off herself.

When would it happen again, he wondered. Tonight? Tomorrow night? Would they be forced to endure a long string of nervous days and tension-filled, sleepless nights before this possession, this change came over Michael again and he could finally be sure — sure that Michael actually was what he thought him to be; sure of the precautions he had taken to keep Michael safe; sure that all these things were necessary and effective. These were the thoughts that had plagued Eli's brain as he lay unmoving and pretending sleep for the last four hours.

He knew that Carolyn could not bring herself to face what he had told her about Michael. Lying here now and thinking about it, the total unreality of it struck him and he found himself doubting everything himself. Well, he thought as he rolled over on his side and forced his breathing into the evenness of sleep, soon the truth would be at hand — and if they were patient, they could solve it themselves.

'Eli, what're we going to do?' Carolyn asked suddenly in the darkness. 'We can't just leave him locked up every night for the rest of his life. What're we going to do to help him now that we have him nailed in his room?'

'I don't know,' he answered truthfully, dropping his pretence of sleep. 'I was just laying here thinking about that. I don't know what we can do.'

'Maybe we could take him to one of them special doctors, the kind that're supposed to help with mental troubles; maybe he could do something.'

'They'd probably put him in one of the crazy houses, thinking he was nuts — us too. Naw, whatever we do, we got to keep this to ourselves — work it out ourselves. Ain't nobody in this world gonna believe our kid's acting like a werewolf — if we told them that, we'd be giving ourselves more trouble than we got already.'

'So I'm asking, what do *we* do?'

'I don't rightly know. Maybe if one of them doctors seen what happens to him — '

They both froze, momentarily holding their breaths at

the sound of something crashing and breaking somewhere in the house. The noise was followed by a long, pitiful moan; the moan of a trapped animal desperate for escape . . . it chilled their blood with its eeriness.

In one swift motion, Eli was off the bed and on his feet, then walking quickly towards the hall. He stopped abruptly, realising Carolyn was not with him. He went back into the bedroom and turned on the light to see her immobile on the bed, the look of fright frozen on her face.

'That's Michael making that godawful noise,' Eli said to her. 'We have to go in to him — he might need us. C'mon.'

'I can't, Eli,' she said, shaking her head wildly. 'If that's Michael moaning like that, and if — ' she stopped and shut her eyes. 'I can't go in there — I can't bring myself to see him like that.'

Eli turned to the bed, and as the plaintive moaning began again he took Carolyn's hands firmly in his. 'Whatever he's doing — whatever he's possessed by — he's our son. Now get up and get going.'

Carolyn hesitated a few seconds more, then let Eli lead her from their bedroom and down the hall. Reaching the bolted door to Michael's bedroom, they paused. Eli, taking a deep breath to bolster his courage against whatever he was about to face, slipped back the bolt and quickly pushed the door open, Carolyn clinging close behind him.

Michael stood at the far end of the room, facing the open window, his hands wrapped tightly around the wooden bars. Another long moan filled the otherwise silent bedroom as he violently pulled and heaved against the immovable bars, his knuckles white with the effort. From the back, in the shadowy half-light given off by the over-turned bedside lamp lying on the floor, he *looked* normal enough.

'Oh, Eli — look!' Carolyn exclaimed, breathing a sigh of relief as she pushed past him through the doorway. 'This godawful cage in here and it's my little boy, having another bad dream.'

'No, Carolyn — I wouldn't go near him yet,' Eli shouted, making a grab for her hand.

'Nonsense, she said, shaking out of his grasp. 'The way you was telling it, I half expected to see him with a furry face, pointed ears and a tail.' She looked back over her shoulder,

'Ain't nothing wrong with him — '

Michael turned quickly from the window to face them; they both stopped where they stood, staring.

'His face,' Carolyn gasped in shock. 'Eli, look at his face.'

Michael's normally angelic face seemed to have undergone a strange transformation. His ears now seemed to be standing out slightly from his head, his nose flattened slightly, nostrils flaring. His lips were drawn back over his teeth, baring them, and a low, rumbling growl emanated from his throat. But the feature that struck the most terror in their hearts was his eyes: wide and staring within red-rimmed lids, bearing within them a chilling presence of animal-like savagery . . .

Carolyn gasped and took an unconscious step backwards, bumping into Eli directly behind her as Michael suddenly crouched and, with a growling snarl, sprang at her, his fingers, curled like tiny claws, aimed at her throat.

Eli stepped quickly forwards, pushing Carolyn roughly out the doorway, and extended his right arm, taking the full impact of Michael's leap against the palm of his huge hand. When his hand struck his son's chest, Eli shoved with all his strength, sending Michael flailing backwards to bounce off the bed and roll onto the floor. Michael was on his feet immediately and springing at him again, but Eli had gone out the door, slamming it shut behind him. As he quickly slid the bolt closed he could hear his son growling and snarling furiously, scratching and beating on it.

'Eli, what — ?' Carolyn began to say, her eyes dulled with shock.

'Shhh,' Eli said, as soothingly as he could manage. 'I think he'll quiet down after a while, if we leave him be. Come on, let's go back to our room.'

She stared at him in disbelief. 'How can you even think about going back to bed — after seeing what we just saw?'

'Nothing we can do — except just love him and try to protect him.' He heaved a long, frustrated sigh. 'We just have to face it — the boy's got the falling sickness or some kind of fits, or he's possessed by something horrible and there's nothing we can do about it. We have to keep him locked up like this for the time being, just to keep him from hurting anybody or getting hurt himself.' He took her

162

hand. 'It's all we can do. I suppose after a while we'll get used to the noise — maybe even learn to sleep through it, in time.' He held her close, his heart sharing her grief. 'But this sickness is something we have to find a way to live with — until it's over.'

Back in their bed, Eli reached out to the table beside him and switched off his light.

'Honey,' he said, 'come on, turn off your light and try to get some sleep. It's late.'

'I wonder.' Carolyn said suddenly, sitting up.

'Wonder what?'

'I wonder how come it only happens to Michael at night. . . .'

18

For Michael, the next few months were spent in a nightmare of fear and uncertainty. Tormented mentally by all manner of ideas about what his parents believed him to be and by the strict rules and conditions for living that were forced on him, he spent most of his conscious hours in a state of acutely painful waiting; expecting at any moment to lose his sense of who he was, changing for all he knew into something horribly grotesque, something beyond imagining, envisioning within his frightened mind that he would be forced by powers he could not control to break through the door, kill his parents, break through other doors, kill his teacher or perhaps the other students in his class — anyone who happened to be near him when this dreaded change overtook him. Life at home was overshadowed by tension and fear; it seemed as though his parents were now constantly watching him. His mother, especially, always seemed to be eyeing him closely, her fear of him and of what he might do or become next apparent in her every gesture.

At school, he stayed aloof, allowing no one to get close to him in any way; ready, at a moment's notice, to bolt from the classroom if that strange feeling he had experienced during his fight in the schoolyard began to come over him again.

After school, he would go home as quickly as possible, almost breathlessly, to the relative security of a controlled if unpleasant and fearful existence.

Dinner for them was usually a strained and uncomfortable affair at best. Michael could *feel* his parents' tension as they carefully watched him eat.

After his nightly bath, still insisted on by his mother, Michael would stand for long minutes in front of the bathroom mirror, looking at himself intently — scrutinising his face, his hands, his whole body — waiting and watching for a telltale sign of *something*, he didn't know what.

Although fear and anxiety filled all the waking hours for Michael and his parents, the dreaded change never occurred during the day. At night, when Michael's consciousness dulled and succumbed to sleep, then and only then did the beast awaken within him, to lope with an unrestrained ferocity through his dreams and night-time reality.

In the morning, after such an occurrence, nothing would ever be said about it by either Michael or his parents; Michael would simply eat his breakfast, get dressed and be driven to school by Eli on his way to work. Carolyn would set to the chore of tidying up Michael's bedroom again and putting the upset and scattered furniture back into its proper place — as if nothing untoward had happened. The three of them would agonise through a day of wondering fearfully what would happen next.

After a few months, Eli began to see that in spite of what he had initially believed, Michael was certainly not a werewolf; at least not in accepted supernatural terms. The change in Michael, when it came, seemed to come strictly from the depths of his personality, with little or no change to be seen physically. His features, for example, never changed in any lasting way; it was more as if they simply contorted to express the brutally savage forces within.

So fearful was Michael of what he thought of as 'the beast,' so completely did his thoughts dwell on combating and suppressing its coming, that in time he succeeded in learning to restrain it in his subconscious. As the months passed, his changes gradually became less and less violent, then the transformations themselves began occurring less frequently. After roughly a year and a half of fear and suffering, the strange comings of the beast within him seemed to have ceased altogether.

Eli and Carolyn were at first sceptical that the dreaded nocturnal spells were over for Michael. Insisting that their strict conditions for him continue, they watched him as closely as ever.

As more months passed, though, they began to allow themselves the hope that, whatever the horror had been, whatever its causes and dark purposes, it seemed now no longer to possess him; what they termed, first reverently and then joyously, as 'a miracle' had truly occurred.

The restrictions and conditions of fearful vigilance were gradually — and gratefully — dropped and forgotten. True, the bars remained for a while on Michael's bedroom window, simply because they were part of the frame to the house, but Eli had eventually made a production out of removing the bolt from the bedroom door and cere-moniously throwing it into the river as his son watched. Soon after, he came home early one Friday and took out the whole array of bars, burning the heavy wooden beams in a small bonfire in the backyard the next night. No more the fear and anxiety of watching and waiting, they all thought; the horror would now be over.

PART 4

19

The MacCleary family gradually settled into a new, more relaxed pattern for living over the next four years, achieving a more or less normal, and certainly happy, family life. Eli and Carolyn unhampered by night-time worries about their son and feeling assured that he would sleep through the hours of darkness peacefully, resumed their marital intimacy with a frequency and ardour they had not known since the early days of their marriage; Eli now seemed to possess an insatiable sexual appetite — something that Carolyn found she did not mind in the least.

The most pronounced change of all, however, seemed to have taken place for Michael. After having been so shy and standoffish, almost secretive in his ways, it came as a pleasant surprise to everyone who knew him that he seemed now to blossom into a new, more self-assured personality; unafraid to seek out warmth and friendship from people around him. It seemed as if a great weight of oppression had been lifted from him, leaving him hungry for the closeness and company of others which he had forgone during the years of his problems. Girls and boys alike could not help but respond positively to his new, more outgoing manner, and in a short time he was one of the most popular boys in school.

As Michael turned thirteen, he had all but forgotten the 'beast' and its horrifying influence on him. He was enjoying his popularity and tried to be friendly with everyone. Only to Jerry Wilson, whom he regarded as his closest and best friend, did he confide his more intimate thoughts — and most of his secrets.

Others whom he knew only as casual friends felt drawn to Michael, who was a little taller, a good deal stronger and certainly better looking than most of them. The girls he viewed as nuisances at best. He had always been mildly curious about their female differences, but it had never gone much beyond that.

Michael had grown and matured over these four years; then, although these physical and emotional changes were extremely slow in coming, the most important effect they had on him came without warning and all at once. A new and initially terrifying influence now entered his life, bringing with it strange new feelings and sensations.

Suddenly, Michael MacCleary experienced the full effects of puberty.

'I smoked a cigarette last night,' Jerry Wilson whispered conspiratorially. 'Smoked the whole damned thing, too.' He tossed a wad of waxed paper from his bag lunch into the air and batted it with his palm into a nearby trash can.

Michael gave his friend a doubtful look and took another bite from his sandwich, then went back to idly watching a group of younger girls playing on the monkey bars in the school playground.

'You don't believe me?' Jerry said, abandoning the whisper.

'Sure I believe you,' Michael said with a shrug. 'Why shouldn't I?' Reluctantly, he turned his attention from the girls to his friend. 'Where'd you get a cigarette, anyway?'

'Swiped it from a pack laying on the table at home. Took it into the garage and smoked the whole thing. It made me cough to beat hell at first, but once I got used to it, it wasn't so bad.'

Michael only nodded, his attention drawn this time to Pattie, the girl who sat behind him in class. He saw her get up from one of the other lunch benches and drop her empty lunch bag into the trash can, then head for the play area.

'Hey Mike,' Jerry said, 'after school, you want to walk home with me or is your mom picking you up?'

'Yeah,' Michael mumbled as he watched Pattie crossing the playground.

'You ain't even listening to me.' Then Jerry noticed the reason for Michael's lack of attention. 'Oh, you watching Pattie, huh?' he said with a knowing grin. 'Well, just keep on watching her. If she knows you're watching, she kind of puts on a little show, you know.'

'What kind of show?'

'Just watch; you'll see,' Jerry said knowingly. 'She does it every time.'

Michael watched as Pattie walked over to a large oak tree a short distance away at the side of the grassy schoolyard. After glancing quickly at the two of them, smiling to herself as if she had thought of a secret, she jumped a few feet off the ground, grabbed one of the low-hanging boughs with both hands, and began swinging slowly back and forth. Each time she made her forward swing, the breeze would catch her dress, billowing it out and exposing her panties. Even across the thirty yards that separated them, Michael could see her buttocks, rounding and maturing with the onset of young womanhood, outlined through the thin cotton material.

Giggling happily, Pattie pulled herself up and hooked both legs over the tree branch, letting go with her hands to hang by her knees, the hem of her dress falling down over her face. As she worked her legs apart slightly for better balance, Michael could see a darker indentation in her panties where her thighs met. A tight, pleasurable yet unsettling sensation spread through his groin; his penis began to grow hard. He adjusted his position on the bench in an effort to relieve the tightness.

'Pretty good, huh?' Jerry said in his I-told-you-so voice.

'Shhh,' Michael hissed, making an impatient gesture with his hand. He had witnessed scenes like this before in the schoolyard, but this time it seemed . . . different. This time he *liked* what he saw. He continued staring at Pattie openly as his arousal grew.

Another sensation began throbbing at the base of his skull, causing him to arch his neck slightly as he watched her. The feeling moved slowly down his spine, spreading out, working like slowly flowing oil through his back and chest, into his arms and hands, growing to an intensity that soon matched the excitement in his loins, mingling with it and, he thought, heightening it considerably. As the sensation welled through his brain, his vision seemed to focus more sharply, his entire consciousness centering on the two mounds of smooth flesh encased in the thin white cotton

171

panties. Suddenly, all inhibition seemed to fall away; fear, simple curiosity and wonder all were replaced by a new, all-consuming desire. He tried to close his eyes against the intense emotion he felt, but something inside forced him to continue staring hungrily at those exposed, tantalising buttocks. His breath slowed and deepened, whistling noisily first through his nose, then through tightly clenched teeth. He wanted to possess that smooth, pink flesh; to touch it, to knead it between his fingers, even to taste it's flavour on his tongue . . . He got slowly up from his seat on the bench, horrified at the images he had created.

'What's the matter, Mike?' Jerry was looking up at him. 'You look kinda funny.'

Michael, only dimly aware that Jerry had spoken, was unable to respond. He was aware of voices talking and laughing all around him, but they seemed distant, wholly disconnected from him; all that seemed real, all that mattered was his driving need for those two − . He started walking towards her, unmindful of the bulge in the front of his pants.

Pattie saw Michael approaching out of the corner of her eye. 'No fair, Mike,' she said impishly. Still hanging in her upsidedown position, she reversed her legs on the bough to turn her body to face him, but still she made no move to cover herself.

As she moved herself adroitly around on the lower branch, Michael gazed fixedly, hungrily, on the small patch of cotton cloth between her legs, saw the indentation widen slightly, then close again. His hands went out to her slowly.

The clanging din of the schoolbell suddenly echoed in his head, cutting through his consciousness; he was simul-taneously aware of a sharp tugging on his right arm. He blinked as voices and outside impressions came flooding back, but the residue of the intense thing he had felt still clung to his brain, still making returning reality seem dis-connected. He shook his head in an effort to clear his mind.

' − crazy or something?' It was Jerry, tugging at Michael's arm. 'You'll get us both kicked out of school.'

'What?' Michael asked, looking at Jerry in confusion.

'Aw, come on. I ain't stupid,' Jerry said disgustedly. 'You was gonna poke her in the ass, then run like hell.'

Michael could only shake his head dumbly.

'Look, buddy. I'd like to put it to her as much as you, but not in the middle of the schoolyard. Now, come on, we have to get back to class.' Jerry started walking towards the schoolroom.

Michael stood there, confused and disoriented. He blinked again in an effort to regain control; his body and mind still reacting to the stimulus of moments before. When he looked up again, Pattie was just climbing down.

'We better get to class before we get in trouble,' Pattie warned, but then stood, openly staring at the bulge that still remained in the front of Michael's pants.

Following her gaze, he looked down at himself, then blushed, his hand involuntarily covering the embarrassing protrusion. He mumbled something unintelligible by way of excuse.

Pattie merely smiled, then turned and walked towards the classroom, leaving Michael to stand by himself a few minutes longer, until his body had finally calmed down.

As he sat at his desk and the afternoon session began, Michael thought about what Jerry had said. Although every thought, every feeling he had experienced earlier was still vividly clear in his mind, strangely, the thought 'putting it to her' had not occurred to him. Something else had been in his mind. He thought about it now in detail.

Michael picked a shady spot beneath a tree outside the school and resigned himself to sit and wait for Jerry.

If Jerry had had sense enough to keep his mouth shut and not talk back to the teacher, Michael thought disgustedly to himself, then he wouldn't be stuck a half hour after school. He shook his head; it was so like Jerry to do something stupid — he just never learned.

Leaning back against the trunk of the tree, he thought again about what had happened to him at lunch. What *had* happened? he wondered, still mystified. It had something to do with sex; of that he was sure. Not only had dad explained to him a little about sex, but he had listened to the whispered conversations between Jerry and the other boys as they expounded their vast knowledge of the subject. He had thought he had understood it, but at the moment he was still not sure what to think of the sticky wetness that was staining the front of his underwear. And that feeling that had come over him; the feeling of completely unrestrained power, the exquisite pleasure — it was like nothing he had ever experienced before. He wondered abstractedly if it was like that for everyone.

'Hi, Mike. What are you doing?' It was Pattie's voice.

Michael looked up to see Pattie standing in front of him with the new girl in class, Suzanne something-or-other — he couldn't remember her last name. 'Hi,' he said. 'Just waiting for old dumb-dumb to get out of school.'

'You gonna walk home today?' Pattie asked.

'I guess so,' Michael answered, nodding. 'If he ever gets out of there.' He gave Pattie a questioning look. 'You walking home?'

Pattie nodded. 'Suzy's not far from me, we're walking home together.'

'Maybe we'll catch up and go with you,' Michael said, 'if he doesn't take too long getting out.'

Pattie gave a little wave of good-bye and the two girls walked off together.

Michael watched them as they walked down the driveway to the main road. Suzanne was much prettier than Pattie, Michael thought. She was the prettiest girl in class, in fact, but her slim figure still had the gawkiness of a child; her body had not as yet attained the gentle roundness that Pattie's already possessed. It seemed strange to be dwelling on such differences; differences that had never mattered that much to him before. As Pattie and Suzanne turned the corner and went out of sight, Michael's eyes swept the street and the bus stop in front of him, comparing other girls with one another. There seemed to be so many differences between them; so many *nice* differences.

Jerry's voice broke in on his contemplation. 'You going to set on your ass all day? Come on, let's get going.'

Michael walked with Jerry for a long time in silence, thinking about the questions that were uppermost in his mind and trying to summon up enough nerve to ask some of them. Looking at the scenery around them, he was surprised at how far they had already walked; they were well out of town and were now passing the old oak tree on White River Road, almost halfway home. He glanced at Jerry, who was idly kicking a rock along the road as he walked;

174

taking a deep breath, he decided now was as good a time as any.

'Jerry,' he began, trying to sound impassive, 'did you ever — you know, do it with a girl?'

'Do what?' Jerry asked, looking at him.

'You know — *it*.'

'Oh, you mean — ,' Jerry made a circle with one thumb and forefinger, then moved the other forefinger in and out rapidly. 'Sure, I screwed lots of girls.' Something about Jerry's answer made it hard for Michael to believe him.

'Come on, Jerry — no bullshit,' Michael insisted. 'This is real important. If you don't know, just say so.'

Jerry looked embarrassed. 'You won't tell the other guys?'

'Promise.'

'Well, I ain't never actually *done* it. Oh, I thought about it plenty, but I guess I just never had the occasion.' He gave Michael a quick look. 'How about you?'

'Naw, never. I never even thought about it, until recently.'

'I been thinking about it for a long time, just never done it.'

'Well, how do you feel — when you're thinking about it, I mean?' Michael asked, probing for information. 'I mean like today, when we was watching Pattie. How did you feel watching her and . . . thinking about it?'

'I got a hard-on. What did you expect?'

'That's all?' Michael asked, disappointed. 'You didn't feel nothing else?'

'That's all,' Jerry answered, sounding embarrassed now. 'I was wishing I could see what was doing under them panties of hers and I got a hard-on.' He gave a shrug. 'So what?'

'I sure felt more than that,' Michael admitted. 'I got a hard-on too, but then I started feeling all funny and strange like it was all mine — mine for the taking and all I had to do is go over and grab her and — '

'Hey, look.'

'Michael looked in the direction Jerry was pointing and saw Pattie coming out of the bushes by the side of the road just ahead of them.

'Hey Mike, I found the neatest little pond, just the other

side of the trees,' she called, scrambling out of the bushes and walking towards them, 'Let's go wading in it.'

Michael turned to Jerry. 'You want to?'

'She called your name, not mine,' Jerry said, giving Michael a knowing look. 'Anyhow, I got to be getting home.' He gave Michael a pat on the shoulder and smiled. 'Good luck.' He walked over to the other side of the road, passing Pattie as he went.

'Where's Jerry going?' Pattie asked when she and Michael met.

'He had to get home,' Michael answered, more nervously than he could explain or even understand. 'I — I should be home too.'

'Oh Mike,' she said. 'A couple of minutes wading in the pond won't hurt. It'll feel good on a warm day like this.'

'Well,' Michael said, knowing at least that he wanted to go with her, 'okay — just for a couple of minutes.' He allowed himself to be led into the bushes, down a gully and through a stand of trees.

'Didn't I tell you it was a nice pond?' Pattie asked, waving her hand towards an irregularly shaped little pond of water, bordered on one side by a pile of uneven rocks and on the other by sparse weeds and bushes. She sat down on a rock and took off her shoes.

Michael stood quietly, unmoving.

'So take your shoes off and let's go,' Pattie bubbled enthusiastically. She waded out a few feet into the water. 'Oooh, it's cold.'

Michael removed his shoes and socks, then rolled his pant legs up above his knees and waded out to join her.

'You know, Mike,' Pattie said matter-of-factly after a few minutes of wading around in the water, 'I seen you watching me today.'

'I wasn't watching you — '

'Being curious is nothing to be ashamed of,' she said, looking at him seriously. 'It's natural enough.'

'I wasn't watching you.'

'Sure you was. I seen the front of your pants.' She giggled 'Did you like what *you* seen?'

Michael blushed deeply.

'Tell me the truth, Mike — have you ever seen a girl naked?'

'Sure, lots of times,' Michael lied.

'I ain't never seen a boy naked,' she said, equally untruthfully.

'So?'

'You want to?' Pattie asked it as if a new game had been introduced.

'Want to . . . what?' Michael asked, fear rising in him.

'Go skinny-dipping.' Before he could answer, she was out of the water and off behind a clump of tall bushes. Then came the sound of clothes rustling.

'I don't think so,' Michael called to her, wanting to now.

'Oh, don't be afraid. It can't hurt nothing.'

'We'll get in trouble. Somebody'll see us.'

'We're all alone out here, nobody around to see us. Now get undressed and we'll go for a swim.'

'Well, okay,' Michael relented, 'but you go in first.' He went behind a bush and started taking off his clothes. He looked up as he heard a happy giggle, then a splash.

Naked except for his shirt, which he clutched in front of him in the uncertain effort at modesty, Michael walked out from behind the bush and down to the water's edge. Out in front of him, he could see Pattie's head and shoulders above the surface.

'It's not as deep as it looks,' she called 'I'm sitting on the bottom.'

Michael stood, mutely staring at her bobbing head. He clutched the shirt tighter to him.

'Put your shirt down and come on in — the water's great,' she called splashing some in his direction.

'I — I can't,' he stammered. 'I ain't never done nothing like this before and I just don't feel right doing it right now.'

'No reason to feel shy, I'm not going to hurt you, for Pete's sake.' She rose slowly to her feet and stood for a moment, the water dripping off her young body.

Michael stood transfixed, his eyes moving slowly down her, hungrily taking in the sight of her young breasts with their nipples erect from the cold water; down across her belly to the freshly sprouted pubic hair. He felt his arousal building quickly within him, hardening his penis under the bunched-up shirt.

She waded towards him, then stopped in front of him, her eyes now holding his. 'Nothing to be scared of Mike,' she said slowly and, reaching down gently took the shirt from his hands and dropped it on the ground. 'Ooh,' she moaned her eyes going to his erect penis. 'Do you want to touch me?'

Michael shook his head dumbly.

'Well, I wanna touch *you*,' she whispered. Reaching out, she gently took the head of his penis in her hands.

With her touch, a sensation of almost painful pleasure shot through his testicles and up his spine. Emitting a low moan, he stood stock-still, captive to the overpowering pleasure that came over him.

Withdrawing her hand for a moment, she wet her fingers with saliva, then began stroking his penis vigorously with them.

Michael closed his eyes against the unbelievable pleasure that coursed through his genitals and up into his belly; wonderfully intense pleasure, like nothing he could ever have imagined. Willingly, he gave himself over to it.

Another sensation began pulsing at the base of his skull, spreading out into his back and arms, filling his mind with fleeting impressions of sound and feeling and untasted new erotic desires — the same sensations he had experienced earlier that day on the schoolground. He was frightened by the speed with which it built in strength and intensity this time, affecting him physically and mentally until it seemed to be separate and tangible, a complete entity within him. He was beside himself with the pleasure of it, as if he were two people. Pattie's delicate stroking of his penis, which had begun as a sensual delight, was now enhanced beyond anything he had ever felt. This, he liked immensely, though the other, accompanying feelings and impressions frightened him. There was a nearly overpowering impression of Pattie now reduced in his mind's eye to nothing more than flesh and bone, no longer with an identity of her own; an impression, too, of *him*, lustfully tearing her to pieces, tasting her, feeding on her warm —

His conscious mind protested at the evilness, the savagery of these urges and impressions. With this conscious denial the images diminished in his mind, and with them the erotic stimuli.

He stopped fighting it for a moment, allowing his thoughts, his errant imagination to run wild. As if bidden, the frightening images and compulsions returned, stronger than before. This time, he let it happen, his senses running free like a loping night animal beside its mate. It seemed to him as if there were something *moving* within his brain.

Frightened, he sought to push back against the cravings of this dream world, concentrated on simple realities like his name, who he was, the day of the week, the presence of Pattie in front of him — until the images began fading. Again he relaxed his mind slowly, in stages. It seemed that by using his consciousness in this fashion, he could establish a certain amount of control; the visions of horror, the compulsions were now at a distance, while the unbelievably heightened sexuality remained in the foreground.

He looked down, eyes glazed with passion, at the girl gently massaging him. He felt a twin sense of abandon and discovery, a new realm within him he felt he could master in the very act of surrendering himself to it — and surrender he did.

Pattie smiled in the sunlight as Michael's penis spasmed in her hand, his warm sperm shooting out into her palm.

20

Michael quickly began to fear that the powers dwelling in his subconscious were no mere element of his imagination. Two mornings after his experience with Pattie he woke up, hands and face smeared with blood for the first time in five years.

After the utter panic he had felt, his next thoughts had been of secrecy. If his parents found out, he knew that the bars would be back on his window. Again he would be watched and put on a leash of suspicion. He needed time to think — figure out what to do, how to drive the genie back into the bottle . . .

He crept into the shower, washing the traces of his condition down the drain.

He soon learned the extent of the beast's influence on him. It was always with him, just below the level of consciousness, taunting him. He found that during the day, if he kept his mind active, it was possible to keep the beast subdued and under control. But at night, when he had finally put a tired body and mind to sleep, the beast dominated him. When the beast took him, he would seem to awaken again, and although acutely alert to everything that followed, he was powerless to reverse or arrest it. His awareness, brought along as an observer rather than a participant, would travel with the beast, looking out through *its* eyes as it stalked the forest in the dead of night in search of prey. Only at the first hint of dawn did the beast's influence seem to abate and his consciousness to reassert control again.

He would return home, hoping to God he had not been seen, clean himself of any evidence of the killing excursion and return to bed and almost immediate sleep. Strangely, upon getting up for breakfast even as soon as half an hour later, he would feel as refreshed as if he had slept the entire night. His days became a contest of temptations, his mind seeking to forget but a part of it wanting, desiring to remember.

Over the next five years, Michael made the most of his daylight hours. He was among the top four in grades at his school, excelled at sports, pursued an active social life — anything that would keep his mind occupied. It was the only way he could try to keep the beast under control. But come the night, he would find himself an unwilling passenger, travelling on another voyage into horror, compelled to share in the primeval cunning and bloodthirsty ruthlessness of the carnivorous entity within him. This, for him, was the ultimate horror; a horror beyond anything he could ever have imagined as they hunted the night together in search of prey, often catching and killing an animal or, on rare occasions, stalking a transient traveller walking the forest roads by night.

At eighteen, Michael endured the day and was terrified by the night.

Michael leaned against the fender of his car, his weight shifting restlessly from one foot to the other. Through the large front window of the Woolworth's he could see Suzanne moving around behind her cash register, counting the money and putting things away in preparation for closing time. He glanced at the illuminated clock in front of the bank: 8:55 — she would be coming out soon.

Earlier that day at school, when she had asked him to meet her after work and drive her home, he had first told her that he had something important to do. She had insisted, though, saying that there was something she had to talk to him about, to ask him. He had agreed, and now he was sorry he had; he was getting the all too familiar feeling, the yearning to be out — out of himself, asleep and at the same time roaming free — building up within him. He tried to suppress it until bedtime.

Allowing his eyes to roam idly up and down the main street, he noted with amusement that all the store lights and overhead neon signs seemed to be going out as if in order on both sides of the street. In a few minutes the only places left open would be the Pig an' Cluck Diner and the Elbow Room Tavern, which catered to the sawmill crews coming off work at the midnight shift-break.

Not even nine o'clock yet, he thought ironically, and already the town is shutting down tight as a drum. Another hour and it'll be like they rolled the sidewalks up . . .

The restless, uneasy feeling was building and he was forcing it back. Soon, he knew, it would become an almost tangible hunger within him. He had to be *out*, giving himself over to the beast totally, prowling the forest by night . . . hunting. At times like this even his frequent trysts in his car on some deserted logging road with the always-willing Pattie could not quell the mounting frustration, the overpowering bloodlust that the beast's influence would evoke in him. It was either submit to pressures beyond his control or go insane from the feeling of being caged by his frustration. Although the uncontrollability of it still frightened him, he had to admit that in some way he looked forward to it.

Inside Woolworth's, the fluorescent lights began going off, and Suzanne came out through an employee exit at the corner of the building. She stopped and checked her handbag, then glanced away down the street before seeing him.

181

'Oh, hi Mike,' she said, surprised to see him. Then she smiled, her even teeth standing out in the half-light. 'I'm sure glad you came. I was hoping I would see you.'

'I said I'd come and I'm here,' he said simply, opening the passenger-side door of his car for her. 'What'd you want to talk to me about?'

'Nothing especially,' she said with a shrug, climbing into the car. 'Just . . . talk.' She looked up at his face, his eyes holding hers with the intensity she had come to find fascinating. Michael said nothing until he was behind the wheel and the car was moving. He knew what she wanted to talk about and was not sure how to handle it. He had been avoiding her over the last few months, declining her invitations, walking off by himself when he saw her at school. He knew that she wanted to get closer to him, but the idea of letting their relationship become anything more serious made him feel cornered and uneasy, for her sake as much as his own. He was afraid to trust himself with her; something terrible might happen if he were to . . . lose control. He liked to be around Suzanne and thought of her as someone quite special, but he would have preferred to put off forever the discussion he knew was coming.

'How was work?' he asked, unable to think of anything else.

'Boring. Don't think I had more than three or four customers all day. It'll pick up a little soon, from right after Thanksgiving until Christmas is done, then — ' She made a quick nose-dive gesture. ' — right back to boring again. I don't see how they can even afford to keep the lights on with the business they do.'

Michael nodded without interest.

'I'm really glad you came by,' she said seriously, moving closer to him on the seat. 'With everything that's been going on, I have to admit I was a little scared to be walking home by myself. They just found a bum about tore to pieces, out in the woods. Makes three they found so far in the last couple of months. The sheriff thinks it was wolves that done it, or maybe wild mountain folk.' She gave a little shudder. 'It gives me the willies, wolves or whatever roaming around out there.'

'Ain't nothing out there in them woods.'

She gave him a dubious look. 'Well, if a big old killer wolf walks up to me some time, I'll sure tell him you said so.'

'There ain't no wolves out there.'

'Well, there's sure as hell *something* out there. Last fella they found had his left arm yanked half out of his shoulder and his throat tore out.' She glanced at him cynically. 'You figure he committed suicide?'

Michael shuddered slightly but said nothing, as her words were lost in a memory of something he must have dreamed two nights earlier. His hands began shaking at the thought of it.

'Oh, I'll be so glad when we get out of that trailer park and into a good solid house,' she continued. 'I never did feel safe in that tin cracker box.'

He glanced at her insurprise. 'You moving away?'

'No, just a little ways down White River Road; not far from you, matter of fact. Daddy bought up some old farm for the price of back taxes. Him and my Uncle Harry been working real hard the last couple of days or so, cleaning the place up and making it livable.' She made a sour face. 'It was a real rat hole, the way I hear. Big piles of rotten garbage and junk all over the house — must have stunk something awful.' She turned and looked at him, her eyes wide with the drama of her words. 'I heard they even found *human bones* down in the cellar.' She gave another little shudder to emphasise her point. 'Spooky sounding, ain't it?'

Michael only shrugged noncommittally as he eased the car to a stop in front of the gate to the trailer park. He switched off the engine and turned to look at her. 'You have to go right in?' he asked tentatively.

'No, it's still early. I can sit a while,' she answered. She then lapsed into a minute of thought before speaking again.

'Mike,' she said finally. 'How long have we known each other?'

Michael nearly groaned. Here it comes, he thought, the big question. He took a slow, deep breath, preparing himself for what he was sure would be an awkward conversation. Above all, he did not want to hurt her feelings. 'I don't know,' he answered finally. 'Last few years, I guess. Why?'

'Well, in all that time, you never asked me out on a date.' She turned and looked at him seriously. 'Don't you like me,

Mike? Don't you like it when you're with me?'

'I like to be with you,' he answered, a little more enthusiastically than he had meant to. He shrugged. 'I'm with you right now, ain't I?'

'Oh, I don't mean just seeing each other at school, or you driving me home from work two or three nights a week. I mean a *date*. I mean being together a whole evening; going to a movie, maybe — or maybe going up to park by Coon's Hollow.' Shyness crept into her eyes; she lowered them demurely. 'I like you, Mike — I like you a lot. If you was to ask me to go parking with you some night, I don't think I'd mind it one bit.'

Michael squirmed on the seat. 'I like you, too,' he said slowly. 'I guess I'm just not much for dating — '

'For someone that ain't much for dating,' she said, her temper beginning to flare, 'you're sure down there visiting that Pattie Herman often enough.'

'Pattie's different, she's — just Pattie. She's there — in a different way, for a different reason, when I want to go see her. Other than that, she don't mean nothing to me.' He put his arm around her shoulder and drew her closer to him. 'I do like you, Suzanne,' he told her truthfully. 'I like you more than I can say. But I got good reason for being kinda scared to be with you, *because* I like you so much.' He paused, trying to choose his words of explanation carefully.

'There are times,' he continued, 'when I'm with Pattie, that I kinda — lose sight of things and hurt her being too rough. I don't care, because she don't mean nothing special to me, and she don't seem to care. Matter of fact, she likes it.' He took another deep breath before proceeding, hoping she understood what he was trying to say. 'I think you're a wonderful girl, but I like you for who you are. Don't go comparing yourself to Pattie; you just ain't that kind of a girl.'

She looked at him steadily, a tear glistening in the corner of her eye. 'Mike,' she said, her voice quivering slightly, 'I could be that kind of girl.' She placed a nervous hand on his thigh and pushed it slowly towards his groin.

'You don't have to do that, Suzanne.' He gently removed her hand with his own and put it back in her lap. 'That's not necessary. Anything that happens between us will be because you want it to, not because you think it's something I want.'

She looked at him with a combination of relief and adoration. She looked ready to say something, then sat back against the car seat, looking deep into his eyes for a moment as if trying desperately to read something hidden there.

'Mike,' she said slowly, her voice shaking with emotion, 'I'm just *crazy* about you, and I'd do anything for you.' She looked at him meaningfully. 'Anything. And willingly, too. Thing is, I want to. Don't you feel anything . . . special for me?'

He looked closely at her face, tilted up at him, barely inches away from his, and it was suddenly as if he were seeing her for the first time. Her blonde hair, which he had always thought attractive, now seemed to be shining iridescently in the moonlight; her eyes seemed to glow blue-green. He suddenly felt such a strong surge of emotion — of love for her, it made him want to cry. He kissed her, slowly and tentatively at first, but her lips softened and parted beneath his, more demandingly.

The familiar feeling began spreading through him, getting stronger, seeking control — something he remembered feeling so many times before, and was afraid of.

'*No*,' he shouted, breaking the kiss abruptly and pushing himself away from her and against the back of the car seat. 'No! Not now . . . not this time . . .'

Suzanne looked at him in total shock. 'What . . . what did I do?' she stammered, staring at him wide-eyed.

Michael fought to find his voice; the beast still warring with his will, pressing itself against his consciousness. 'You . . . didn't . . . do . . . nothing,' he managed to say through gritted teeth, perspiration standing out on his forehead. 'It's me. Just . . . give me a minute . . . to calm down.'

'Are you sick or something? Should I go in and get daddy?'

Michael could feel the power weakening, relenting in its assault. 'No,' he managed. 'Another . . . minute and I'll be just fine.' He tilted her head back and concentrated on controlling his breathing. Suddenly, it was as if the beast had been there, but had never been there; he was in control again. He turned his head on the seat and gave Suzanne a weak grin. 'Sorry,' he said simply. 'It happens to me sometimes.'

'*What* happens to you? You looked like you was throwing some kind of fit.'

'It ain't nothing like that,' he assured her. 'It ain't nothing serious. It's more like I kind of . . . lose control of myself.' He took another deep breath, then smiled at her. 'Sorry if I scared you, honey.'

'Well, you did,' she admitted, looking away from him.

'Sorry.'

'You feel better now?'

'Yeah.'

'Then answer my question.'

'What question?'

'How do you feel about me?'

'I thought I told you. I never kissed a girl like that.'

'Say it. I wanna hear it.'

'I love you, Suzanne,' Michael said as matter-of-factly as he could.

'You do!' she squealed happily, throwing her arms around his neck and hugging him tightly. She gave him a long kiss that literally left him breathless.

'Don't go telling anyone about this,' he said. 'Leastways until we see what happens between us.' He gave a little shrug. 'Who knows, tomorrow you could change your mind about me.'

'No chance.' She kissed him again.

'I know one person won't be happy about it when he hears,' Michael said thoughtfully. 'Eddie Mathews.'

'Why him?'

'He's got the idea you're *his* girl. At least that's what he tells everybody.'

She laughed. 'I dated him − once. He's a slob and a bully. He probably eats with his hands. I couldn't wait to get home. I hardly even talked to him since.' She looked at Michael seriously. 'Mike, anything between him and me is strictly in *his* mind.'

'Well, he's always making muscles and telling the guys to stay away from you; that you're his girl.'

'So?'

'I don't pay much attention.'

'Then the hell with him. You better kiss me again, because it's late and I have to be in.'

He reached out to her again.

'Good evening,' Mr Harvey,' Michael said politely as they entered the trailer. Suzanne's parents got up from their place in front of the television to greet him. The Harveys had been friends with his parents for years; her father worked for his dad at the sawmill. Her parents were not attractive people; both of them were short and squat, and Michael had secretly wondered for a long time how two such homely people could possibly have borne such a beautiful daughter.

'Well, Mike MacCleary,' Clarence Harvey said cheerfully. 'It's good seeing you again. How you been, boy?'

'Just fine, sir.'

'Appreciate you seeing Suzy home. We been having some trouble around these parts lately.'

'Happy to do it, sir,' Michael said, smiling at Suzanne. 'Intend to be doing it a lot more, from now on.'

'We're going steady, daddy,' Suzanne announced, her smile radiant. There was no mistaking the happiness that showed in her eyes.

Mr Harvey looked at Michael appraisingly. 'Well, that's just fine,' he said finally, nodding to his wife. 'Just fine. I always did like you, Mike.'

'Glad to hear that, Mr Harvey, and I've always liked you.'

'It's sure getting disgusting around here, the way everyone likes everyone,' Suzanne said, taking Michael's hand. 'I like him, daddy. That's what counts.'

'I hear from your dad that, after you get out of high school, you might be coming to work down at the sawmill,' Mr Harvey said. 'Just want you to know, there's always a place in my crew for you, anytime you want.'

'Thank you, sir,' Michael said, suddenly feeling cornered by the conversation. 'Yeah, my dad and me talked about it, but I really don't know what I'll be doing. But, thanks for the offer.'

'Anytime, boy.'

'Well, better be going,' Michael said, suddenly wanting to get out of the boxlike trailer. He went to the door with

Suzanne. 'I'll see you tomorrow,' he said, then whispered, 'When you go to sleep tonight, dream of me; I'll be dreaming of you.' He kissed her quickly on the cheek and left quickly; afraid that she would plant one of *those* kisses on him in front of her parents.

Michael was relieved that the evening had turned out as it had. He shivered involuntarily at the grisly thought of what could have happened.

I can't live like this, he thought anxiously as he envisioned an existence forever overshadowed by his dark inner spectre, never knowing when or how it would again take control of him.

He realised he had been lucky tonight. If his concentration had been just a little weaker, if the beast had pushed an ounce harder . . . He tried desperately to push it all out of his mind.

At least now, he thought as he pulled his car onto the road through the forest, he could get the sleep he so desperately needed.

Nancy Fischer was eighteen going on spinsterhood. She was too tall and much too thin – almost no figure whatsoever. She had a large, slightly bent nose and prominent buckteeth. Poor eyesight compelled her to wear thick glasses, and her hair was completely unmanageable. In short, she was popular with all the girls at school and ignored by every boy who saw her.

Her reputation in the Pea Ridge community, aside from being perhaps the loneliest and most frustrated girl in town was that of the community's resident baby-sitter. She took any and all jobs offered to her – jobs the prettier, more popular girls turned down – and was known by the mothers of Pea Ridge for availability and reliability.

Tonight, though, was a very important night for her as she walked Greenbrier Road along her usual route home from the Blackburn house. She had been invited to a Halloween party taking place in two weeks; the first party, besides her own birthday parties, to which she had ever been invited. The babysitting job she had just finished gave her enough money to buy a dress she had seen in the front show window at Lynda's Boutique, the most expensive dress shop in town. Her mind filled with fantasy pictures of a crowded party, young men, eager ones, crowding around her and vying for her attention . . .

Fate laughed at Nancy Fischer.

The beast crouched low in the thick underbrush that bordered the road, his body tense. He had heard the lightly scuffing footsteps of the figure walking quickly up the road before seeing its outline against the moonlit sky. He sniffed the air, his senses identifying the gender of the approaching prey. A tremour of excitement shook his naked body, making his mouth salivate heavily, making his penis swell and stiffen to full erection.

Licking his lips in anticipation, eyes never leaving the approaching figure, the beast shifted more weight to the balls of his feet.

As she came abreast of him on the road, he let out a fierce growl and sprang, his body colliding with hers. His hands, fingers held on like talons, gripping and tangling in her hair, as the force of their collision knocked her sideways, down onto her back with him on top. For a split second, he looked into her wide, terror-filled eyes and saw recognition there. She knew him! As she opened her mouth to scream, he wrenched her head back and sank his teeth into the side of her neck.

The sticky-sweet taste of up-pumping blood sent him into a new frenzy of excitement. Releasing his hold of the struggling girl's tangled hair, he reared back on his haunches and began tearing at her clothing; the material ripping and parting in his hands. As the last thin traces of wispy nylon came away in his fingers, he forced her thighs wide apart, unmindful as the hip joint in her right leg popped from its socket, then fell on her again, penetrating her, hips moving in an urgent, rhythmic cadence, his face nuzzling the blood-smeared side of her throat, sucking at the blood as he did. He was close . . . then, as the orgasm came to its full intensity, he let out a growl of animal pleasure and sank his teeth again into the girl's throat, tasting the blood, drinking it in, taking pleasure in the gurgling sounds she made as she drowned in it.

Spent now, the beast rolled off the dead girl and onto his side, where he lay breathing heavily through his mouth. Quiet minutes went by. The moon had moved. Gradually, his breathing slowed and his pulse rate returned to normal . . .

Michael got slowly to his feet. He looked down at his bloody hands and the long, red smears down his chest, then at the dead girl at his feet. How could he have done *this*, he wondered with growing revulsion, to someone he *knew*, someone who had sat next to him in school for . . . as far back as he could remember. The beast had not waited, as it usually did, until he was asleep, but had overtaken him while he was still awake, while he was still driving home. He remembered the receding red taillights of the truck ahead of him, like the glowing eyes of a fire-lit animal backing away from him into the darkness, then his car was slowing, stopped on the side of the road, then . . .

He was suddenly aware of the intense October chill on his bare skin and began shivering uncontrollably. He stumbled into the underbrush a short distance away, where he found his clothes and dressed quickly, using his undershirt to wipe the blood from his hands and face and then burying it.

He came back to the place where the dead girl lay and searched the area as best he could for any evidence of his presence. Finding none, he turned and began walking slowly down the road towards his car.

He realised how horrible was the sickening taste of blood in his mouth. He hated the killing of animals and now it all seemed so unutterably worse — this time he knew, as it was happening, that he had killed a *human being*. He decided that his terrible secret could not be kept much longer.

21

Eli sat wide-awake in the darkened living room, waiting. He had been in the same position on the couch, nearly unmoving, for over an hour, half of his mind listening abstractedly to the house creaking in its night-time repose and the sound of chirping crickets that filtered in from outside, the other half filled with a thousand thoughts and perplexities. Could what he suspected be true? Could the whole nightmare of years ago have begun all over again? When he remembered that hellish ordeal they had all once lived through he wanted to cry out in terror at the thought of its recurrence. But, what other answer could there be? he asked himself. All the signs were there.

Carolyn, at first, had been impossible to reach. Even in the face of what was now becoming undeniable, still she had maintained that her son was a good boy who had left those horrible things behind. Eli knew better and had not let it rest. It had taken him a great deal of talking, but now it seemed she was beginning to understand.

Tonight, he resolved, he would put an end to all the uncertainty; tonight, he would have his answers.

He looked at the luminous dial on his watch. What *other* reason, he asked himself again, could Michael have for being out in the forest at two-thirty in the morning?

He was truly sorry that his relationship with his son had deteriorated so much over the last few years. Where once they had been quite close, now he felt he had lost touch with the boy. Although he loved Michael very much and still worried about him constantly, now it seemed he no longer knew things about him; where he went, what he did, what his feelings or his worries were; all the things he felt a father should be in tune with in order to have a close relationship with his son. It was now as if they were total strangers, living in the same house but in different worlds. Where once they had been brought closely together by the horror and trouble of those past, earlier years, now . . . He held his head in despair. If the trouble *was* starting all over again . . . something had to be done, and he couldn't say what.

He heard the sound of a car coming down the access road, then of tyres crunching in the gravel out front. Keys jingled, then one was inserted in the front door. He sat quietly in the dark as Michael came into the house, closing the door behind him. He watched silently as Michael shrugged off his coat, took off his shoes and started quietly towards his bedroom.

'Where you been, boy?' Eli said, breaking the thick silence. He knew immediately that he had startled Michael by the way the boy spun to face him.

'Oh, hi dad,' Michael said, his voice shaking a little from the surprise. 'What you doing up, setting here in the dark?'

'I asked you a question, boy,' Eli said firmly. 'Where you been?'

'Ain't been nowhere,' Michael said, silhouetted by the moonlight in the window behind him. 'Just been — out.'

'That's not good enough,' Eli rumbled angrily. 'I want to know where you been.'

'It ain't none of your concern where I been,' Michael answered lightly. 'I just been out a while is all. 'Night, dad.' He started for his bedroom again.

'Look, boy,' Eli pointed an accusing finger at Michael. 'You still ain't too big to get thumped across the side of your head for talking sassy to your father. Now I want to know what you was doing . . . *out there* — ' He made an abrupt sweep with his hand. 'Until two-thirty in the goddamn morning!'

Michael stood staring at his father.

'This time you answer me, boy.' Eli got to his feet and looked down at his son menacingly. 'Or, so help me, I'm gonna — '

'What's going *on* in here?' Carolyn's sleepy voice asked from the doorway. 'What's all that shouting?'

'Now you see what you done?' Eli said. 'You woke your mother up.'

'Just look at you two,' Carolyn said, shaking her head. 'Standing there, hollering at each other in the dark.' She turned the switch on the table lamp, illuminating the living room. 'There. At least you can see who you're shouting at.'

'*I* ain't shouting at nobody,' Michael said. 'I just got home, and right away dad jumped on my ass — '

'You just watch your mouth in front of your mother,' Eli said. 'Don't go using no dirty talk around her.'

'I just can't win around here,' Michael said in exasperation. 'Whatever I do, *he* tells me it's wrong.'

'But, Michael, what *is* this all about?' Carolyn asked quietly.

'Remember what we were discussing about a week ago?' Eli asked, giving Carolyn a knowing look. 'Well, here it is, three in the morning, the kid just got home, and he won't tell me where he's been or what he's been up to.' He put a hurt look on his face, hoping to gain her support. 'I figure I got a right to know — under the circumstances.'

'What circumstances?' Michael asked.

'Well,' Carolyn began, choosing her words carefully, 'you remember, back years ago, when you was possessed by whatever that was, and you used to go out at night?'

She paused, watching for a response. None came.

'Well,' she continued slowly, 'with everything that's been happening around here recently — first them finding dead animals in the forest, all tore up and looking half-ate — now they're finding people, tramps and bums all killed and mutilated something terrible. Everybody says it's wolves doing it, but — ' She looked at Michael almost apologetically. ' — well, how can you expect me and your dad to be happy about you running around at this hour of the morning?'

Michael stared intently at his parents, his expression hard to read.

Eli took a deep, tired breath. 'Let's cut through the bullshit, boy,' he said slowly, 'because your mom and me, we just gotta know. You know anything about all these things happening out there in the forest? Is that possession thing back inside you again?'

Michael continued studying his parents for another moment, as if coming to some terrible decision, then his features seemed to soften slowly into a portrait of intense sadness. Tears filled his eyes. 'It . . . it never really went away, dad,' he answered slowly, his voice cracking. 'I guess it's been with me, one way or another, all the time.' He shrugged helplessly. 'Whatever had me — possessed before, I guess it's still got me. Only now it's stronger and meaner, it's — worse.'

The confession, once it had begun, seemed to have a therapeutic effect: the release of agonies and frustrations he had kept locked inside him — locked away even from himself — over the years. Pacing back and forth, he told them nearly everything, beginning when he was thirteen and bringing them up to the present. He held back the events of that evening, but even so the words flowed like a torrent released after being dammed up for too long.

193

Eli and Carolyn exchanged horrified looks as Michael spoke; each comtemplating the new aspects of an old nightmare.

'Oh, my poor baby,' Carolyn said when Michael had finished, her voice breaking. Tears glistened in her eyes as she moved close to her son and put her arm protectively around him.

Eli said nothing. He continued staring at his son, numbed by what he had heard.

'Don't go feeling sorry for me, mom,' Michael said, shrugging off her embrace. 'Sympathy's not what I need. I need — ' He sat down desolately, unable to find the words. 'I don't know what I need.'

'I'll tell you what you need,' Eli said with finality, breaking the silence. 'You need to fight this thing inside you — all of it. You can't just give in to it.' His voice became gentle, almost pleading. 'You know your ma and me, we'll do all we can to help you, but you have to *try*.'

'You think I ain't tried, dad? Do you know how many nights I fought sleep, forcing myself to stay awake, trying *not* to let this — thing get hold of me?' He dropped his hands to his knees and shook his head. 'Just comes on, stronger and stronger — I can't do nothing about it — sure as hell can't stop it.'

'Then your ma and me, we'll stop it for you — like we done before.' The more Eli had thought about it as he sat waiting for Michael to come home, the better an answer it seemed. 'You say you're okay in the daytime, so we just build us some new bars for your bedroom window — '

'I can't live like that. You want to lock me up in a cage? Well, you ain't *gonna* lock me in no cage again!'

Michael's mind raced wildly. He could see the direction the conversation was taking, the conclusions being too quickly formed. He needed time to think. If there was one thing he feared more than the beast, it was the thought of being caged up with it for the rest of his life. He had an inspiration. 'It ain't *me* we have to stop.' He pointed to himself. 'I'm your *son*. It's the *thing* that's inside me — *that's* what we gotta stop.' He looked at his parents forlornly. 'Why should *I* have to suffer by being locked up like that again?'

'People'll find out,' Carolyn said desperately, 'come get

194

you — put you away somewhere or maybe kill you. Nobody would understand.'

'No, they won't,' Michael said, sounding as matter-of-fact as he could. He shrugged. 'Who would believe it?' he asked, putting the truth before them. 'You wouldn't have, if you didn't know better.' He looked at his parents for a long moment. 'Anyhow, I — uh, did kind of exaggerate a little on what I told you before,' he said, trying his best to look guilty, as if he'd been caught telling a lie. 'It don't come on me half as bad as I said, and it only happens when I'm around the forest. Maybe, if I could get away from the forest around here and go somewhere else — a big city, maybe — then this thing won't come on me no more.'

'You don't really believe that, do you?' Eli challenged, doubt written on his face. 'My God, you say you may have been killing people.'

'Yeah,' Michael said, picking up on it, 'but it always happened *in the forest*. If I could just get away from this damn place . . . maybe . . . it's the *forest* doing it to me — '

'We can't let you go running off somewhere.'

Now Michael sounded resolute. 'That's what I *gotta* do; can't you see that? If I can just get away from the forest, I'll be all right.'

'You *won't* be all right!' Eli shouted, banging his fist down on the arm of the couch. 'Can't you understand what it all means? You're dangerous — a killer. We have to make it so you can't go hurting nobody — or yourself — no more.'

'Now, do I look dangerous to you,' Michael asked, smiling at both his parents in turn. 'Yeah, I got a — something in me, makes me do terrible things sometimes, but it ain't something we got to settle here and now. We can talk about it again tomorrow, when we all had some sleep and feel better.'

Eli relented, too tired to continue anyway. 'We'll talk more about it tomorrow. But you put that idea about leaving out of your head. You ain't going nowhere.'

'I ain't talking about going tomorrow,' Michael lied. 'I mean in about two weeks or so, when school lets out for vacation, and then just for a day or two, to see if it makes any difference.' He smiled again, trying to look as coopera-tive as possible. 'I know you two just want to help me, and I

195

appreciate it. Suzanne'll help too − '

'Suzanne who?' Eli cut in suddenly. 'You mean Suzanne Harvey, Clarence and Emma's girl? What does *she* have to do with this?'

'She's my girl,' Michael said simply. 'We love each other. When I tell her about this, the sickness I got, I'm sure she'll − '

'Don't you understand, boy,' Eli cut in, looking at his son incredulously. 'You can't tell no one 'bout this, specially her.'

'Yeah, well, we can start doing something about it ourselves tomorrow.' Michael got up and stretched his arms over his head in an exaggerated yawning gesture. He could see the conversation going around in a circle again and didn't want to repeat himself. He saw he was getting nowhere in convincing them and he had a lot of thinking to do. 'I figure we should all get to bed already. I got school tomorrow.' After saying a quick good-night, he went into his room and closed the door.

'What're we going to do, Eli?' Carolyn asked, after a few minutes of silence.

'Stop him,' Eli said with conviction. 'Stop him from hurting anyone else − including himself.'

22

The small parking lot at Samuel R. Curtis High School was full, as usual. Michael drove his car through the main gate, then stopped, looking at the crowded rows of parked trucks and cars. With a shrug of resignation, he put the car in gear again and nosed it into the tight space on the edge of the lot, halfway onto the shoulder of the driveway.

After going to bed the night before, he had lain awake for the hours remaining until dawn, thinking and weighing possibilities. One fact was obvious: he had to get away from

Pea ridge and everything connected with it. There was nothing, no one, including his parents, that could help him; of this he was sure. Therefore, he reasoned, staying in such a small community, being what he was, kept him in constant danger of being discovered. It was horror enough, he felt, living under the dark shadow of the beast, without having the threat of discovery, capture, a life of imprisonment hanging over him.

The more he thought about it, the better it sounded: move to a large city where he could live, for a while at least, in a cloak of annonymity. He knew now that he loved Suzanne, hoped that she would go with him to help him master this. The problem would be to convince her to go away with him — in other words, given the kind of girl she was, to marry him — on such short notice.

At first he had intended to skip school today, maybe quit entirely, but had decided that by going one last time he would have an opportunity to talk with Suzanne, on and off, for the whole day.

Gathering up his notebook and books from the front seat, he locked his car and began walking across the schoolyard to his English class.

Entering the two-storey building, Michael was saddened by how totally disconnected, how estranged he felt from the other students that filled the hallway. These were people he had known all his life, his friends — yet now he felt like an outsider.

Michael stopped suddenly in mid-stride, surprised by the sight of Sheriff Flynn, the local law, in the hall ahead of him talking with the principal, Mr Larsh. Sheriff Flynn was a large, round man, usually wearing a good-natured grin; opposite in character to the small, sour-faced Larsh. This morning, Sheriff Flynn was not smiling.

For an instant, Michael was frightened, frightened that the sheriff had somehow found out about him and was here to arrest him. Then the sheriff, still in the midst of conversation, let his eyes roam around the hall, looked directly at him without even noticing him, and turned his attention back to the principal. Breathing a sigh of relief, Michael suddenly found himself very curious as to why the sheriff *was* here.

Michael positioned himself in front of the last wall locker

in the row on the right, not three feet from where the two men talked, and while fiddling with the combination lock in front of him in a pretence of opening it strained his ears to overhear their conversation.

' — found her up on Greenbrier Road early this morning, raped and murdered,' Flynn was saying. 'This one changes a lot of things. This one was definitely murder.'

'I don't think I understand, Hector,' the principal said. 'You said before that this one's just like them others. I thought you figured it was wolves. Now you're saying it was murder.'

'That's just the point,' Flynn explained, 'It's *exactly* like the others, in almost every way, except this girl was sexually assaulted and her right hip joint was broken. According to the coroner's report on her, she was chock-full of human sperm and her hip was busted not by claws or teeth but by hands — human hands, prying her leg out like a goddamned drumstick.' He shook his head, as if doubting his own words. 'Yet she was *killed* by having her throat tore out, and the coroner thinks it coulda been done by human teeth.' He shook his head again. 'I'll tell you, Walt, we got us something or somebody mighty strange prowling around in them woods, and we have to do everything possible to catch whoever the hell it is, before there's any more killing.'

The hall bell suddenly gave two short rings; class was to begin in five minutes. Reluctantly, Michael had to leave his eavesdropping to hurry on to class; it was either that or, perhaps, draw suspicion to himself by being the last person standing in the hall.

Michael slid into the seat behind his desk just as the bell rang announcing the beginning of first period. Sitting back in his seat, he folded his hands in front of him.

Class came to order and Mr Stewart, the English teacher, stood up and cleared his throat. 'Before we begin today, class,' he said, pronouncing every word clearly, 'Sheriff Flynn would like to address you.'

Flynn came in and strode to the front of the room. 'How y' all doing?' he asked good-naturedly, glancing around the classroom and smiling broadly at all the expectant faces. Then his face turned serious. 'I suppose you all heard about what's happened,' he began, his tone sombre.

As if on cue, all eyes turned to Nancy Fischer's vacant seat. A heavy, ulmost tangible tension hung over the classroom.

'We got us a really dangerous situation out there in them woods,' Flynn continued, the seriousness of his words seeming to etch new lines on his face. 'Anybody knowing anything about it, anything at all, y'all come and see me.' He slowly studied all the faces again, searching almost pleadingly, it seemed to Michael, for signs of some suppressed knowledge. 'Anything at all will help. In the meantime, the sheriff's department's imposing a nine o'clock curfew on the woods and all roads leading to and from it.' He held up his hands against groans of displeasure. He added, in an effort to lighten the tension he had caused, 'That'll only mean you kids'll have to find yourselves a different place to park and do your necking.' He turned serious again. 'But, I'm telling you all, this is important. Anybody caught out after nine o'clock — well, you'll be in big trouble, and I wouldn't want to see that happen.' He turned to Mr Stewart. 'That's all I got to say. Thank you for your time.' He turned and left the classroom with a jangle of keys and handcuffs to repeat his speech in the next class.

'Well, the situation appears to be much more serious than we had anticipated,' Mr Stewart said. 'I do hope that all of you will cooperate as the sheriff asks.' He then reached behind him on his desk and picked up a thick English book. 'Now, to the business at hand,' he said, adjusting his glasses. 'Please turn to page forty-three in your text — '

Michael watched the clock impatiently for the last ten minutes of English, waiting for the period to end. Next was history, and he couldn't wait to get there. He sat next to Suzanne in history and would make a date for tonight. The instant the bell rang, he was on his feet, gathering his books.

'Oh, Mike,' Pattie's voice called from somewhere behind him. 'Wait up a minute. Please . . . '

'Ain't got time to talk now,' he said over his shoulder as he moved quickly out the door. 'I can't be late for history.'

'I have to talk to you, Mike,' Pattie called after him, her voice worried. 'Something's wrong . . . I didn't get my — ' She stopped as the other students stared at her, and when

199

she got out in the hallway Michael was already disappearing around the bend in the corridor on his way to history class.

Eli sat on a stack of freshly cut pine boards, his head in his hands, stunned by the news he had just heard. He leaned back against a higher stack of boards behind him and shut his eyes, willing away nausea. For long, agonising minutes, the feeling stayed with him, making him break out in a cold sweat and twisting his stomach into a knot.

They had found Ernie Fischer's daughter, Nancy, raped and murdered out on Greenbrier Road.

Although the grim announcement had come only minutes ago, speculation was already sweeping through the sawmill, as the news, coupled with personal opinion, travelled and spread. Everyone was confused and appalled as to whoever or whatever could possibly have done such a horrible thing to such a sweet girl.

Everyone but Eli.

Eli was afraid he knew who had done it.

As the shock-induced nausea slowly passed, it gave way to a desperately conceived feeling of hopeful doubt: it just couldn't be true. Michael had known that girl for most of his life; had gone to school with her; had been her friend as much as anyone, which Eli guessed wasn't much. Still, Michael couldn't possibly have . . . even with everything he already knew about his son, *that* seemed inconceivable . . .

But Michael could have done it, he realised suddenly and undeniably, and the realisation turned his last spark of hope into an attack of deep, mind-numbing anxiety. Michael could have killed her, with no remorse, no conscience at all if that thing got hold of him. The boy talked about it the other night . . . what had he said, that it had never left him? What in God's name had he been trying to tell them? Eli's eyes filled with tears for the first time he could remember in fifteen years.

'Hey, Eli. What's the matter, pal? You sick or something?' Clarence Harvey asked, sitting down on a wooden box opposite Eli.

'Huh? What?' Eli mumbled incoherently, blinking to clear his eyes of tears. 'Oh, hi, Clem. What did you say?'

'Well, shit,' Clarence said, looking at Eli with concern, 'you set there, white as a ghost, and I just ask you what's the trouble.' He shrugged. 'Less you figure it ain't none of my business.'

'Naw,' Eli answered with a dismissing wave of his hand, 'I appreciate your worrying about me. It's just that — ' He stopped in mid-sentence as a hundred thoughts suddenly shot through his brain. He saw a series of brief impressions: Clarence — Emma — Suzanne — the old house they had just moved into — Michael. The images solidified into a picture. That was the answer; he had been there, years ago, almost bought the house himself, seen the layout — it was exactly what they needed.

Clarence was staring at him again. 'Eli, for Chrissake, what's the matter? You look like someone just stuck a knife in you.'

'Clem!' Eli half-shouted, putting his hand on his friend's shoulder. 'Clem, I got to talk to you about something important. You have to help me.'

'Sure, anything. You just name it.'

'It's about Michael. He — '

'Clarence's face relaxed into a toothy grin. 'Love him like a son, that boy. To hear my girl tell it, we gonna be in-laws before you know it.'

'No,' Eli said, 'that can't never happen! I got something to tell you about my boy — something you won't want to believe, but it's true.'

Eli took a slow, deep breath. He knew he had to choose his words carefully. 'Clem, my boy's got a sickness, a sickness in his head that makes him lose control of himself from time to time, makes him violent. The doctors we talked to say he can beat this thing, eventually snap out of it — but it'll take time, maybe quite a while.'

'Gosh, Eli, we never knew he was sick, never figured — '

'That's just the point,' Eli explained slowly. 'Carolyn and me been keeping this thing secret, we ain't let nobody know about it because there're people want to take him and put him in a hospital or something. Then he'd never get well and never lead a normal life.' He looked at Clarence intently. 'That's where you come in. That's where I hope I can count on you.'

'We know you people a long time,' Clarence said simply,

201

'we think of you like kinfolk, and now my girl says she's in love with your boy.' He sat back and smiled at Eli. 'You just name it — if I can do anything to help.'

'Well, when this sickness comes on him,' Eli began, the unaccustomed taste of deception bitter on his tongue, 'he gets a little wild and dangerous, and he has to be kept locked up so he's safe and can't hurt no one.' He paused, taking another deep breath to bolster his courage for what he was about to suggest. 'Now,' he said, eyeing Clarence fraternally, 'here's what we have to do — '

23

Michael sat on the bench between the rows of gym lockers, tying his shoes. He had taken his time getting dressed after his sixth-period gym class in order not to have to leave the gym with everyone else. He had already made up his mind to cut his seventh-period maths class; cut out of school completely, as a matter of fact; to finally get away from the life — or lives — he had been forced to lead up until now. Tonight would be the end of it all, and the beginning; tonight he would convince Suzanne to run away with him, and he would then be free to find, with her help, a way out of the cage that imprisoned him within himself.

He had already spoken to Suzanne and, during a hurried, whispered conversation before the beginning of history, had reinforced the fact that he loved her more than ever. He was telling her that there was something very important he had to discuss with her when the teacher handed out a test and he had to stop talking, but she had agreed to meet him that night after she got off work. Knowing that his father would be at work all day and mother always shopped for food on Fridays, this afternoon would give him an opportunity to go home and pack up undisturbed all the things he wanted to take with him and load them into his car. He had considered waiting around to say good-bye to

202

his parents, but then realised that it would only be painful for all three of them. Another meeting would only invite another confrontation and argument. Dad might try to stop him from leaving . . . No, he decided, it would be better this way. He would simply leave, and later write and probably come back before too long —

'Hey, asshole! I been looking for you!' Eddie Mathews's belligerent voice came from somewhere behind him, echoing hollowly off the tiles in the shower room.

Michael groaned inwardly. The last thing he needed was to get into a tussle with a jerk like Eddie Mathews. 'Go away, will you?' he said over his shoulder in a tired voice. 'I ain't got time for your bullshit.'

'You ain't, huh?' Eddie snarled, putting a hard hand on Michael's shoulder and forcibly twisting him around on the locker room bench. 'Well, I'm just gonna tell you once: you stay the fuck away from Suzanne!'

Michael got slowly to his feet and stood there for a moment, his eyes boring intently into Eddie's. 'Don't screw around with me, Eddie.' I don't want to hurt you, so don't push me.'

'You don't want to hurt me?' Eddie was half a head taller than Michael and at least twenty pounds heavier. 'Well, let's just see about that right now.' He got into a fighting stance, his hands balled into callused fists.

Michael remained silent and motionless, staring into Eddie's eyes with an intensity that unnerved the older boy.

'Well, come on, asshole!' Eddie shouted. His right fist shot out suddenly, catching Michael on the left cheekbone. He laughed to himself as Michael stumbled backwards onto the bench again, his eyes seeming to roll up into his head. This was quicker than he had thought it would be. He had this fight already won . . .

The smile disappeared from Eddie's face when he saw Michael's eyes again. They seemed drastically different, wide with the unfeeling savagery of a jungle animal. As he watched, the face before him grew taut and hard, then the lips parted slowly and drew back with a snarl, exposing slightly parted teeth, dripping with saliva. Now it was his turn to take a step backwards as an unreasoning fear gripped him.

With a low, guttural growl, the beast sprang, the force

and momentum of his attack sending Eddie flailing into the bank of gym lockers behind him. He tried to scream, but it was stillborn as the beast attacked his now exposed throat, the cartilage collapsing and tearing between his teeth.

With inhuman strength, the beast held the now limp body pinned against the wall of lockers and bit fiercely into his victim's neck and shoulders, tearing and mauling the flesh and pulling both collarbones loose. Finally, satiated and nearly choking on the blood and tissue that filled his mouth, the beast released his hold and allowed the body to fall to the floor . . .

Michael collapsed onto the bench, sapped of strength, concentrating for almost a minute on slowing his breathing and pulse rate. When his body was functioning somewhat normally again he sat up to face the grisly scene around him and began speculating as to what needed to be done.

His first instinct was to try to hide the body, but he had no idea how. In a few more minutes — he had lost track of the time — the seventh-period gym class could start filing in. Then what? He looked around at the blood-spattered wall lockers and floor, at the widening dark red pool spreading out on the tiles from the crumpled body.

He caught his reflection in the long mirror over the sinks and was shocked by what he saw. Blood stained his face and still ran from the corners of his mouth; his shirt was saturated with it. Buttons popped in all directions as he tore the front of his shirt open and rolled it up into a soggy wet ball; he threw it into the back of his open locker. Moving to the sink, he turned on the tap and plunged his head into the flow, vigorously scrubbing at his face, neck and chest with both hands. Drying himself with a towel, he put on his purple gym shirt and inspected himself in the mirror. Good enough, he thought, even though he was now wearing a dark purple T-shirt with light grey pants.

Hearing the boisterous sounds of boys entering the front of the gym, he slammed his locker shut, gathered up his books from where they had been scattered on the floor and left the shower room through a side exit, blending into the stream of students on their way to seventh period until he came to the side door and walked out.

24

Time dragged by for Michael at an agonisingly slow pace as he sat in his car on the dark street outside the now closed Woolworth's, waiting for Suzanne. He had been home to pack up his belongings, leaving a short letter of good-bye to his parents with the liquor his father kept hidden — where he guessed his father would run across it after he was gone. Then he had driven into town and stopped at the bank withdrawing the entire $1,635.82 in the savings account his mother had opened in his name soon after he was born and had added to faithfully every week since. It was what she had always referred to as his going-to-college money.

While in town, he had half expected to see his father cruising his truck up and down the streets searching for him. He realised that meeting his father now could ruin his plans completely, so he had taken whatever steps he could to avoid the confrontation.

There was now only one last thing, or rather person, to see about before he could leave — Suzanne. He had decided that if she refused to go with him, he would go without her. He suspected that he would miss her at first, but in time she would become another part of the past he had left behind.

Michael sucked in his breath as a sheriff's patrol car rolled quietly to a stop behind him, its bright spotlight shining through the rear window of his car, reflecting off his rear-view mirror, directly into his eyes. In the fifteen minutes he had been parked, waiting for Suzanne, he had seen the car twice, cruising up and down the main street. It had only been a matter of time before they would decide to check him out. Assuming his most innocuous pose, he sat quietly and waited as the deputy got out and sauntered over.

'Evening, boy,' the deputy said in a deep monotone as he

shined his flashlight in Michael's face, then swept its beam across the front and back seat of the car. 'You planning on going somewhere?' he asked seeing the battered suitcase and stuffed laundry bag resting on the back seat.

'Evening, officer,' Michaeel replied politely. He couldn't miss how tense the deputy seemed to be and how his right had rested casually on his gun belt, not two inches from the butt of his revolver. With everything that had happened in and around town lately, the police seemed suspicious of everyone. Michael kept his hands on the steering wheel in front of him. 'Just setting here, waiting for my girl to get off work.' He nodded towards Woolworth's. 'Figured we'd maybe get away together for the weekend.' He gave the deputy a knowing wink.

'You got some identification?' the deputy asked, all business.

Michael dug into his back pocket, producing his wallet. He handed over his driver's licence.

'MacCleary?' the deputy said, examining the licence carefully. 'You Eli MacCleary's kid?'

Michael nodded.

'Worked with your dad at the sawmill, back a few years ago,' the deputy said, relaxing a little. 'He's a good man, your dad. I always liked him.'

'Here comes my girl now,' Michael said, seeing Suzanne come out of the building and anxious to break away.

'This ain't a good night to be loitering around town,' the deputy advised, handing back the licence. 'You make sure you get gone before the curfew. With everything that's happened, people are calling in with monsters and such like hiding behind every bush and tree.' He glanced at Suzanne, walking towards the car. 'Mighty pretty gal you got there.' The radio in his patrol car crackled with a call. 'Well, 'night, boy,' the deputy said, smiling. 'And — ' He glanced at Suzanne again. ' — good luck.' He walked back to his patrol car and got in to answer the radio.

'What was that all about?' Suzanne asked, sliding onto the seat next to Michael and closing the door. 'What did the cop want?'

'Just reading me my rights,' Michael answered, his face expressionless. He saw the look of concern that crossed her face and he hurried on. 'Seems I love you so much it's a crime,' he offered with a smile.

She smiled back at him, obviously pleased. 'Well, if that's a crime, I guess we're both guilty,' she said. Sliding closer to him, she put her arms around his neck and gave him a long, sensuous kiss.

'Where were you when all hell broke loose today?' Suzanne asked, as they drove down the deserted main street.

'What hell?' Michael asked, already knowing the answer. The thought made him shiver. Of all the things on his mind, he had been most worried about his incident with Eddie Mathews.

'At school. Seventh period,' she said. 'I was taking a test in home ec when we heard sirens. And I don't mean just sirens, I mean *sirens*, coming from every which way. We looked out the window, and, my God, there had to be every cop in the state out there, all running around, shouting at the kids, shouting at each other. I don't think any of them cops knowing what the hell really happened.' She paused to take a breath, then continued. 'Boy, bet you that's the biggest thing to happen at that school in fifty years — and *you* didn't hear 'bout it?'

'I left early — right after sixth period. I had a lot of things to take care of today. Yeah, I heard something about it when I was in the bank, about Eddie Mathews getting killed.'

'Not just killed, Michael — *murdered.*'

'Yeah, well . . . I guess he finally picked on someone his own size.' He took a deep breath. 'Suzanne,' he began, suddenly feeling nervous, 'you remember I said I had to talk to you — '

'And I heard they found him in the boys' locker room, his head was all the way off, blood all over the place.'

'Dammit, Suzanne!' he shouted, turning towards her. 'Eddie Mathews can just go to hell — and he probably did. Now hush up a minute and listen to me. I got something to ask you.'

'Michael,' she said reproachfully, unnerved at his shouting.

Michael hesitated. He had rehearsed this a dozen times during the afternoon, but now it seemed he couldn't find the proper words. 'Suzanne — ,' he faltered, then suddenly blurted out, 'I want you to marry me.'

'What?'

'You heard me,' he said, gaining courage. 'Marry me. You know I love you with all my heart, and you said you loved me, so — let's get married.'

'I do love you,' she replied, her face softening, 'I've loved you for a long, long time, but really, this is so sudden . . .'

'Sudden?' Now it was Michael's turn to be surprised. 'You mean you haven't been thinking this whole time what it would be like being married to me?'

'Sure I have, lots of times. But it always seemed — I don't know, like just dreams. What you're asking me now is for real, and it's all happening too fast. I need time to think about it.'

'Nothing to think about,' Michael said, urgency creeping into his voice. 'We love each other; what else counts? We'll be happy together, and I promise life will never be dull.' A quick glance at his watch told him it was nearly a quarter to nine. If she did turn him down, he estimated that he would be gone and well on the road to — wherever — by ten o'clock.

She sat for a minute, looking at him intently as if trying to memorise every feature of his face. 'Well,' she said slowly, as if still weighing her decision, 'maybe, if you was to ask me again, real nice and proper — '

Michael saw his mistake and corrected it. 'Suzanne Elizabeth Harvey,' he said reverently, 'would you do me the honour of becoming my wife?'

'I will,' she said, putting her arms around his neck and kissing him on the lips.

'Suzanne,' he said as they broke the kiss, 'I already have my stuff packed and in the car. We can go by your place so you can pack — '

'Pack?' The confusion was back on her face. 'Tonight? Pack what? What're you talking about?'

'We're getting out of here. We're leaving. We're going to make a new life for ourselves — ' He put his arm out the window of the car. ' — out there.'

'Leave Pea Ridge? We never talked about that.'

'But there's a whole world out there to see. A world chockfull of cities; big, beautiful cities that'll make you forget a little hick town like Pea Ridge inside of a week. Anyway, our home'll be wherever we are at the time – long as we're together.' He watched her reaction. It was getting late.

'I don't know.' She scrutinised his face closely. 'What if I say I just can't go away like that?'

'I wouldn't never go without you,' Michael told her. 'We'd stay right here forever and ever, if that's what you wanted.' He made his face serious and miserable. 'But, I'll tell you right now, I'd hate it. Think of everything we'd be missing.' He had banked on the fact that she loved him deeply and wouldn't refuse him if she thought it would make him unhappy.

'Oh, Mike,' she said slowly, a touch of doubt still in her voice, 'to just pick up and leave like you're suggesting – I mean, there's still so many things to see about, to do, before we can go; like finishing the last two weeks of school and graduating; our folks arranging a wedding; saying good-bye to everyone – '

'Suzanne,' he said as persuasively as he could, 'the only thing that's really important is that we're together. Everything else will take care of itself. We can write letters to people, explaining that we didn't want to wait. They'll understand – they'll be happy for us. We'll get married when we get to Little Rock, or maybe as far east as Memphis.' He shrugged his shoulders. 'Your folks can't afford a big wedding any more than mine can. We'll be doing everybody a big favour by getting married on our own. And all that other stuff, well, once we're married and we start a new life, you'll see that it just isn't all so important.' He looked at her, his eyes pleading. 'Please, darlin', say yes. You won't be sorry.'

Silently, she nodded, yes.

'Great!' he said exuberantly. 'I'm already packed and ready to go. I've been to the bank and drew out my sixteen hundred dollars; that'll keep us going until we settle somewhere and I get a job – '

'Wait a minute,' she said, confused again. 'When did you plan on leaving?'

'Tonight,' he answered matter-of-factly. 'Soon as we can get you packed and ready to go.'

'Oh, Mike – '

'Tonight,' he said firmly. 'If we're gonna to it, let's do it. Okay?'

She was silent for a few more minutes. Finally, almost grudgingly, she nodded. 'Okay,' she answered slowly. 'If that's what you wanna do, we'll do it, as long as we come back for graduation.' She leaned over and kissed him lightly on the cheek. 'I just hope we're not sorry.'

'We won't be, you'll see.' In his heart, he thanked God. With Suzanne, perhaps he stood a prayer of a chance of working his way back to a normal life.

Taking Suzanne home, Michael took his usual left turn onto White River Road.

'Where're you going?' Suzanne asked.

'Taking you home so you can pack.'

She gave him a disapproving look. 'You see?' she said reproachfully, 'you didn't listen to a word I told you this morning. We don't live in that trailer park no more. My Uncle Harry helped us move into the new house this morning. That's why I was late for school, remember? We're living on the farm now.'

'Sorry, I had a lot on my mind this morning . . . guess I wasn't listening.' He shrugged. 'So how do we get there?'

'Just turn yourself around, then go out about three miles past the turnoff to your place, and there it is.

Michael slowed the car, then swung a U-turn and took off in the opposite direction.

'Oooh,' Suzanne breathed, as a new, troubling thought occurred to her, 'you know, one of the reasons why my folks bought this house was so we could all have more room to live. They're gonna have a living fit when we tell them we're planning to get married but won't be living at the new house . . . ' As they drove, Suzanne began talking about their leaving, getting married, and all the foreseeable problems of making a new life for themselves. She rambled on, almost without taking a breath, finding a positive answer for every negative point that occurred to her.

Michael drove along quietly, nodding or mumbling something in assent when he had to.

Michael slowed the car to a crawl as they passed the access road leading to his house, then came to a complete stop. He could see the house clearly through the windbreak of trees that bordered the highway. One light burned in the kitchen window, and from time to time he could see his father's hulking shadow pass across it, as if he was pacing back and forth. The pickup truck stood by the side of the house, its loadbed piled high with freshly cut lumber. When he had seen his dad driving the truck earlier that day in town, the truck had been empty.

He found himself filled with feelings of sadness and remorse. He loved his parents, he realised, and was sorry to be leaving like he was. Why, he wondered, couldn't they understand about him, what he needed, what he was, instead of trying to stop him, fight him all the time . . .

'Do you want to go in and say another good-bye?' Suzanne asked gently.

For a split second, Michael considered it; he wanted to desperately. Then his eyes fell on his dark bedroom window, newly refitted with wooden bars, and he knew that he could not. That house and everything in it represented all the restrictions and confinement he was so desperate to get some distance from. He could not go back — ever.

'No.' He shook his head slowly. 'Best we just be on our way. Leave things as they are.' Stepping hard on the accelerator, he drove quickly away, continuing down the highway.

'You better slow down a bit,' Suzanne warned as they went around a sharp turn in the highway, 'or you'll miss the turnoff. It's not much of a road, and it's hard to see at night.'

Michael slowed the car to twenty miles per hour and still almost missed the narrow wagon road that led off to the left.

'Told you so,' she teased as they backed up and he made the turn.

The house stood about a quarter of a mile down the wagon road. Michael stopped the car beside a pile of rotted timbers that had once been a split-trail fence before and had just been replaced by a new picket fence that now bordered the property. They sat for a moment, looking at the house, each of its windows illuminated brightly.

'Well, what d'you think?' she asked.

For no apparent reason, Michael took a deep and immediate dislike to the house. He didn't know what, but there was just *something* about it he found extremely unpleasant.

'It looks old,' he said noncommittally.

'Oh, it is. Daddy says it's over a hundred years old. Built by the pioneers back in the late 1800s. Isn't it something?'

'Yeah, really something,' he agreed as he got out of the car to open her door for her. He stopped for a moment; there was a tight knot of tension in the pit of his stomach. That was silly, he realised; he supposed he had plenty to be nervous about, but he told himself that Suzanne would go with him even if her parents screamed their heads off. He knew her that well. So why the strange, tight feeling inside?

By the time they had gone up the path leading to the house and had reached the wooden porch, the tight feeling inside him had intensified and spread, until now it felt like an attack of his worst fears. He couldn't explain the intense feeling of foreboding building within him. His skin felt clammy and a thin film of perspiration stood out on his face. He stopped and leaned against the porch railing as a mild case of dizziness made his head swim — and there was something else: a dark stirring with his brain. It was a stirring he had come to know all too well; the beast had awakened — this time without warning, without his wanting it to.

'What's the matter?' Suzanne asked, looking at him with concern. 'You don't look so good.'

'Just a little dizzy.' He smiled apologetically. 'I guess it's just the excitement of going and all. Go in and say hello to your folks. I'll be in there in a minute.'

'Well, okay,' she said reluctantly, 'if you're sure you're all right.' She kissed him lightly on the cheek. 'But come in as soon as I tell them the news.' She opened the front door and stepped into the house.

Her father was trying to get a book rack to hang straight against the bumpy, uneven stony surface of a living-room wall. Hearing Suzanne come in, he turned and a relieved look went across his face.

'Honey, I'm glad you came straight on home from work. I need to talk to you — ' Then he saw Michael standing in the shadow of the porch behind her and the smile disappeared. Without finishing his sentence he went to the newly installed telephone and dialled a number. After a few seconds, he said simply, 'He's here now. Yeah, I'll try. Okay, soon's you can.' Then he hung the phone up.

Suzanne, hearing the cryptic message and seeing her father's mood change so dramatically, turned quickly to Michael.

'Mike!' she called sharply. 'Come on in here.'

The beast was now fully awake within Michael and was at that moment trying to gain control. But this was not the usually subtle urge towards dominance that he was used to; this time the attack came with a desperate, almost frenzied urgency that he had never felt before. *Something* was enraging the beast, and it was taking every ounce of his will to keep it from taking control of him . . . Hearing the urgency in Suzanne's voice, he pushed himself away from the railing and stumbled into the house on shaky legs.

'What's the matter?' he managed to mumble, as he stood for a moment, his body quivering and jerking under the terrific mental strain. He managed two more steps before his legs finally gave out and he collapsed onto the couch. Inside the house, the beast's power seemed immediately to multiply and redouble, until it seemed ready to completely overwhelm his struggling consciousness. Not now . . . not with all of them here, his mind screamed as he fought back. He was only dimly aware of sounds and impressions around him as he lay sprawled across the couch, his mind straining, doing battle with itself. Somewhere far away in the limbo of realities and fantasies he heard Clarence Harvey say, 'Your pa told me about you . . . ' He heard Suzanne shouting, 'Leave him alone, daddy! Can't you see he's sick? Look how he's shaking.' There were other words, other sounds around him; a flurry of activity as Suzanne was forcibly pushed away from him by her father as he shouted, 'Stay away from him, he's dangerous when he's like that' – but it all now sounded distorted and disconnected to him and carried no definition as his will weakened and his grip on his mind began slipping away. His heart pounded wildly with a sudden sense that if he lost this battle, *he* would be lost, his rationality, his identity – everything that made him a conscious, loving human being – gone forever, pushed back into oblivion. For a brief instant, before the savage grip had him completely, the last grain, the last speck of his rational consciousness called out once in terror . . .

The beast slowly opened his eyes, and the room seemed to freeze in its three dimensions. Suzanne and her father were held motionless, staring mutely into those eyes, seeing for the first time the cold ruthlessness and unspeakable savagery behind them. The hypnotic quality of the scene fell away as the beast's lips drew back, exposing glistening-white teeth, and a low, guttural slurp escaped his throat. Chaos broke loose as the beast sprang, seizing Clarence, the one closest to him, by the neck with both hands and flinging him bodily with a bone-crushing thud against the stone wall of the living room.

The beast turned quickly on Suzanne, still standing rooted to the spot, her hand pressed tightly to her mouth. Crouching low, he began moving slowly to the left around the large oak table that blocked his path to her, his movements liquid and instinctive like those of a stalking animal.

Suzanne started to counter the beast's moves, keeping the table between them while slowly backing away towards the corner by the front door.

With a roar, more out of frustration than anger, the beast leaped easily over the obstructing table, his right hand whipping out savagely. Most of Suzanne's dress came away in his clutching fingers as she screamed and jumped back out of reach, trapping herself in the corner. Behind the sound of her scream was the noise of a truck screeching to a stop outside.

The beast lunged again. Suzanne tried to step past him, but he had her left arm and now pulled at it viciously. There was a loud pop as her arm was dislocated from her shoulder; the force sending her onto the floor beside the couch.

A low growl of pleasure escaped the beast's lips as he advanced on his victim lying nearly naked on the floor. Saliva trickled freely from the corners of his mouth at the sight of her exposed legs and throat. He could sense, almost taste the warm, rich blood that pulsed there.

Heavy boots sounded only an instant on the porch before the front door was opened with force enough to embed its doorknob in the wall. Eli's enormous frame filled the doorway. His eyes found his son crouched over Suzanne's prone body, and his features hardened into a mask of grim resolution.

'Michael, no!' he shouted, taking two steps into the room, then bracing himself for the expected attack as he watched his son rise halfway out of his crouch, his body tense, ready to leap at him.

With a growl of defiance, the beast sprang, hands held before him like claws, teeth bared for the attack; the lust for blood in his eyes unmistakable.

Eli caught his son by the shoulders in mid-leap, and for a moment held him off the ground at arms' length as the boy twisted and squirmed, snapping his teeth like an animal. Both hands came up between Eli's massive arms, raking both sides of Eli's face, gouging and slicing open his right eye. Blinded by the pain, Eli released his grip, but immediately struck out with his fist, catching his son squarely on the jaw and sending him toppling backwards.

Wiping the blood that oozed from his burning right eye, Eli was taken by surprise; with a snarl of rage, the beast sprang at him again. He brought his left arm up in front of him for protection, but the teeth sank into the fleshy forearm. Eli shot his right hand out again, the palm hitting his son on the forehead hard enough to make him take a wobbly step backwards. He got both arms around the boy, then wrapped his right arm around his son's neck, locking his elbow beneath the jaw. He squeezed slowly, applying pressure to both sides of the neck. He could feel the pulse pounding against his arm. He continued applying pressure until the struggling weakened, then ceased completely.

Eli slowly released his stranglehold and allowed the limp body to sink gently to the floor. He looked at his son's face, the face he loved, now calm and relaxed in unconsciousness. Tears welled up in his eyes, then ran slowly down his face, mixing with the blood dripping onto his shirt.

'There wasn't no other way, boy,' he said, deep sadness evident in his voice. 'No other way,' he repeated again, as if trying to justify, at least to himself, what had to be done. 'I had to stop you — any way I could. Now you'll be kept safe from yourself — so you can't hurt no one else.' He could not talk through the hard grief that choked him. He looked up at the sound of Suzanne's moan, then heard Clarence call out in pain from what looked like a broken leg.

Sinking slowly to his knees, he gently kissed Michael's

215

forehead — then began to tie his hands and feet with the cord of an overturned lamp before looking for the telephone.

25

Eli and Carolyn sat sombrely on the couch in the Harveys' living room, Clarence and Emma sitting in chairs across from them. It was a bleak gathering.

'Well, it's done.' Eli drew a tired breath. 'Ventilator is installed, floor is laid down, the partition and bars are all up — ' He shrugged. 'I only hope it holds.'

Clarence nodded in agreement, painfully shifting the cast on his right leg to a more comfortable position. The entire right side of his face was one large bruise. 'Oh, it'll hold all right,' he said reassuringly. 'Only wish I could've done more to help, but — ' He gestured apologetically at the heavy cast stretching from his hips to his toes.

'I didn't have no trouble tending to it myself,' Eli said, 'and I'll tend to the damage he caused in the barn, too, soon as I rest up a little.' He felt for the bandage covering his injured right eye. 'This thing just makes working a little hard, is all.' He looked at them seriously through his good eye. 'You two are doing enough just allowing us to use your place like you are until we settle on what to do. And, well —' he stammered slightly. 'I can't find words enough to tell you two how much we appreciate what you're doing.'

'Don't need to say nothing,' Clarence said simply. 'Our girl loves him and wants to take care of him.' He shrugged. 'Even with everything that's happened, I guess we love him too.' He looked over at Emma, who nodded in agreement.

Suzanne hobbled into the living room from the kitchen, carrying a tray of food. A thick cast crossed her left collarbone, encasing the entire shoulder in plaster and stretching down to just above her elbow.

'Even after you told us about him, what's wrong with him . . . ' she said, 'and even after I saw him like that myself, I still can't believe it.'

Eli spread his hands in a desolate gesture. 'We told you what he was like when he was a kid, after his great-grandma told him all those legends and stories about werewolves. He ran around the house for the longest time, pretending to be one. After a while, I guess, in his mind he just stopped pretending and started believing it. How else can you explain it?'

'Will he ever — you know, be all right again?' she asked hopefully.

'Sure he will. It comes and goes with him,' Eli assured her, knowing he was only buying time.

Suzanne put the tray down. 'He really scares me sometimes, though, and he hasn't seemed to come out of it. Like when I take his food down to him, he just growls and snaps his teeth at me and throws everything around. He tries to reach out and grab me through the bars.' She shook her head sadly. 'I'd sure like to see him back again just once the way he was.'

'I'm sure he will be, Suzanne,' Carolyn said, 'but we been through this before. You got to be patient, it'll take time.' She caught Eli's eye and they exchanged an apprehensive look.

'Well, I guess I'll get on with it,' Suzanne said half-heartedly, limping across the living room to the trap door, now fitted with new steel hinges and a heavy sliding bolt. Drawing back the bolt and easily swinging the trap door open, she picked up the tray again and began making her way carefully down the cellar steps. As soon as the trap door had been opened, the cellar under the house began echoing with the sounds of furious growling and the thud of fists and feet hitting against the wall.

26

The maternity ward at the Bentonville Community Hospital seemed unusually quiet and uneventful the night Pattie Herman was wheeled into the delivery room. The other three women present in the ward had each given birth some time earlier that day and were all sleeping soundly.

'She's pretty far along, doctor,' Nurse Stevens, the delivery room scrub nurse, informed Doctor Gowens. He completed his surgical scrub and she helped him slip into a pair of thin surgical gloves. 'She's already three inches dilated, and contracting at two minutes, steady. She's prepped and ready to go.'

'Extremely large, active foetus for such a small girl,' the doctor said as she tied his mask over his nose and mouth. 'It's going to be at least a ten-pounder, unless I miss my guess.' Holding his hands up in front of him to keep them antiseptic, he backed through the large double doors into the delivery room.

The anaesthetist had already done his job. Pattie lay on the delivery table, her nose and mouth covered by a clear plastic mask, her thighs spread wide and fitted into metal stirrups.

'I never could get her to tell us the name of the father this morning,' the doctor told them. 'It sounds like whoever it was ran out on her as soon as she told him she was pregnant.' He shook his head. 'When will these kids learn?'

The doctor took his place on a rolling stool at the far end of the table and raised the sheet covering the patient's splayed legs.

'The head's coming!' he said suddenly, reaching for a set of forceps on the towel-covered table next to him. 'Aid her bear-down with vertical push at five-second intervals.'

The nurse began pushing hard on Pattie's abdomen, beginning just below the rib cage and moving down across her stomach.

'There . . . the head's coming nicely,' the doctor said. 'Now for the shoulders, and we'll — ' He stopped in mid-sentence as the baby's head emerged.

'What is it, doctor?' the nurse asked, startled. 'Continue the push?'

'Uh — no,' the doctor answered, his voice stunned. 'That will be sufficient. The shoulders are free.'

The nurse moved over beside the doctor to see the baby. 'Doctor, look at its — his face,' she gasped. 'The shape of the eyes — the nose, like a snout. Doctor, he's got — teeth!'

The doctor looked up at her, his eyes wide, confused. An unspoken message passed between them.

'Doctor, we can't,' she admonished. 'It's — it's still a life.'

Shock faded from the doctor's eyes as sensibility returned. Skilfully severing the baby's umbilical cord, he then applied a plastic clip to both cut ends to stop the bleeding. Lifting the baby by his heels, he administered a quick slap to the baby's buttocks.

Instead of the first crying-breath of life, a long, high-pitched howl echoed through the delivery room.

Fiction

GENERAL

☐ The House of Women	Chaim Bermant	£1.95
☐ The Patriarch	Chaim Bermant	£2.25
☐ The Rat Race	Alfred Bester	£1.95
☐ Midwinter	John Buchan	£1.50
☐ A Prince of the Captivity	John Buchan	£1.50
☐ The Priestess of Henge	David Burnett	£2.50
☐ Tangled Dynasty	Jean Chapman	£1.75
☐ The Other Woman	Colette	£1.95
☐ Retreat From Love	Colette	£1.60
☐ An Infinity of Mirrors	Richard Condon	£1.95
☐ Arigato	Richard Condon	£1.95
☐ Prizzi's Honour	Richard Condon	£1.75
☐ A Trembling Upon Rome	Richard Condon	£1.95
☐ The Whisper of the Axe	Richard Condon	£1.75
☐ Love and Work	Gwyneth Cravens	£1.95
☐ King Hereafter	Dorothy Dunnett	£2.95
☐ Pope Joan	Lawrence Durrell	£1.35
☐ The Country of Her Dreams	Janice Elliott	£1.35
☐ Magic	Janice Elliot	£1.95
☐ Secret Places	Janice Elliott	£1.75
☐ Letter to a Child Never Born	Oriana Fallaci	£1.25
☐ A Man	Oriana Fallaci	£2.50
☐ Rich Little Poor Girl	Terence Feely	£1.75
☐ Marital Rites	Margaret Forster	£1.50
☐ The Seduction of Mrs Pendlebury	Margaret Forster	£1.95
☐ Abingdons	Michael French	£2.25
☐ Rhythms	Michael French	£2.25
☐ Who Was Sylvia?	Judy Gardiner	£1.50
☐ Grimalkin's Tales	Gardiner, Ronson, Whitelaw	£1.60
☐ Lost and Found	Julian Gloag	£1.95
☐ A Sea-Change	Lois Gould	£1.50
☐ La Presidenta	Lois Gould	£2.25
☐ A Kind of War	Pamela Haines	£1.95
☐ Tea at Gunters	Pamela Haines	£1.75
☐ Black Summer	Julian Hale	£1.75
☐ A Rustle in the Grass	Robin Hawdon	£1.95
☐ Riviera	Robert Sydney Hopkins	£1.95
☐ Duncton Wood	William Horwood	£2.75
☐ The Stonor Eagles	William Horwood	£2.50
☐ The Man Who Lived at the Ritz	A. E. Hotchner	£1.65
☐ A Bonfire	Pamela Hansford Johnson	£1.50
☐ The Good Listener	Pamela Hansford Johnson	£1.50
☐ The Honours Board	Pamela Hansford Johnson	£1.50
☐ The Unspeakable Skipton	Pamela Hansford Johnson	£1.50
☐ In the Heat of the Summer	John Katzenbach	£1.95
☐ Starrs	Warren Leslie	£2.50
☐ Kine	A. R. Lloyd	£1.50
☐ The Factory	Jack Lynn	£1.95
☐ Christmas Pudding	Nancy Mitford	£1.50
☐ Highland Fling	Nancy Mitford	£1.50
☐ Pigeon Pie	Nancy Mitford	£1.75
☐ The Sun Rises	Christopher Nicole	£2.50

Fiction

HORROR/OCCULT/NASTY

☐ Death Walkers	Gary Brandner	£1.75
☐ Hellborn	Gary Brandner	£1.75
☐ The Howling	Gary Brandner	£1.75
☐ Return of the Howling	Gary Brandner	£1.75
☐ Tribe of the Dead	Gary Brandner	£1.75
☐ The Sanctuary	Glenn Chandler	£1.50
☐ The Tribe	Glenn Chandler	£1.10
☐ The Black Castle	Leslie Daniels	£1.25
☐ The Big Goodnight	Judy Gardiner	£1.25
☐ Rattlers	Joseph L. Gilmore	£1.60
☐ The Nestling	Charles L. Grant	£1.95
☐ Night Songs	Charles L. Grant	£1.95
☐ Slime	John Halkin	£1.75
☐ Slither	John Halkin	£1.60
☐ The Unholy	John Halkin	£1.25
☐ The Skull	Shaun Hutson	£1.25
☐ Pestilence	Edward Jarvis	£1.60
☐ The Beast Within	Edward Levy	£1.25
☐ Night Killers	Richard Lewis	£1.25
☐ Spiders	Richard Lewis	£1.75
☐ The Web	Richard Lewis	£1.75
☐ Nightmare	Lewis Mallory	£1.75
☐ Bloodthirst	Mark Ronson	£1.60
☐ Ghoul	Mark Ronson	£1.75
☐ Ogre	Mark Ronson	£1.75
☐ Deathbell	Guy N. Smith	£1.75
☐ Doomflight	Guy N. Smith	£1.25
☐ Manitou Doll	Guy N. Smith	£1.25
☐ Satan's Snowdrop	Guy N. Smith	£1.00
☐ The Understudy	Margaret Tabor	£1.95
☐ The Beast of Kane	Cliff Twemlow	£1.50
☐ The Pike	Cliff Twemlow	£1.25

Fiction

SCIENCE FICTION

☐ More Things in Heaven	John Brunner	£1.50
☐ Chessboard Planet	Henry Kuttner	£1.75
☐ The Proud Robot	Henry Kuttner	£1.50
☐ Death's Master	Tanith Lee	£1.50
☐ The Dancers of Arun	Elizabeth A. Lynn	£1.50
☐ The Northern Girl	Elizabeth A. Lynn	£1.50
☐ Balance of Power	Brian M. Stableford	£1.75

ADVENTURE/SUSPENSE

☐ The Corner Men	John Gardner	£1.75
☐ Death of a Friend	Richard Harris	£1.95
☐ The Flowers of the Forest	Joseph Hone	£1.75
☐ Styx	Christopher Hyde	£1.50
☐ Temple Kent	D. G. Devon	£1.95
☐ Confess, Fletch	Gregory Mcdonald	£1.50
☐ Fletch	Gregory Mcdonald	£1.50
☐ Fletch and the Widow Bradley	Gregory Mcdonald	£1.50
☐ Flynn	Gregory Mcdonald	£1.75
☐ The Buck Passes Flynn	Gregory Mcdonald	£1.60
☐ The Specialist	Jasper Smith	£1.75

WESTERNS

Blade Series – Matt Chisholm

☐ No. 5 The Colorado Virgins	85p
☐ No. 6 The Mexican Proposition	85p
☐ No. 11 The Navaho Trail	95p

McAllister Series – Matt Chisholm

☐ No. 3 McAllister Never Surrenders	95p
☐ No. 4 McAllister and the Cheyenne Death	95p
☐ No. 8 McAllister – Fire Brand	£1.25

Fiction

CRIME

☐ The Cool Cottontail	John Ball	£1.00
☐ Five Pieces of Jade	John Ball	£1.50
☐ Johnny Get Your Gun	John Ball	£1.00
☐ Then Came Violence	John Ball	£1.50
☐ The Widow's Cruise	Nicholas Blake	£1.25
☐ The Worm of Death	Nicholas Blake	95p
☐ The Long Divorce	Edmund Crispin	£1.50
☐ Love Lies Bleeding	Edmund Crispin	£1.75
☐ The Case of the Sliding Pool	E. V. Cunningham	£1.75
☐ Hindsight	Peter Dickinson	£1.75
☐ King and Joker	Peter Dickinson	£1.25
☐ The Last House Party	Peter Dickinson	£1.75
☐ A Pride of Heroes	Peter Dickinson	£1.50
☐ The Seals	Peter Dickinson	£1.50
☐ Gondola Scam	Jonathan Gash	£1.75
☐ The Sleepers of Erin	Jonathan Gash	£1.75
☐ The Black Seraphim	Michael Gilbert	£1.75
☐ Blood and Judgment	Michael Gilbert	£1.10
☐ Close Quarters	Michael Gilbert	£1.10
☐ The Etruscan Net	Michael Gilbert	£1.25
☐ The Final Throw	Michael Gilbert	£1.75
☐ The Night of the Twelfth	Michael Gilbert	£1.25
☐ The Blunderer	Patricia Highsmith	£1.50
☐ A Game for the Living	Patricia Highsmith	£1.50
☐ Those Who Walk Away	Patricia Highsmith	£1.50
☐ The Tremor of Forgery	Patricia Highsmith	£1.50
☐ The Two Faces of January	Patricia Highsmith	£1.50
☐ Silence Observed	Michael Innes	£1.00
☐ Go West, Inspector Ghote	H. R. F. Keating	£1.50
☐ Inspector Ghote Draws a Line	H. R. F. Keating	£1.50
☐ Inspector Ghote Plays a Joker	H. R. F. Keating	£1.50
☐ The Murder of the Maharajah	H. R. F. Keating	£1.50
☐ The Perfect Murder	H. R. F. Keating	£1.50

NAME ....

ADDRESS ....

....

Write to Hamlyn Paperbacks Cash Sales, PO Box 11, Falmouth, Cornwall TR10 9EN.

Please indicate order and enclose remittance to the value of cover price plus:

U.K. CUSTOMERS: Please allow 55p for the first book, 22p for the second book and 14p for each additional book ordered to a maximum charge of £1.75.

B.F.P.O. & EIRE: Please allow 55p for the first book, 22p for the second book plus 14p per copy for the next seven books, thereafter 8p per book.

OVERSEAS CUSTOMERS: Please allow £1.00 for the first book plus 25p per copy for each additional book.

Whilst every effort is made to keep prices low it is sometimes necessary to increase cover prices and also postage and packing rates at short notice. Hamlyn Paperbacks reserve the right to show new retail prices on covers which may differ from those previously advertised in the text or elsewhere.